GODHEAD

WALTER HARRIS

Patagonia Press

Published by Patagonia Press

© Walter Harris, 2014

ISBN: 978-0-9928649-0-3

Formatting for ebook: KindleMonster.com

Cover art by Angela Jane Swinn
www.angelajaneswinn.com

FOREWORD

How many claimants to be the Son of God have there been? Could faith ever be as powerful as proof for anyone to be accepted as the Son of God? Could there be a worse curse than to be granted immortality, and could that curse be removed by anyone but the Son of God, held to be responsible for it?

Nathaniel ben Ezra, who accidentally tastes Jesus' blood as he hangs on the Cross, finds himself confronted with these questions as he begs for death from a twenty-first century Jesus claimant who has become his friend and client in modern America.

DEDICATION

To Alison, who came into my life so unexpectedly, and
inspired me into an increasingly long and joyous old age.

Published novels by Walter Harris

Clovis
The Mistress of Downing Street
Droop
The Day I Died
The Fifth Horseman
Saliva
Creature from the Black Lagoon (written as Carl
Dreadstone, UK edition as E.K. Leyton)
Werewolf of London (written as Carl Dreadstone)
The New Avengers: To Catch a Rat

PROLOGUE

I have so far encountered four men claiming to be the Son of God who seemed to me to possess some significance. One was crucified for his claim, a second was burned by the Inquisition, and I am pretty sure the third was murdered for his, not officially but by a stiletto slipped stealthily into his heart in a Venetian backwater.

It is the fourth, whom I met only recently, who most intrigues me. There is something about him, a quality of gravitas combined with the ability to communicate, an obvious humanity melded with something that is not obvious at all, which give him such a degree of conviction.

Against all my scepticism and hatred for Jehovah, I find myself considering it just possible the latest claimant might indeed have a degree of godhead.

Ever since I encountered the first of the three, hands nailed to a cross-piece of rough wood, feet impaled by a large nail to a timber upright, I realised how urgently faith in godhead is demanded by the claimant and how insistently proof, the enemy of faith, is demanded by the hoped-for believer.

For my part, I have little time for faith. There have been times when I longed for a great universal Abstract to which or whom I could attribute an explanation for the creation of the cosmos and for qualities of altruism and benevolence, but faith has usually demanded more in the way of acceptance than I could supply. I have seen it so many times fail to avert catastrophe or mitigate disaster, as a result of which those who claim to possess it spend an inordinate amount of time trying unconvincingly to rationalise its failure.

The manifestation of cruelty in answer to prayers for divine mercy, the failure so often to deliver a victim from evil in exchange for sacrifices claimed by the divine recipient of prayers, have always combated any inclination towards faith that I might have had.

Faith, like temptation, can only be measured by extremes. For example, it was not unnatural that when the storm burst over the three crosses that long ago evening in Golgotha, it was claimed by his disciples that Jesus lost faith and cried out to the God he alleged was his father not to forsake him; agony was close to destroying his self-belief, a worse punishment for a martyr than the agony itself.

It was also claimed that Jesus had earlier in the day shouted at the heavens, as his executioners were hammering in the nails: "Forgive them, Father, for they know not what they do!" which completely contradicted the Jewish belief that an eye should be claimed for an eye, and a tooth for a tooth; the plea for forgiveness was equally incomprehensible to the Romans, who, like the Jews, were not forgivers.

I myself have no answer even though I was there, standing in the rain below the crosses and the men stapled to them, as the storm broke. Perhaps Jesus had, like myself, been startled by the lightning and a roll of thunder louder than the roar of a Coliseum lion.

There are so many things to which, even now, I have no answer even though I have for so long been the victim of a philosophy that has rendered me devoid of most qualities of the human spirit. I am perfectly balanced and astronomically remote. Whatever else may constitute philosophy: history, logic, culture, discipline, it is essentially the wisdom of the bystander.

I seldom suffer the ravages of emotion; in fact I am emotionally mummified. Of course I deplore the human race's insatiable brutalities but it is a long time since I felt impelled to storm the barricades.

As for love, I have had a surfeit of it, being unable any more to feel it or undergo being the object of it. What has been described as 'sweet torment' imposes a responsibility I can no longer bear, and I am equally remote from the stimulus of hatred. I cannot help regarding such friends as I have as garments, to be donned or discarded, according to mood.

They, on the other hand, are kinder, more tolerant, towards me, perhaps because they are so much younger–they have no idea how much younger. That sets me apart from them, as does my appalling wealth. Money has so little meaning for me it never enters my consideration—I take it utterly for granted.

Today is the first of July: the Julian Calendar, Caesar, Augustus, Tiberius, Nero, the Sanhedrin, the Roman Senate, the Temple, my father, the sloe-eyed women of Antioch, are all droplets in the wake of my memory.

It is my birthday next week, and there is a hideous but chastening inevitability to it and the burden it imposes on me.

Give or take a few decades, I shall be two thousand years old, and even though I long to die, death is still beyond my reach. I suppose I know everything there is to know about human frailty but alas, I am too bored to want any longer to succumb to it.

Chapter 1

I have just been shaving, and as always, peered into my bathroom mirror to look for any signs of ageing. As always, there are none. My hair is coarse, curly, and completely free of white or grey. My face is unmarked by the experiences and travails of life, its skin looking tanned and smoothed. A bulbous-tipped Semitic nose plays the referee between brown eyes under thick black brows. I look like a man in his early thirties.

After shaving, I went out, still dressed in my bath robe, to the terrace, and stood looking across the East River to Brooklyn Heights, obscured by early morning cloud. My penthouse is usually just under the cloud line or just above it; I turned and walked along the terrace which encircles the building, and after a circuit, during which the July sun seemed to leap into the sky and at the same time release its heat like a weapon, went indoors.

My valet had laid out my clothes for the day but was not present; I hate being dressed by anybody else. Breakfast was steamed scrambled eggs, cooked in a flanged soup plate above a saucepan of boiling water, with cream, paprika, pepper, and chopped tomatoes and seasoning. As soon as I had finished, Mia, one of my personal secretaries, came in to retrieve yesterday's tapes in order to transpose them into print.

She has a habit of looking at me as if I am not so much a normal man as strange, a little unreal, possibly a myth that she has imagined.

She calls me Sir, there is none of to-day's first name familiarity, at least not on her part. I call her Mia, never Miss Sanderson. She is not afraid of me, I am

1

convinced, but she always gives me the impression that she can't wait to get out of the room.

. I do my best to live in the present, but the years of my past so heavily outweigh it that it is difficult to adjust. History is as fickle as the women of Antioch, of Rome, of eternity. History has a random beauty combined with an evil that was planned and whose tragedy has been that it is so much more a strategy than a tactic, although whose strategy or whose tactic only god—if there were one—could know. Did the god of Abraham suffer a second lapse of morality and decide it would be a good idea to beget his own son in order to slaughter him, albeit by proxy? He had no one to answer to, no one to worship, as Abraham did. Yet the strategy involved faith, and plenty of it.

My most implacable memory of what became known as The Crucifixion was the smell of blood permeating the meadow and hill of Golgotha, which looked like a skull but breathed out the scent of jasmine from its absent nose and staring eye-sockets.

I remember too the silence of the woman who stationed herself in quiet dignity at the foot of the cross from which her half dead son leaned forward, by now almost immune to the agony which was suffocating him. She was in her way suffering as much as he was. The centurion guard had told me she was the mother of Jesus, and that whereas the other women who came and stood vigil with her for a while cried out and wailed, his mother simply stood as she was standing now, without moving or crying.

Perhaps a stranger to pity, but not entirely hostile to it, the centurion had given me permission to come back with a pitcher of orange juice to offer Jesus. "It might help him live a bit longer," was his comment, "if that's what he wants." He looked at me curiously, wondering no doubt why a young Jewish boy should want to help an unruly blasphemer whose own people had demanded his death.

In fact I was impelled not only by kindness, but to a greater extent, perhaps, by curiosity. I knew the view of Pontius Pilate, who had judged Jesus and regarded him as innocent of the blasphemy attributed to him by the Pharisees, who were outraged by his criticism of them. It didn't take much to outrage a Pharisee.

The Hill of Golgotha was considered by the Romans, artists in the protraction of dying, as an appropriate location for crucifixion, elevating the condemned to stare into the distance for which they would be heading and giving the spectators an uninterrupted view of the agony on display.

As crucifixion was the customary method of execution, I had no idea at the time why there was such an uproar about the crucifixion of Jesus, could not guess at the power of the event's imprimatur on future history. Had the Romans thrown him to the lions, no doubt the churches and cathedrals which rose in his name would have featured a lion on their altars, whilst the noble beast would also have peered down from their steeples. If he had been hanged, I expect an elegant representation of a gibbet would have been used as a sovereign protection against the menace of the ungodly.

As it happened it was Jesus' followers, such as Paul, with whom I was to become friendly, who later on endured the many Roman ways of death, which were also circus entertainments. The ordinary crucifixions were designed only to be lingering punishments devoid of glamour or excitement. After the nails had been hammered in and the screams subsided to moaning, there was nothing for the victims to do but to die.

As I was about to press a full goblet to the lips of Jesus, the ladder lurched and I had to save myself by grabbing at him, gashing my fingers on the crown of thorns which the crowd had placed lopsided on his head. The thorns were already sprinkled with blood from the deep scratches on his forehead, and I put my damaged fingers in my mouth and sucked them.

"God bless you," murmured Jesus' mother, as I climbed down. I muttered something and went over to a second man, who had died. I remember his smell, but not his name. Men have their individual smells in death as women have in love; there is a pot pourri pungency and scent, light and dark, sunshine and the pit.

A third crucified man hung inert, eyes closed, and I was eager to leave the garden. The sky was heavy with cloud, and without warning the air had evaporated. I fought to breathe, looking back at Jesus' mother for some sort of comfort. I could not see her at first; she was standing without movement behind her son's cross.

Thunder roared savagely, and lightning tore at the sky. Even the centurion guard stood petrified, like something white seared on to a deep purple background.

I fought to move, burst free of my shock at the onslaught of the storm, and left that place; as I started to run there was another jagged flash of lightning like an earthquake in the sky, and a piercing cry. I ran home as quickly as I could through the furious night.

When Golgotha was used for a crucifixion the birds fled. They stayed away whilst the sun rose high, but returned when the brief twilight brought out the scent of jasmine, the other sweet but entirely different smell of blood being quenched by the coolness preceding the rising moon.

4

Some of the birds sang as if to comfort the condemned; others, the carrion-eaters, circled in patient hunger, knowing that soon they would be able to sate their appetites. The Roman soldiery were in their barracks, or wenching in the wine-shops, and if a vulture wanted a meal they were not going to hurry back to Golgotha to foil it with a spade and a winding-sheet.

I was a child of twelve, and learned a good deal through temple gossip but more from knowing Pontius Pilate. Apparently Jesus had offended Annas the high priest and his acolytes by blasphemy, subversion and irreverence in throwing out the temple money-changers, especially as Annas owned the money-changers' franchise and received a percentage of the profits.

Jesus also appalled the high priest and Sanhedrin by claiming to be the son of God and enraged the body politic by claiming to be King of the Jews. These claims aroused the suspicions of the Romans as to possible sedition and rebellion against authority.

In fact, this man with fire on his tongue was a dangerous nuisance whose subversive views placed every subject in danger of Roman wrath. To avoid that wrath Annas and several senior members of the laity, the Pharisee sect and the Sanhedrin, had pre-empted Roman action against the community by going themselves to the Roman governor to complain.

The Pharisees complained about pretty well everything and thought they were nobler than anyone else and more worthy of celestial consideration; Jesus' calling them 'whited sepulchres' had enraged them further, especially as the phrase caught on and was mockingly used by the masses.

The Romans' only concern was to keep order; the fact that a carpenter's son was claiming to be King of the Jews did not strike them as anything to laugh at. He was more than a nuisance – he was articulate and, it seemed, unruly. They were infuriated too by his claim to be the son of the Jewish god because of its possible effect on the people, although the idea of an invisible god instead of gods like theirs, which had a physical presence and could be looked at, was beyond their understanding.

Had the Jews, like their one-time Egyptian masters, worshipped Ra, Osiris and the rest of the pharaonic pantheon, the Romans would have perhaps been more lenient towards their unwilling vassals, being able to relate them to Jupiter, Venus and so on. As it was, they regarded the abstractions of monotheism and its claims to supremacy as verging on the impertinent.

I remember my father saying that Jesus' claim to be the Son of God was not only blasphemous but an extraordinarily arrogant interpretation of the humility Jesus liked to praise as a necessary virtue. Pontius Pilate was tolerant of him as a human being but not as a god; he had expressed his opinions over a few goblets of wine both before and after the trial, and I was curious about this self-proclaimed god-man, which was why I had gone to see him at Golgotha.

The stories about the death of Jesus further baffled both the Jews and the Romans. His pupils, known then as disciples and later as apostles, spread it about that the storm had not been a normal one at all, but a manifestation of the wrath of God, Jesus' proclaimed father. Obviously, if that had really been the case, the cross would have been split into fragments by the outraged Almighty, Jesus' wounds healed, and his oppressors slain. The God of the Jews certainly wouldn't dream of turning the other cheek and forgiving his son's murderers.

6

Even more extraordinary was the claim of the disciples that the body of Jesus disappeared from the tomb after he died, and that he later returned and talked to them, which struck us all as absurd. The people he was alleged to have thus addressed were those closest to him, and of course they tended to show off about being honoured by these post-mortem confidences.

To give these disciples their due, they did show sincerity and bravery in the maintenance of their faith in Jesus' holiness. Paul was a particularly impressive man, who once helped to save the lives of my father and myself. Years afterwards, I tried to save him from becoming a Circus attraction when he was in prison awaiting Nero's summons to the arena of the Coliseum. Nero died in May, before his decree had been carried out, but the Romans carried out the death sentence anyway.

Chapter 2

My father was a spice merchant. To me he was the incarnation of knowledge, and smelled of it. He smelled of his knowledge of the world he knew well, and which I had never seen, of saffron and cinnamon and the hasty blandishments of black pepper. He smelled also, before he bathed on his return, of camels and leather and sweat, of alien and exciting cultures and their practices. While he was away I thought of him often as putting on a cloak of cultures, of the hot, passionate cultures of Egypt, of Samarkand and India which he traversed so diligently on his way to romance and profit. He would tell me on his return of the mysterious places he had visited, and I wondered what exactly mystery was, for I was at an age when I had not had the experiences which gave words their meaning, and instead had to compensate for my lack of understanding by drawing on my imagination.

To me mystery was a place of cloud-swept darkness, of light with black hounds tearing at its edges, of a sky like the surroundings of a vast market, whose stars were smoky lanterns peering through rolling incense whose impact built a temple of dreams.

My father had a voice of honey when he described his travels, the gutturals of Aramaic undulating gently instead of sounding, as they did in the mouths of other men, harsh and unforgiving. My mother, who was to die young of malaria, also enjoyed listening to my father, her eyes sparkling as he spoke; he would always bring her back something beautiful from India or the lands beyond the Euphrates, as I would later for the women in my life. The presents were often brooches and pendants carved in the form of wild animals, snarling Chinese jade lions and ivory elephants, or faceted rubies that glowed in glossy malevolence.

It was said by Jesus' disciples that his birth had been welcomed by three kings bearing gold, frankincense and myrrh, but I was sure that nothing they had brought could have excelled in its wonder the treasures I watched being unloaded from my father's camels, and those he tenderly placed round my mother's neck.

Beautiful artefacts were something I encountered often and therefore could compare with each other, because my closest friend at the time was Lucullus Quintus, the nephew of Pontius Pilate. Lucullus had a sister, Julia, of whom I was also very fond, and who had begun to arouse feelings in me beyond ordinary friendship. The three of us shared the same tutor, and I had learned to think of Pilate in the same terms of address as Lucullus and Julia: Uncle Pontius. It was hearing him talk about Jesus before he reluctantly sentenced him to be crucified, and after the event when he regretted it that had aroused my sympathy and curiosity about the self-styled Son of God; it seemed hard to have to die because your judge was a man who would do anything for a quiet life. "But he did ask for it," Pilate repeated often, "he more or less insisted on being condemned, because he wouldn't shut up about being King of the Jews and insulting the High Priest and other Elders." He would shrug with self-pity and gulp wine.

The Governor and his family lived in a marble palace on the outskirts of Jerusalem, a place that reminded me of a vast, multi-flavoured fruit, with its skirts of lemons and oranges, figs and limes. There were olive trees drawn up like centurions on parade, casting their slightly bitter fragrance on the breeze, and peacocks whose finery outshone everything, strutting proudly and picking at the fallen fruit as they expressed themselves in voices that were in hideous contrast to their gorgeousness.

Indoors, slaves in white tunics attended on the feasts that Pontius held in huge, sumptuously furnished salons. Although the Romans were an army of occupation, feared by most, I felt at home with my Roman friends, and my father's trading connections had given him a sophistication and understanding lacking in most of those who criticised me.

I was not, in the modern sense of the word, 'collaborating'; Rome occupied us, but we were not at war with her. The Romans had their spears and their armour and their supreme military discipline, but there was no weapon to match the fear they wielded.

Lucullus was a tall boy with a face like that of one of the eagles that scowled down from the legions' standards. His skin was sleek and golden, his large eyes the colour of mulberries. If his head was like an eagle's, his body had the suppleness and grace of an antelope; he was like myself only twelve years old, but already a respected athlete.

Julia had a similar noble beauty, and liked to run through the desert in the early morning, when the dew was heavy and turned the rocky dunes to purple. She regarded me at that time as a brother, and treated both Lucullus and me with the same slightly contemptuous condescension. I no longer thought of her as a sister, and as she was just beyond the cusp of puberty, and I was approaching it, I am sure she knew I desired her, and looked forward to being able to use her new power over me.

In the salon beyond the atrium, with its mosaic floor flecked with azure and gold and stylised, scintillating dolphins, there was a cool inner chamber in the middle of which was a fountain. The divan beside the fountain, of crimson leather tooled in gold, was Pontius' favourite place to relax.

He would return to the house where a slave waited for him with a crisp, freshly laundered toga. After bathing, Pontius donned the new toga and lay back on the divan, which was flanked at each end by small bronze tables. One of the house slaves would plump cushions behind his head and in the small of his back whilst Sarda, a huge Circassian, brought an amphora of crystal wine with which he filled a goblet.

Before he had drunk, Pontius said nothing; a smile was his only form of recognition till his thirst had been satisfied. He was *in loco parentis* to Lucullus and Julia, whose father, being a senator, could not stay away from Rome for long. He had promised to make a quick visit with the children's mother in the near future, but that near future had been some time ago, and Lucullus told me that he and Julia would probably be returning to Rome with Uncle Pontius before their parents had got round to coming out to Judea.

I tried not to think of that time, hoping it would never happen, that somehow the three of us would be able to carry on as we were, regardless of the world beyond ours.

The day after Jesus' death, I was playing in the garden with Lucullus. Julia was reading a scroll, rather self-consciously lifting it up occasionally to show us that she was engrossed in it and needed to raise it against the sun to decipher an unclear word. Sarda stepped into the garden and gestured to us to come indoors. Lucullus and I obeyed at once, Julia paused to

11

roll the scroll carefully and tie it round with a purple cord.

"I need to be entertained. I thought perhaps you would play to me, Julia, and you boys can sit with me and tell me later what you have learned today." Pontius was flushed, his large face smooth and with sweat lining a crease just below his lower lip. "I have had a difficult day," he went on, "justice is as tiresome to administer as it is tiring. By the gods I want to forget justice for the rest of the day." He sighed, as a slave handed Julia a lute. She began to play, the melody of plashing water, and Pontius, smiling at her, called for Sarda to fan him.

"How I would like a cool posting for a change – I find this heat boring. Though perhaps not as unpleasant as it can be to criminals." He smiled at me, and there was something about the smile I found discomfiting. "I understand, Nathaniel, that you went to Golgotha yesterday evening with a pitcher of orange juice for the prisoners I condemned to death."

My stomach felt hollow. "Yes, Sir."

He sighed again. "It is often kinder to be callous than concerned, Nathaniel. Nobody likes to see suffering, least of all myself, but it cannot be regarded in isolation, only in the context of why it is being inflicted.

"A man doomed to die and suffering from thirst during the dying, will be put out of his misery sooner than a man suffering from thirst and given something to drink so that the agony is prolonged. I believe the centurion on guard mentioned that to you." He sighed again, a man bearing all the tribulations of the world. "Do you understand what I have told you, Nathaniel?" I hesitated before answering; he did not ask me why, and if he had I would probably have not been able to answer him.

Instead: "How did you reach the men to give them a drink?" asked Lucullus, as Julia continued to play softly and Pontius smiled fondly at her and sipped his wine as the slave girl dabbed at his chin.

"There was a ladder nearby which I managed to prop up against a cross. Just after I reached the top the ladder slipped and I nearly dropped the pitcher. I had to save myself by grabbing at Jesus, and gashed my hand on the crown of thorns."

Lucullus laughed, and Pontius added plaintively: "I didn't sentence the man Jesus to wear a crown of thorns. That was an extra humiliation thought up by the crowd. Why did they have to be so vindictive – isn't justice enough for them?"

"I'm not sure exactly what justice is, Uncle Pontius," said Lucullus.

Pontius gave another of his sighs. "Neither am I, dear nephew." He settled himself more comfortably against the cushions and closed his eyes.

Augus Semiramus, our tutor, was a tall, thin, doleful artist whose father had been a Recorder to the Senate. According to Augus his father had been learned but timid, a man who never courted trouble and was always surprised at some new depth of perfidy dreamed up by those jousting for political influence so as to attract the baleful eye of the emperor. Nevertheless he had been killed in a back street brawl, and his body never recovered from wherever it had been taken—Augus had heard unsettling rumours that his father's corpse had been sold to Scana Decatus, Caesar's senior cook, to be fed to Tiberius' lampreys to improve their succulence and flavour. Usually they were fed on live slaves.

Although they were risking the caprice of a tyrant, the place-seekers were confident of their value in his eyes, and that he would regard their political and administrative skills as more important than their potential as his playthings. They were not always right.

With the ghoulish curiosity of children we pressed Augus to tell us about the Court of Tiberius, and demanded to know if it were true that one of his pleasures was to ply his male guests with wine and then, before they had time to relieve themselves, command his slaves to tie their penises with cord and watch them till their bladders swelled up and burst.

Augus started to tremble and begged us not to mention such things, so we naturally concluded that the rumours were correct. Certainly the name of Tiberius inspired as much fear among the Romans as the Romans did among their vassals, and yet there was to me something exciting about being accepted by Pontius' family, a sense of being central to things.

In addition to Greek and Latin our curriculum included history, divinity, architecture and arithmetic and the basic elements of civil administration. We learned also grammar and elocution, and practised oratory and rhetoric. Lucullus and I pretended to be senators, and made impassioned speeches about the wine we had just drunk or the food we had eaten, praising or blaming its quality – although we did not do the latter in the hearing of the kitchen slaves and their overseers, the chief of whom was called Celina, a fearsome woman of Gaul, whom Pontius had bought from a legionnaire who had captured her and brought her to Rome. She had biceps like thighs and the temper of a leopard.

Pontius had felt safe in making her a freedwoman, as Gaul was a long way away and she could only return by ship. She was tolerably happy in her authority, and looking back I suspect she must have been bedding Augus, perhaps the reason he was so thin and apparently a prisoner of melancholy.

Sometimes I was invited to accompany Pontius' entourage when he visited his seaside home in Caesaria, on the shore of the Mediterranean. It was a large white villa, crouching behind tall, slender columns like the bars of an elegant prison. There was a narrow white beach in front of the house, and a barge with a gold-tasselled canopy and room for a dozen oarsmen each side lay beside a jetty.

Pontius could be Roman in his rigour, but on these occasions was usually content to let the slaves ply their oars to the rhythm of the overseer's gong without having them struck with a whip to encourage them. Sometimes Pontius even gave them a goblet of wine, a practice we could see greatly displeased the overseer.

When we drew into shallow water near the beach the slaves would ship their oars whilst we children jumped into the sea, wearing loincloths, and splashed each other.

Lately, I had been embarrassed, not by the risk of my excitement being noticed by Julia, but of displaying my condition to Lucullus. She looked at me sideways with a sly smile; instinct told me he would disapprove of the effect his sister had on me.

After we had finished bathing we frolicked about on the beach while Celina and her underlings set out our provisions on linen cloths. Pontius was rowed ashore in a small boat with rugs and cushions which were arranged by a slave for his comfort – his wife, Aurelia, never came with us, disliking the sun and everything else. She could grumble like a Pharisee and seemed to have been inflicted on Pontius as a sort of permanent punishment. I seldom saw her, as she liked to hold court in her own rooms, enjoying her status as First Lady of the province while the slaves served her gossiping guests.

My father thought I was associating too much with the family, and warned me gently that no matter how close our friendship seemed to be, the Romans did not make real friends of those they had subjugated, and never forgot they were the masters, not hesitating to discard those who ceased to amuse them.

I therefore gave nobody in my family a hint of my growing passion for Julia. It was not only the Romans who discarded people; the Jews did not hesitate to forbid their children to associate with anyone they deemed unsuitable.

I knew my father would shortly take me along on one of his journeys and start my training in business, which would effectively cause a long interruption in my relationship with Julia, which I dreaded.

Chapter 3

After the disruption caused by the Jesus episode and its aftermath, the Temple reverted to its usual practices. The money-changers shouted and clamoured for business, the Pharisees behaved as arrogantly as before and spoke angrily of the disciples, who now called themselves apostles and kept alive Jesus' claim of sovereignty and godhead.

Now and again these apostles and those who believed their stories of the resurrection of Jesus and his address to them enraged Pontius to the extent that he would affront the whole Jewish community by having coins with pagan symbols minted and distributed. He compelled the money-changers to deal in them, and also hung images of the emperor on the walls and sacred places of Jerusalem.

Sometimes, when I grew older, I wondered if I should have warned Pontius about antagonising the Jews and their leaders, but I have no doubt that if I had he would have been angry enough to forbid me his house.

As it was, the governor's provocations were to prove a significant factor in his downfall, for the Jews discovered that Pontius owed his governorship to a patron called Sejanus, a favourite of Tiberius. When Sejanus became a victim of his master's caprice, the Jews seized on Pontius' vulnerability and avenged themselves on him for his insults by reporting his actions to Rome. They accused him additionally of executing an illegal death sentence on Jesus and this destroyed him, for the Romans wanted to rule without strife and also believed in punishment of guilt through association.

I personally did not believe that Jesus had been more than a teacher and prophet, a messiah in other words, and my visits to the Temple with my parents did nothing to reduce my religious scepticism, for I found the God of Israel just as difficult to accept. Over the years I was to become convinced that he was simply Celestial Box Office, the Invisible Ruler who disdained to give any proof of his existence.

Observance of the Sabbath and the prayers which were dispatched like lances towards the Temple roof seemed to me a complete waste of piety and time, as the prayers were never answered. Sick children continued to die, and when I prayed beside my father for the life of my desperately sick mother, both of us blinded by tears, those prayers were answered, after many hours, by a dreadful rattle deep in my mother's throat as she tried to reach out to us in a final gesture of love. That attempt at benediction had a quality of poignancy I have never encountered in a professional prayer house, it is the only time I have ever felt really blessed. God, on the other hand, had at the moment of her dying cursed me by being deaf to my prayers, and my rage at him for that only subsided when I ceased utterly to believe there was such a being.

Even before the death of my young and loving mother, the official words of praise in the Temple had struck me as sycophantic and in conflict with what I suppose was my arrogant self-respect – I have never been good at grovelling. Self-respect, I had been taught by my father, was the best defence against oppression, and it seemed to me that God was more oppressive than the Romans, and in his way demanded far more. It was not simply a question of rendering unto Caesar what was Caesar's and unto God what was God's; what was Caesar's was claimed by God too.

Half drunk with incense, trying to believe in the God my parents believed in, I sat next to my father on the hard wooden bench and stared at the Tabernacle, wondering what it must be like to be God. Could he really respect this congregation, all his congregations, praising him and crediting him with all power? I thought such abject and overwhelming praise was more likely to make Jehovah impatient with his worshippers rather than want in any way to comfort or reward them.

Surely too, those who administered God's decrees should be in some way in the image of God? It was difficult to attribute any such quality to the cantor, for instance, who had a face like a goat, with a pure high voice coming out of a fledgling's mouth set in a straggly nest of beard which twitched assent to each expression of worship. The men of the congregation sat together, pure in their gender, whilst the women remained apart—menstruation risked defiling the men and nullifying their prayers. The cantor performed solo in cabritic splendour, face powdered with dust mites in the intrusive sun.

The Temple was a place of torment in various ways, not only the sitting and standing and repetitious orisons, but also the flies. The flies of Judea had hot feet, and clung to the skin as if the insects too were pleading for favours. Now and again an especially strong smell of ordure was wafted in from outside, fighting the incense and sweat for our nostrils' attention. A camel went mad on one occasion and dashed into the Temple with its owner in pursuit; it snapped at a man sitting near the Tabernacle, its great yellow teeth shining in the candlelight as he screamed, then dashed on its way, saliva trailing behind it, the cantor too outraged and frightened to protest till the beast had stumbled through the doorway into the dusty street.

Unfortunately we did not enjoy such distractions very often, and I took refuge in my imagination again, about what it might be like to be God.

Why did he inhabit such unlikely places? Couldn't he have found more congenial accommodation, for instance, than a burning bush? And what did it feel like to be surrounded by the frantic pulsing of a human heart? I found God's evil practical joke on Abraham and Isaac shocking, and could not forgive him for it. What was the point? He had proved Abraham's love and obedience without considering the hatred he must have engendered in Isaac for his father, for how could a son forgive his father for loving anyone more than himself, let alone for agreeing to murder him to prove that love?

Was it lack of self-confidence that impelled God to keep proving his supremacy, or was it simply egotistical malice?

As with so much else, it was far easier to ask the question than to find the answer.

Chapter 4

It was a Judean afternoon, gaudy with sunlight, at Pontius' house. We had just eaten, and were relaxing during what Pontius called the *hora post prandia*. As usual, Aurelia had not joined us; she evidently preferred other company, no doubt her own, as there was no sign of any visitors. Pontius was lying back on his divan and feeling benevolent. When Pontius felt benevolent, he often went in for gentle teasing, but with Pontius you never knew. Behind the jest, there was often a touch of malice.

Today he looked at me with his eyes half shut, sweat as usual glistening on his chin just beneath his lower lip. A slave girl dabbed at it with a linen cloth, and went off with her trophy.

"Tell me, Nathaniel, why do your people so rigorously maintain that to eat pork and shellfish is to offend your God? Do you think he peers down from above and shakes his head and curses you if you swallow an oyster or taste the succulence of a sucking-pig?" Lucullus and, to my chagrin, Julia, took up the question. "Yes, why do the Jews not eat such delicacies?"

"Perhaps your god is offended by such things because he has no stomach," suggested Lucullus

"That is perhaps why he is a god who cannot be seen," added Julia. "I would certainly not like to be seen if I had no stomach."

"And where does food go if you do not have one? Straight on to the floor? How difficult that would be—one would have to have a slave with a golden trowel in attendance all the time." Lucullus chuckled.

21

I knew perfectly well why there were dietary laws against eating pork and shellfish – in Judea it was common sense not to eat food which could kill. I had seen a tape worm ooze out of a man's mouth after he had ignored those laws and spent days in agony with stomach cramps, but I could not understand why they had to be part of our religion. My later experience convinced me that the mixing of dietary law with holy law was unacceptable, for once religion is involved in custom dissension is sure to follow.

Still smiling but remorseless, Pontius went on: "Don't you like pork, Nathaniel?"

"I don't know, Sir. I have never tasted it."

"Of course you have, boy. You've just had it for lunch. " He roared with laughter, as did his niece and nephew.

Pontius went on to tell us how great civilisations may be judged by the way their leaders fart. In Rome, for instance, the public lavatory available to Senators was lined with marble and warmed by central heating. There were comfortable couches to stretch out on after the bathe in the nearby pool which followed the morning's mass peristalsis, which induced a feeling of companionship.

"A man who has just emptied himself likes to share his sense of wellbeing with others who have done likewise," Pontius told us, "and the pleasure of the emptying is enhanced if the surroundings are aesthetically enjoyable.

"We void ourselves in the annexes to bathhouses which are heated during the winter and display fine marine figures of dolphins. Good food deserves comfortable disposal." Something as natural as defecation had been changed by oligarchic Romans into a rite. Slaves paced considerately among their masters with amphorae of wine and trays of goblets, whilst others dried the senators' glistening bodies and arrayed them with crisp fresh togas.

This, Pontius explained, was the hour of gossip, before the time of serious debate began in the nearby Forum, and the noisy strife between reluctant bowel movement and colonic insistence had died down.

"Speaking of gossip," Pontius went on slyly, "it was said at the Dolphins by some who know him that our Emperor, who of course is also a god, resents having to defecate, for defecation is the great leveller. Apparently – and of course I am only quoting—Tiberius feels that his godhead is diminished by having to engage in it. Because of that he hates even having to succumb to the mortal frailty of passing wind."

Pontius started to laugh. "The Emperor, it is maintained, resents the whole post-digestive process. He told a friend of his that he suspected Jupiter did not have to go through it, which made Tiberius himself feel like a lesser god. Next day, when he realised how much he had confided in his friend, he had him slain, but by then the story had got out".

Foolhardy men who had heard the story had inevitably embroidered it, saying that Tiberius tried to console himself by maintaining that rain was Jupiter urinating, and added that thankfully there was no meteorological equivalent of what the god-Emperor was doing as he squatted above his gilded *cloaca.*

Because he was always in a bad temper when defecating, Pontius went on with sublime and, as it turned out, fatal indiscretion. It was believed by his courtiers that Tiberius regarded his Defecatorium as the ideal place to contemplate the imposition of a death sentence or some amusing atrocity with which to regale himself. In fact he sometimes summoned a slave with a *stela,* or for greater pleasure a senior member of his household, to record his orders as, with accompanying bursts of intemperate thunder, he emitted clouds of imperial stench.

As Pontius turned on his side and began to snore, there was a shriek from the distant slave quarters and the sound of a blow, followed by Aurelia calling for the giant slave Sarda. She came in, pulling a slave girl by her hair. Sarda was not far behind.

"Flog her!" commanded Aurelia, releasing the girl's hair and almost throwing her into Sarda's arms.

"Must you wake me up?" Pontius glared at her. "Whatever the girl's done doesn't warrant your screeching like a fishwife."

Aurelia returned the glare. "She broke my mother-of- pearl mirror! The clumsy slut just dropped it."

The girl, terrified, said nothing.

"I have enough of physical violence every day," grumbled Pontius. "Show the girl some mercy."

"Mercy?" Aurelia was outraged. "That was my favourite mirror! Go, take her and do not let me see he again until she is well blooded!" she again commanded Sarda.

Sarda dragged the girl out, almost carrying her.

"Now can I get back to sleep?" Pontius closed his eyes again.

Aurelia transferred her glare to me. "Why do you come here so often, boy? Is your own home not comfortable? Do your mother and father starve you, that you are always here? I do not like a Jew being treated as part of my family. You are our subjects, not our equals!"

I had never hated anyone before, but I hated Aurelia then. I had to turn my head away, otherwise she would have been speared by my hatred and forbidden me the house there and then.

"He is our friend, Aunt," Julia said.

Her defence of me made up for her joining in the teasing of me earlier. I loved her as much as I hated Aurelia.

"Friend!" snorted Aurelia, "Romans do not take subject peoples as friends!"

"At least they do not keep us awake," Pontius said, eyes still shut. "Leave explosions to Etna and Vesuvius, in the name of Jupiter!"

Aurelia flounced out; as she went through the archway we heard the screams of the slave girl she had ordered Sarda to flog, and the sinister slapping sound of a heavily wielded strap. It was only much later that I discovered that Sarda had been merciful, and that the strap had been applied to a table as the girl screamed realistically to its rhythm.

"I'd better go," I said. Aurelia had spoiled the atmosphere, and put my future visits in doubt. I was near to tears, because whatever happened, I would never feel as comfortable and as at home as before, and I had been humiliated irrevocably in front of the two people I valued most, apart from my parents.

"Come again tomorrow, Nathaniel." Lucullus was smiling. "It is not for Aunt Aurelia to say who comes here and who is banished."

"Thank you, Lucullus." I embraced him and walked through the archway into the atrium. Behind me I heard a loud fart, and a peal of laughter from Julia.

"Uncle Pontius is dreaming of dolphins," she called to me. She had come to stand in the archway; she smiled at me and waved, her high-cheek-boned face framed by her glossy hair. She had the effulgent beauty of a full moon. "*Vale.*"

Lucullus appeared beside her. "*Vale,*" he echoed, "don't worry about Aunt Aurelia. You are under our protection. You are our little Judean province."

I had to continue coming to this house, which, with Julia and himself, had become an integral part of my life, but at his final words I felt demeaned.

Chapter 5

One of the most memorable things about my ancient childhood was the inflexibility of the prevailing culture. There was humour and there was a wry sense of perspective that was forever being frustrated by circumstances— after all, we were an occupied country. However, the framework of society was rigid, as though God and the Gorgon were one, petrifying us.

Those were harsh and unforgiving days when the lonely call of the jackal in the desert arced at night over the urban babble of a Roman-dominated provincial society, speaking vulgar Latin, Greek and Aramaic.

The harsh profiles of the bearded and authoritarian leaders of the Sanhedrin signified little alongside the impressive silhouettes of our Roman occupiers; it was the emperors whose visages decorated the coinage, the emperors whose engraved heads peered into every personal recess, loitered on every dresser, spied on every relationship as a lover's purse was opened. Those heads seemed alive, their eyes as all-seeing as the God of the Hebrews.

Even though the heads of the Caesars were minted in metal, whereas our god was minted in men's imagination, who was to say which gods were the more powerful: the invisible and abstract who reigned in an invisible place among the stars, or those who lived in our purses and governed our economy?

When we paused in the bazaar to buy something, the emperor paused with us. One could not escape that all-seeing gaze, and it was impossible not to respect and be in awe of the severe and in a way beautiful profile of a Caesar. Hail Caesar and his faithful servant, Pontius

Pilate, Governor of Judea, who did not understand that, no matter how powerful a governor may be, he owed allegiance to Caesar, and that if there is one person superior to us, it is that person who is sovereign, not the subject, no matter how exalted. It is the sovereign alone, or those acting in his name, who has the ultimate power of life and death.

That was what Pontius forgot.

Chapter 6

Not long after my *Bar Mitzvah*, when a few months after my thirteenth birthday I officially and ceremoniously entered the world of manhood, I arrived at the Governor's house and realised at once that something was wrong.

There was nobody at work in the garden, and beyond the silent atrium the room where Pontius loved to lie beside the fountain, was empty. Even the fountain seemed lacking in exuberance, its water rising wearily, to fall back even before it had reached its crest.

The smell of apprehension was in the air too, sour and feral as the stink of a caveman. I began to feel apprehensive myself, and sick at the thought of what might have befallen the family.

Pontius came into the room. The sweat was not only on his chin; the whole of his face seemed to be liquid, and I could tell from his eyes that he was fearful.

"Nathaniel, this is not a good time for you to be here. I do not want to seem discourteous but you must leave now." He sank on to the divan but did not lie back, and no slave came to attend him. I could hear the voices of women in the distance, their words indistinct but their tone clear in its dismay.

"Are Julia and Lucullus in good health, Sir?"

"We shall all be leaving tomorrow. Now go, boy."

Manhood was no armour against tears, and the atrium shimmered with them as I made my way out. I was in emotional shock, utterly unprepared to lose the two people who had become so dear to me, and with one of whom I was falling in love.

She was waiting for me in the garden. "We have to leave tomorrow, Nathaniel."

"Your uncle has just told me. Why, what has happened?"

A bird burst into inappropriately happy song.

"Lucius Aelius Sejanus has just been put to death."

"Who ?"

"Uncle Pontius' friend and protector, the Praetor Sejanus. Apparently a conspiracy has been discovered to murder a number of eminent citizens, including the husband of Sejanus' mistress Livilla."

I gaped at her. "What does that have to do with you and your uncle?"

"The husband of Sejanus' mistress is Drusus, one of the sons of Tiberius. Now do you understand?

"And not only that," she went on, "Sejanus is accused of plotting to overthrow Tiberius and take over the Empire. So because of Uncle Pontius' relationship with Sejanus we too are suspected of being disloyal and subversive". She looked at me angrily. "It is all so unjust!

"So now we have to return at once to Rome, and perhaps die ourselves. I do not want to die!"

"Die? You die?" I was appalled. She had spoken in a fury, but beneath it I could sense that she was as afraid as her uncle, and desperately I took her into my arms and hugged her.

"Caesar is vengeful. I only recall meeting Lucius Aelius once, and then for less than a full afternoon, but Uncle Pontius knew him well, and we are Pontius' family. Our father is his brother, and being a senator will prove rich prey for Tiberius' suspicions." She bit her lips. "We are all likely to be purged."

"Then you must not go back!"

"And add rebellion to our other offences? The boat sent to fetch us is waiting at Antioch, and the order recalling Uncle Pontius was delivered by a praetor, who rode up to the house with half a dozen cataphracts." She managed to smile. "You should have seen how their armour weighed down their labouring horses. They are camped nearby, pretending to be an honour guard, but of course in reality we are their captives."

I tried to draw again on my newly attained manhood. "I can hide you and Lucullus somewhere. My father —" but I knew as I spoke that my father would never agree to risk our lives by hiding two Roman fugitives in our house.

"There is nothing to be done, Nathaniel. There, look!" A cataphract had ridden up and was staring through the archway at us. He was a big man on a black horse and was wearing a helmet with a red crest. His face was not that of a Roman, for his nose was short and turned up, and his head square; he was probably a locally recruited barbarian.

The sound of more hooves approached, and we realised that the house was surrounded.

"You had better go before they force you to come with us. Pray to that strange invisible god of yours for our survival, Nathaniel."

"I'll come to Rome and find you," I babbled. "I love you, I won't let them harm you."

She put her hands on my shoulders and without warning kissed me on the mouth with brief chaste passion, before she walked into the house without looking back.

I watched the slaves loading Pontius' furniture into oxcarts, their great wheels digging into the sandy dust as the axles creaked under the weight of couches and silver and gold artefacts. There were bronze and marble statues and figures carved in ivory, ebony, marble, and onyx, and piles of linen and silken robes and vestments. One cart after another was filled and set off on its squealing way, as if the axles were protesting on behalf of Uncle Pontius and his family at the injustice of being accused of abetting another's crimes.

The family appeared next, Aurelia and Pontius in litters borne by strapping Nubian slaves supervised by Sarda. Lucullus and Julia were on ponies. The only notice taken of me was a bitter look from Aurelia, as if I were to blame for her misfortune.

Behind the family came the cataphracts, armour glittering remorselessly, horses sweating and blowing dust from their nostrils. A Roman eagle glared angrily from its perch on top of a standard carried by one of the horsemen. It seemed ironical to me in such circumstances that Pontius belonged to the order of equestrian Knights, the Pontii, hence his family name.

I watched in despair as, riding straight-backed, Julia and Lucullus disappeared into the dust. One of the cataphracts turned and gave me a sinister grin, as if daring me to do something rash, then contemptuously spat before looking again to his front.

The small, poignant cavalcade turned the corner, and I stumbled home.

Chapter 7

It was the Sabbath. I sat beside my father in the Temple, wishing more than ever that I could confide in him my feelings about Julia, and the depth of my sorrow and apprehension. He smelled as usual of the unguents in which he traded, his eyes concealed behind hooded closed lids as he prayed.

It was by now common knowledge that Pontius had been recalled to Rome in disgrace, and the Pharisees particularly were gloating about it. Anything that caused any sort of fissure in the Roman administration of the province called for rejoicing, and Pontius' unwise goading of the population had aroused general resentment.

The prayers, irrelevant to my feelings, echoed through the building, which resounded with the Thirteen Articles of Faith:

"Extol the living God! His praises sound!
Whose being unbegun no time can bound,
A unity is He, beside Him none."

Surely He could help. My father, my uncles, the rest of this huge congregation, were devout in their belief in the might and comfort of God – why couldn't I be? Surely I was infected with Roman arrogance, but even the Romans were humble before their gods and prayed to them as all here were praying.

So I prayed in my mind: Dear All-Powerful God, Help Julia and Lucullus who are in such danger. Please rescue them and enable me to see them again soon." I saw in my mind Julia's face, her smile, the swan's curve of her neck, the way she held her lyre and caressed it

33

like a lover. Like a lover! I longed to be caressed by her as she caressed that instrument, and felt an immediate sexual response. Passion was the music her caress would arouse in me, and the desire which without warning surged through me obliterated my own prayers and those going on about me, overcoming and erasing the cantor's chant.

I longed to sing to Julia The Song of Solomon, but my throat was too dry to sing anything, and anyway she was not here, but on her way to an irresolute and perhaps fatal destiny.

I turned my face from my father so that he would not sense my anguish, and continued to pray silently for Julia's deliverance from the encompassing vengeance of Tiberius.

Chapter 8

The Dolphins Building on East 84th and Lexington was my latest contribution to the Manhattan skyline. Pontius' references to the public lavatory in which senatorial defecation occurred whilst gossiping and discussing the policies of the Empire had amused me, and as over the centuries I created my banks and trading companies, I used the word 'dolphins' as their title and distinguishing feature. When trademarks came in, my dolphins logo was one of the earliest.

My penthouse was designed by me to have powerful links with my early history, a sentimental nostalgia for old Judea. It rests on top of the Dolphin Building, which houses a number of my companies.

The mosaic floors keep the place cool in the summer heat; I do not like the chill of air conditioning which seems impossible to adjust to a comfortable temperature.

I lie on divans whose silk covering reminds me of the bales of the material which my father brought back from Samarkand, and whose shape is like those on which Pontius would lie, his greasy chin being cleaned by a slave girl as Julia's lute plashed softly.

I stopped speaking into my computer a little while ago to stare out over the East River and try to bring back the taste of Caesarian wine. Rough as emery paper, it scorched the gullet as one drank it, and had a bouquet that owed much to mildew, but at the same time it tasted of sand and sunlight and, I suppose, of childhood.

Chapter 9

My father was a man of courage. Although oriental luxuries that made sybarites of all who could afford them had long been discovered and exploited by merchants and traders, journeys to the sources of supply could take weeks or months through terrain hostile in both geography and population.

Like the Roman army, traders often employed barbarians to protect their caravans; such men were brave and aggressive fighters, and excellent horsemen. Sometimes nip and tuck operations would be mounted by bandits against the returning columns of camels which were often a mile long, and could consist of a thousand beasts or more, an armada of slowly pacing, gently rocking cargo vessels, accompanied by attentive crews.

I had never felt comfortable round camels, especially after the incident in the Temple, but of course I could never admit to any apprehension. Riding a camel was a vital part of my education, and I had first been placed on one when I was about four. Held on its back by one of our Persian dragomen as it rested on the ground, I grabbed his hand tightly as he spoke to it and applied a thong to its ragged haunch, whereupon in a series of angular and contradictory movements it unfolded itself and lurched to its feet.

The arrogance of the camel matched that of the legionary; camels expressed disdain by spitting in one's eye. Perhaps they knew by instinct that without them, the Silk and Spice Roads to Samarkand and far beyond would probably not have come into existence.

My father took everything literally in his stride, being a fine rider of both camel and horse. He had a piratical face, with a high- bridged nose and large dark eyes. Even now I remember my pride at riding on his saddle, perched in front of him as he scrutinised the landscape. "Look over there, Nathaniel, what do you see?"

I squinted in the remorseless sunlight, raw on the brilliant rocks. "I can only see the cave, Father," afraid that I was letting him down. There was movement beside the cave-mouth. "There's an animal, – I think it's a jackal."

"It is indeed a jackal, Nathaniel, and tomorrow it may be a lion. Or bandits. Always be ready for anything, my son."

"I will, Father."

White teeth above his black beard. "Good. What about up there?"

I raised my head to follow the pointing finger. "A boulder on the hillside, Father."

"And what is sitting on the boulder?"

"I can't see anything sitting there, Father."

"It was a vulture," he said, as a big bird flapped into the brazen air. "That could have been a lookout, Nathaniel. Remember – always be ready for anything. Observe with your eyes and also with your mind. Never accept what seems to be there, always make sure you know too what is hidden." His smile, his hand ruffling my hair.

My father had two brothers, Elijah and Saul. Elijah was in charge of administering the business and its finances, and to his credit realised that whereas slaves could keep costs down to a minimum, they in fact

37

were a false economy. Slaves kept those who would have enjoyed work from employment, and having no money, further paralysed the money supply, which was largely thrombotic. Instead of circulating it collected in turgid lakes, which never passed from one sector of the population to another.

The slave was below everyone else, society resting immovably on top of him. The social strata were fossilised, and this stasis was not beneficial to the state. Uncle Elijah therefore never employed slaves. "The Children of Israel were slaves – how then could we inflict slavery on others? If anyone thinks slavery is not an affliction to men's consciences, come and try to explain that view to me. No slaves."

Elijah was a gentle man, and no fool, and his gentleness could evaporate in outrage if he felt he had been taken advantage of, or if his philosophy conflicted with others' perceived reality.

"I'll kick you on the ankle, Nathaniel," was his gravest threat, and he laughed as he said it, or if I scratched my arse in his presence, he would ask: "Got something in your eye, boy?"

Saul was quite different, an uncle I could never quite bring myself to like, though as he was my father's brother I suppose I felt some love for him. He was our architect and building administrator. It was his task to design and set up our entrepôts, the great warehouses in Antioch, Tyre and other ports which we were adding to our distribution locations all the time.

Uncle Saul combined a sense of personal vulnerability with extreme distrust of everyone else's motives, seeming to be suspicious of even his brothers on occasion. He spent his life negotiating with builders and labourers, and poring over scrolls of papyrus covered with drawings and figures.

His offices were hard by the Temple, and when confronted with some logistical or arithmetical problem that seemed beyond resolution, he would leave his scrolls in the care of his wife Ruth, almost the only person he trusted completely, and go to the Temple to pray for guidance.

Saul and Elijah loved to argue, and it had become a convention that when my father had had enough of their sparring, he would decide what to do and they would agree.

When he announced, not long after the removal of Julia and her family, that we were going to Greece to develop our business, Uncle Saul at once suggested that the African shores of the Mediterranean might offer better trading possibilities. As I was on fire to leave for Greece in the idiotic hope that we might somehow intercept Julia and Lucullus, I was filled with hatred at that moment of Saul, who of course was immediately contradicted by Elijah.

"Sailing to Greece gives us a much wider, if more competitive market. Carthage has never recovered from its defeat by the Romans, and Cyrene offers little but sand." He looked at my father, who smiled approvingly. "The northern shore of the Mediterranean gives us access to Cyprus, Crete, Comagene and Pamphylia," he went on, "and beyond those the other trading routes which have been in use for centuries, to Ostia, Rome, Spain, Tarraconensis and Gaul."

"Of course, no one is disputing that," put in Saul, at once disputing it, "but the potential of trading along the African littoral—"

As usual, my father put an end to the argument. "We are going to Greece, Saul. If you wish to trade along the north coast of Africa, please do so. All I ask is that the money you invest in the venture be your own."

Uncle Saul showed little enthusiasm for this suggestion, and gave his usual grunt of acquiescence in my father's decision.

A few days later I was doing my best to ride, rather than simply cling to its hump, a white camel my father had selected for me, a female of arrogant beauty and, for a camel, reasonable disposition. We set off for Antioch in the heavy grasp of morning.

Chapter 10

Just outside Antioch was a vast caravanserai, which could accommodate several camel trains at once. In its huge courtyard the supply carts spent their days, as the Romans would only allow cities to be provisioned by them at night, owing to the immense congestion they caused in daytime streets.

Horses, oxen, flocks and herds of animals ruminated over fodder as though meditating on the most profound questions of the universe, whilst encamped beside them were their masters, men of every race and inclination, Syrian grain merchants, Phoenicians, piratical-looking like my father, Greeks, Phrygians, the dark, angry-looking people of Pannonnia, fair-skinned, taller travellers from north of the Danube.

My ears hummed with these languages of Babel, supplemented by the bellowing of cattle and baaing of sheep, and the occasional roar of a bull camel, while my nostrils could scarcely cope with the reek of ordure, human sweat, urine, and general waste.

My father was building our own serai alongside our new warehouses, in the port area. Here carts and camels were unloaded by swarms of porters, drivers and bystanders ready to earn a few drachma. They worked until dark, when my father's clerks paid them off and they disappeared until the morning, perhaps to enjoy the vice and degradation whose scent had reached out to us when we were still quite a distance from the city. I knew that Antioch was the third largest city in the Empire, after Rome and Alexandria, and had a reputation for depravity. The very word stimulated my imagination, so far nurtured on innocence.

We settled down to cook spiced lamb over wood fires whose scent helped overcome the offensive smells of nature and settled down to sleep, cloaks covering us against the bitter desert cold which had replaced the heat of day.

I lay on the edge of sleep, listening to a silence that was never entirely unbroken; a camel's snort, a woman's distant laughter. I had already seen women black-eyed with kohl move aside their veils to smile at my father and me as we rode at the head of our caravan; my father had stared straight ahead, affecting not to have noticed them, but I could not help a surge of lust at their hint of lascivious promise, and lust kept me awake as I tried to quell it.

As soon as dawn broke, legions of porters reappeared to start toting the bales of goods down to the two ships which my father had chartered for the next stage of our journey. As he and I went down the steps to the quayside, a man in a grubby, tattered cloak and disintegrating sandals hurried to stand in front of us.

"Greetings. Do you go to Greece?"

"We do." My father held his head back like an Assyrian and fastened his intense black eyes on the man. The stranger looked straight back into my father's.

"I seek passage, Sir."

"Have you money?"

The man lifted his upper lip in a grin that was also a sneer. "I was once as rich as you no doubt are. I gave up all I had to follow the Way."

"A man should not give up all he has to follow anything, if having given it up he has to ask a favour from someone who has kept what he has."

"I am a Christian," the stranger said defiantly. "I wish to enter the Kingdom of Heaven."

"And whereabouts on the map is Heaven?" asked my father.

"You mock me, Merchant."

"I do not mock you, but wherever Heaven is, you presumably need money to get there."

"The whole point of Heaven is that it is the poor and humble who are welcome there, not the rich and arrogant."

"I am not especially arrogant, I think. But I am conscious of the fact that you are asking me for money in order to reach a place where being without it is a virtue."

The man's eyes were lambent in dark sockets. He looked tired and ill-fed, and I wondered if it had been Jesus and his preachings that were responsible for his condition. If so, Jesus was either as expert in rhetoric as any Roman senator, or the stranger was excessively gullible to allow himself to be effectively swindled.

"You may not be a believer now, but you shall believe. One day, as Our Lord said, the meek shall inherit the earth."

"And what would they do with it?" asked my father, patient and gentle.

"Keep it for the Lord, and spread His word throughout so that all may worship God and his Son Jesus Christ."

My father turned to me. "You met Jesus Christ, didn't you, my son." He lightly emphasised the last word.

The stranger looked at me, eyes burning. "How did you meet the Lord?"

"I offered him some orange juice when he was on the cross."

"For that you will enter the Kingdom of Heaven, rich or poor. You are blessed."

"Only the God of Israel can give His blessing," said my father. "But for telling my son he is blessed, and because I would indulge in discussion with you, you may come with us to Greece."

"Thank you, Merchant," with a slight smile. "For giving me passage and for the opportunity to convert you to the path of the believer."

"I shall give up nothing to follow anyone, Teacher. Your God will have to wrench it from me."

"If it is His will, Merchant. When do you sail?"

"At dawn tomorrow."

"I shall be here. Thank you."

"What is your name?" my father asked.

"These days I am called Paul."

"Very well, Paul," staring into the avid eyes that shone like those of a bear in its cave. The man turned and walked quickly away.

"For a young man you are already rich in blessings, Nathaniel. You have God's and mine and now you have Jesus Christ's." My father ruffled my hair as he had always liked to do and we went aboard the plump, heavily laden vessel to check that all was properly loaded and secured before going to the Temple to pray for our safety at sea.

The temple at Antioch was even more informal than the one in Jerusalem. Dogs urinated against its pillars, market traders bickered with each other at the rear of the building, and someone who wanted to hawk and spit did not hesitate, even when the congregation sat silently in prayer.

Given that the merchantmen of that time were so difficult to manoeuvre, with only one main sail and sometimes an auxiliary sail on the bowsprit, prayers for safe passage were well warranted, especially if the worshipper believed they would be answered.

Our Jewish prayers tended to mix poetry, philosophy, praise of the Lord and a certain amount of chimerical natural history. We sat, heads covered, and begged for deliverance from the turbulence of the waves, the roaring of billows and the raging storm. We prayed too for 'carking care' which I understood meant that God would assume our burdens, and from 'confusion of times, and change of seasons, and from the destructive monsters that abound in the sea'.

My father was not, I believe, an especially religious man, but he prayed with ardour when it came to calling on God 'to cause a prosperous gale to issue from thy treasure-houses to guide our vessel'.

It was therefore hardly surprising that the prayers for safety at sea – and prosperous voyages – should be so conscious of shipwreck and disaster. At least it was summer – winter voyages were notoriously dangerous.

"Guard thou my soul, and deliver me; I shall not be abashed for I trust in thee." I was to see many results along the Mediterranean coasts of that trust, the hundreds of wooden marine tombs smashed to splinters.

The final philosophic touch: "And as for us, we will bless the Eternal, from now until evermore. Hallelujah."

So man blessed God, and God in answer frequently destroyed him.

Chapter 11

Paul was waiting for us the next morning. We went aboard, and made a last inspection to ensure that everything was properly secured. The boat smelled of its exotic cargo, and was low in the water under its weight. The crew were of various nationalities and colours, from blue-skinned Nubians to blue-eyed Greeks and golden-haired men from the North, who refused any man's dominance and obeyed orders for financial motives only. There were also black-eyed Phoenicians, who had sailed the seas for centuries and regarded their waters as divine.

Paul sniffed the air and helped cast off; a slight breeze inflated our sail and we began to move away from the shore.

Trading vessels of the day were almost female in shape, rounded and with slightly curved sides; perhaps that is why, in English at any rate, ships have been traditionally referred to as 'she'. We carried a few sheep and goats as provisions, and they bleated mournfully as we began to rock in the swell. The land grew distant, and the warm smell of it faded in our nostrils as salt and iodine replaced it.

As we proceeded further, we began to come across merchantmen from Alexandria and Ostia trading between the two cities.

"Egypt has the best quality wheat in the world," my father told me. "Without it Rome would go hungry, as the farms of Campania cannot produce enough to feed the growing number of people. In fact, there have been cases of generals commandeering grain ships when the city was running out of supplies."

"Some of the ships carry lions for the arena," Paul put in. "To the Romans, wild beasts are as essential for entertainment in the Circus Maximus as grain for their bellies."

"True," my father agreed, "but they also carry such cargoes as lumber, olive oil, pottery and wine. We have a few amphorae of wine and oil aboard ourselves." He gestured at the cargo stacked across the broad beam of the vessel. "Of course," he added with a smile, "one or two amphorae of wine are for our own consumption."

Paul's lips were cracked; he looked the picture of deprivation. My father poured wine into goblets and offered him one. Barely pausing to thank him, Paul raised the goblet to his lips and gulped.

I began to get used to the up and down, side to side movement of the vessel. The breeze continued warm, the sea fairly calm. More wine was distributed to the sailors, and as I looked over the blue water towards the West I thought of Julia and her family and wondered if they had yet arrived in Rome, and whether Tiberius had avenged himself on Pontius for his connection with Sejanus. The ship seemed appallingly slow, and I wished that a powerful wind would come from astern and thrust her forwards until we reached Ostia – I hated the idea of simply stopping in Greece.

"What lies beyond the horizon, Father?" I thought if I could get him to talk about Rome, I might be able to discuss going there without arousing his suspicions.

"The horizon moves with the ship, my son. Beyond our present horizon lies Cyprus, and further beyond Rhodes lies Athens. From Athens the horizon conceals Corinth, horizon after horizon moving with us towards Sicily and the cities of Rhegium and Syracuse."

"And through the Straits of Massena towards Ostia, and Rome," put in Paul. "In Rome I shall continue to spread the Word, as I shall in Athens and through the Greek islands." He was not a man who ever passed up the chance to deliver a homily.

"Geographical horizons are, however, like horizons of the spirit – who knows what new thoughts will enter our minds, unsuspected till we think them, or what awaits our spirit ? The soul too has many horizons."

My father proffered another goblet of wine. "That is so, Paul. When we have time to think we can become aware of such horizons, but most of us have little time for thought."

"There is no life without thought," Paul said sternly, "just as there is no life without feeling. Or", he added, "belief".

"Belief can be mistaken, Paul, though I agree that life is little without it."

"True, Merchant." He gave a harsh smile. "You have allowed me to join you for the voyage – should I not now take advantage of my captive audience and persuade you to share my belief in the Divinity of the Son of God, whom the Greeks call Christ?"

"No, I believe in the God of Israel instinctively and because I am a Child of Israel, and with that I am content. If you could spread a sail or calk timber you would assist us rather more than trying to impose your beliefs on us." My father spoke gently, not wishing to rebuke a guest, even a self-invited one.

"I can do both those things, and I too am a Child of Israel, as well as being a citizen of Rome."

My father was surprised. "A citizen of Rome?" Paul looked more like an escaped kitchen slave.

"Certainly. I too believed that Jesus was an impostor and liar, but it dawned on me, after I had persecuted a number of those who believed in His Truth, that they were right. Since then I have tried to atone for my cruelties and disbelief, by following His teaching and exhorting others to follow it also."

"But *we* do not have to atone for your cruelties, having not committed them," my father pointed out. "Therefore it is unfair and illogical to try to redeem yourself by insisting that we share your beliefs."

"It is neither unfair nor illogical to try to steer men towards Salvation, Merchant, to award them with redemption from sin and Eternal Life."

"Only God has Eternal Life," answered my father, "and the power to redeem man's sins."

Before Paul could reply we were hit by a burst of wind, which almost tore the sail from the mast. The boat lurched, while the sheep and goats moaned pitifully.

"We're in for a storm," Paul announced, "the sail should be furled." My father nodded, and Paul climbed the mast and, helped by two sailors, began to undo ropes and take down the sail before the increasing wind.

The sea still looked calm, although clouds began to drift across the sky towards each other in the casual manner of people congregating for a gossip. Without further warning the sun disappeared and the sea took on an urgent, heaving motion.

"I suggest we put into Cyprus," Paul said. "The storm is going to get so bad I don't think we shall weather it."

My father looked thoughtful. "You do not think our prayers for safety will be answered?"

"I think God will be more likely to help us if we help ourselves. There are so many calls on His mercy." Paul seized the steering oar which the helmsman was already barely able to control, and another powerful gust sent the vessel staggering into a trough. It began to feel as if divine vengeance rather than mercy was being shown to us. The impending sacrifices might not be burnt offerings, but to me the shouts of men and the bleating of animals conspired to turn the sea into a rolling, heaving altar on which we were prostrate.

My father seized my arm and together we managed to reach the sheltered part of the ship where the bales of goods were; I crouched down and lost my breath in the screaming gale which now filled our ears. The terrified animals were trying to rear up against their halters and began to kick the side of the vessel in their agony, and the boat bucked and spiralled as the horizon yawed and tilted.

We did not dare to tie ourselves to the ship's rails in case she sank, which seemed likely at any moment.

"Look down on us, O Lord, and quell the winds and waves that we may survive!" Paul bellowed, trying to stand and spread his arms. He was glaring upwards, angry rather than terrified, almost rebuking whichever God he was addressing rather than begging him for deliverance. "We cannot serve you, O Lord, if we are to die in this storm which you have sent!"

God did not heed him, as the winds shrieked and the vessel keeled over till the tip of her mast was almost embedded in the waves. A goat's halter broke and the animal was wrenched from the boat; it soared over us as it rode the gale like Lucifer himself before being flung forward in a butting movement into a rolling wave.

The wind screamed continuously, a universal, embracing insanity; our own shouts and cries had died away, for we could scarcely breathe. The clamour from the tormented animals had ceased as well; I couldn't believe any still lived.

It was during a moment when the wind had lost its voice that Paul yelled and pointed.

"There!" Following his outstretched arm we saw a small beach between black rocks covered with huge bursts of spray. The vessel ran straight ahead, her prow hitting the sand at right angles. A mountain of water astern hurled us forward, wrenching us partially round, then pulled us straight as it receded. We scraped backwards towards the sea and stopped.

"Quickly – haul her up the beach!" We all seized ropes and heaved as the next great wave tore into the small cove, thrusting the vessel forward so violently that one sailor was cut in half by the prow as it sheered through him. The ship lay on the beach quietly after that, as if exhausted, and the wind died down. Soon the fierce, atavistic attack by the weather had turned into the innocence of a golden afternoon.

We buried the dead man and allowed the animals to disembark so that they could recover a little, though there was no forage for them nearby.

"Bless you, Jesus, for our safe delivery." Paul had dropped to his knees on the sand.

"Blessed be the God of Israel, the Eternal is our God: the Eternal is One!" my father's prayer promptly contradicted.

They looked at each other, Paul without humour, determined to convince my father and convert him to his belief in the divinity of the man whom I had tried to solace as he hung on the cross.

"What about *our* seamanship?" demanded a Phoenician sailor. "Don't we get any credit for *our* skill? Maybe we delivered ourselves, without help from anyone else."

"What do you think about that, Paul?" asked my father.

"I think perhaps your crewmen should learn to give God the benefit of the doubt. Whatever we claim to be our skills and attributes, including our lives themselves, derived from Him in the first place."

"Jesus Christ apparently derived from Him too," my father said slily.

"God the Father, God the Son, and God the Holy Spirit."

"Three Gods instead of One? I cannot allow you that, Paul."

"Three Gods *in* One," Paul corrected.

"God is invisible," said my father, "and indivisible." There was a sudden hostility between the two men. "Get the animals back on board," my father ordered, as the crew gathered round, sensing trouble. "We'll relaunch on the high tide."

Reluctantly, terrified of repeating their experience, the surviving animals were pushed and dragged aboard and again tied to the rail, and as the waves began to lisp up the beach towards us the crew made ready to steady the ship and float her off.

It took three attempts before we lifted clear; the small bowsprit sail picked up just enough wind for us to turn about and the mainsail was unfurled and began to carry us before the breeze on our original course.

My father stood, keen-eyed as always, staring towards and beyond the horizon, and Paul stood away from him, looking slightly upward as though expecting a celestial hand to descend and pat his shoulder.

The waves were no longer crested with aggressive spray but behaved as though the sea was always calm and benign, and a school of dolphins appeared and frisked round our bows.

It was not till we reached Rhodes that we learned that Tiberius was dead.

Chapter 12

I had to renounce thoughts of going on at once to Rome. Before I could head for that city with my father's blessing I had to continue my apprenticeship with him, which meant travelling with him after Greece to Kabul, and then spending some time in Antioch. I felt I could die from impatience, and almost went to the Temple to pray that Julia had not fallen victim to Tiberius' all-encompassing malice before he died, but there was nothing I could do that would really at the present time be of any use.

It was winter, and the high mountain passes were cracking with cold. The cold brought a new brittleness to our world; it seemed that all flesh and tissue had been turned to wood. To melt snow took a fire the size of a signal beacon; a horse's eye became a minute brown pond encrusted with sedge. The cold eroded soul and spirit, turned the mind rigid; it was difficult to think of anything else, impossible to feel anything but the bitter lack of feeling.

We began to move along a narrow, icy pass through the high mountains that divided Persia from Afghanistan; we looked like cavemen on the march, a long, etiolated line of the newly dead, teeth made of frost baring themselves against our dark faces and purple lips. Everyone wore furs, and my father seemed to be sharing his with the original owner, a large bear whose huge claws reached down over his shoulders. I wore a cap and cape of wolf fur, and our muleteers and guides were swathed in sheepskin or yak hide, and in one case mountain leopard. We had exchanged our camels for mules as we began to depart from the warm lowlands, leaving them and our porters in the serai at

Samarkand. Hopefully, laden with goods, we would pick them up on our return.

My father and I rode horses at the head of the column, my father leading. The track was narrow, with a sheer drop on one side of thousands of feet to a river, which from our altitude looked like a silver cord. To our left, mountain rivulets flowed down and turned to ice, giving the sun-splintered track a surface as hard and coruscating as a diamond. The air sliced into our lungs, and the sky was empty except for the occasional eagle.

"Try not to look at the snow," my father told me, "it can blind you like the sand of the desert." The sun was reflected on the ice and the summit of the mountains glittered with it, their remoteness giving them a sort of shining chastity.

"Be especially careful here," he called again, as we sidled past a fall of rock that had almost blocked the road. A stream previously flowing over it had turned to ice as it reached the edge of the precipice.

Very slowly, my father coaxed his nervous mount round the boulders and back on to the track, and I followed as closely as I could. We were almost clear when my horse lost its footing.

For one paralysing moment we were braced at the lip of the abyss, but the horse was badly balanced. For a second, an age, it fought to remain upright before the two of us, both screaming, plummeted over the edge.

Through the wind roaring in my ears I heard my father's bellow of horror, and a second later I bounced off an outcrop. My horse was falling below me, a shrieking Pegasus whose wings had been torn off by the wind. It too bounced off an outcrop, and I heard its bones break before it hit a tree. I crashed into it, knocking it clear.

The sky was whirling like a dervish, and the river windmilled even faster as I plunged towards it.

The silver cord had changed to a frigid blue ribbon bordered by foaming lace as the water broke against rocky banks.

Just above me was my horse, pulverised by its encounters with rocks and tree; I caught a glimpse of its bloody open mouth, huge teeth, and bulging, desperate eyes.

I was about to be smashed to pieces and crushed; there was a tremendous impact and bitter, unimaginable cold immediately afterwards. Although conscious, I could feel nothing else, and in a moment or two even the sensation of cold faded. The current bore away the horse, and flung me towards rocks. There were distant shouts, and almost at once a brown, bearded face peered down at me from a small, spinning boat, like a coracle. A hand seized my arm, the boat tilted, and I was dragged ashore. My rescuer was speaking vigorously, but I couldn't understand a word.

Soon other people from the nearby village arrived, surrounding me as I lay on the flinty ground; they gesticulated at each other and pointed at me.

I felt my strength returning and managed to climb to my feet. Everyone leaped back, including my rescuer, shocked that I was still alive. There were probably a dozen men by then, and three or four children. They were all staring at me, before the adults prostrated themselves, pulling their children down beside them. They started to chant what sounded like a prayer, evidently worshipping me, so that the exaltation I was beginning to feel at having survived began to turn to embarrassment.

What remained of my horse was, I could see, beached downstream, with so many broken bones it looked like a sack. Shading my eyes, I stared upward, but the sun was so bright I could see nothing. All I could do was wait for my father, who was doubtless already mourning me. How had I survived?

The great wall of rock stretched up towards the clouds hanging high above the canyon. There had been no clouds earlier, and I wondered if, after all, I were dead, and that the clouds concealed the throne of God. Ridiculous notion—even if God existed, why should he want to reveal himself to *me*?

I felt a sudden and intense hunger, and wondered what the villagers might have to eat. I pointed to my mouth and rubbed my stomach, and the patriarch who was the headman slowly climbed to his feet.

Everyone else remained prostrate, and there was alarm on the headman's face.

Looking down, I saw through the tattered remains of the wolfskin I was wearing that I was covered in dried blood, as if I had been flayed. I knelt by the river bank and clenched my teeth against the cold as I dipped a hand in the water and did my best to wash. The headman continued to look alarmed; there were no abrasions or cuts of any kind to account for the blood— my skin was as smooth and unblemished as before the fall.

I looked at the villagers and motioned them to get up, as I gave thanks for my deliverance to the God I did not believe in.

There was movement between me and the clouds as a flight of vultures swooped and circled, shrieking in frustration as they realised that I was still alive. The horse presented a safe feast, but they were afraid to settle so near me.

I had been lucky, but could not analyse that luck. All I knew was that the air was sweet with the scent of flowers and young trees, the fragrance of life. The villagers slowly scrambled to their feet, ready to fling themselves flat again if I willed it, and I pointed to my mouth and rubbed my stomach; their new god was demanding a votive offering.

Shortly afterwards, when the people had returned to their yak-hide homes, an old man brought me a platter of fruit, and was about to kneel and place it on the ground in front of me when I took it from him. A god should not eat like a wolf, but I was ravenous, and stuffed oranges and peaches into my mouth, hardly pausing to peel the oranges in my haste. The juice poured down my throat, and I raised my arms in what I hoped they would consider a benediction.

I had been scornful of miracles and inexplicable events as attributed to the God of my people in the Temple, and had been reluctant to beg favours from a god whom I had such difficulty accepting, yet it seemed churlish, when the villagers were still eyeing me with the reverence due to a deity, not to accord my own God his due. I found myself putting on a show as an avatar, flinging my arms wide and shouting thanks for my deliverance, and for once it seemed to me that I was not simply addressing empty air.

In fact, at that moment I was convinced, briefly, that there *was* a God, that prayers actually were sometimes answered. There was a shout and my father on his horse waved at me, the animal balancing delicately on the rough rocks as it advanced. He shouted again, with incredulous, uninhibited joy.

It had taken him three days to ride down to me, never dreaming that I had survived. He looked at me disbelievingly and, as we embraced, burst into tears, his strong face convulsed with joy and wonder as, head thrown back, he shouted thanks to God, hugging me close as he did so.

He then took out his purse to reward the villagers for looking after me, but instead of accepting the money they came towards us with small gifts of pomegranates, fish and unleavened bread, which the headman put on the ground in front of us, after which he placed both hands together in salutation and bowed.

Not long afterwards, the villagers' newfound god was gone. I sat as I had done so often in childhood, between my father and the pommel of his saddle, both of us too overwhelmed to talk.

It took several days to catch up with our caravan, which my father had placed under the supervision of Mirza, our Indian dragoman, who spoke Urdu and Pushtu as well as Hebrew and Greek. I watched my father bargaining for goods in the bazaars of Kabul and later in the spice and silk markets of India, until like him I smelled of saffron and turmeric and coriander and the sacks of other spices he bought and helped load into the panniers of the animals, together with hundreds of bales of silk and packages of amber and precious stones.

We arrived back in Jerusalem four months after leaving it; during this time I became aware that my father regarded me in a subtly different way from before. There was something almost reverential in his attitude which made me feel uncomfortable. Like any child I had always wanted my parents to think well of me, but respect is desirable and reverence embarrassing.

I had overheard my father discussing my escape with Saul and Elijah, and neither scoffed when my father suggested that I owed my deliverance to some mysterious holy purpose, which might be revealed in due course.

Even the rabbi looked at me as though I were under divine protection, and the cantor sang ardently about God's mercy in saving me.

If indeed he had, I couldn't help wondering what he had in mind. After so many aeons, I still can't see the logic of it.

Chapter 13

Meanwhile my young manhood flourished on the fertilising dunghill that was Antioch. I was sixteen, nearly halfway through the normal lifespan of the times and when I arrived in that city, still a virgin. My father and Elijah had taken the risk of installing me among so many beguiling fleshpots in an effort to purge me of Julia, a big gamble. Love can be sidetracked by lust for someone else, but not necessarily obliterated. Julia was not only the focus of my love, but of my anxiety. Although I had been forced to repress it, it was as powerful as before. Even so, temptation had become irresistible.

I took a room above a sandal-maker in the *souk*. The house was small and noisy, and not far from our *serai* and new *entrepot* beside the port, where sailors left their ships in search of the pleasures unavailable on shipboard, and the taverns and girls were on hand eager to gratify it.

Any man wishing to investigate the arts of love had only to return a sidelong smile to be invited to a house where the secrets of love were slowly and with delicious agony revealed by the kohl-eyed specialists in what has been called 'unendurable pleasure indefinitely prolonged', and no matter how much a man might try to concentrate on his beloved, they tried to seduce him from all thought of her.

During the hot, sensuous days I continued to study our business and how to assess markets and make provision to supply them, how to barter and buy and, of course, how to sell. I learned too how to discover where rare things were to be had, and how to cost them. The method of presenting them was also important—

aristocratic Romans liked to buy things in a dignified way, disdaining to show emotion, no matter how excited they might be at what they thought was a bargain, or an extreme rarity.

With the abrupt collapse of day into night, I would hurry across the neighbouring roofs to that of Saphira, a *houri* who had just emerged from childhood. She confined her favours to only half-a-dozen lovers, including myself, and relished her power over us and the way she attained it. Her serpentine arabesques were carried out with unhurried grace and merciless skill.

Instead of rewarding her with her normal fee, a silver denarius which was enough to buy ten asses, I gave Saphira an occasional flask of rosewater, an amber necklace from India, or perhaps an intricately worked bejewelled bracelet from Afghanistan. She was a creature suited to rare and unusual things, fine-boned and beautiful with the grace of a Grecian wood nymph. Her cool mouth could stir me with the heat of a dragon's flame.

My thoughts of Julia refused, however, to succumb, and I was aware that I was becoming soft, and that too much time on Saphira's couch and too much wine were replacing the practical realities of life.

I was putting on weight like a eunuch, fat replacing muscle; and resolved to leave the epicene life of Antioch and go at last to Rome. Having finished my long apprenticeship I would from on now be an asset to the business.

When at last I sailed for Ostia, accompanied by three ships loaded with cargo, it was with my father's blessing.

Chapter 14

I heard Paul's voice before I saw him. He was addressing a crowd in the *pomaerium* at Ostia, the open space inside the city walls consecrated by the *pontifex,* a member of the Roman College.

Paul's gift for oratory and rhetoric dominated the crowd; he was inviting them to follow what in Roman eyes were the footsteps of anarchy, to worship a felon who had been punished with death under Roman law. I began to understand that what Paul preached was almost irrelevant—he could have created a religion of camel-worshippers and attracted large numbers of supporters. He had the power to persuade others that he spoke truth, that the crowd gathered in front of him should adopt this new religion of Christianity and the perversities and sacrifices it demanded.

Paul's God was mighty in Paul's mouth, although he was in fact a tamed God, more gentle than the traditional Hebraic God. Having allegedly been born to suffer at men's hands, he had spoken of turning the other cheek and forgiveness, instead of demanding vengeance.

Catching sight of me, Paul came up to me after his address, accompanied by several men and two women of affluence who had obviously been captivated by him. These women wore gold bracelets and one had a necklace of amber studded with rubies. She went so far as to tell Paul how much she had enjoyed his address, and what a fascinating speaker he was.

Paul glared at her and she became silent. When her companion began to speak Paul turned away from her to nod at one of the men in his entourage, who smiled at the women and suggested that, as they had appreciated Paul's speech so much, they were welcome to become Christians. All they had to do was to renounce their riches and possessions, and follow Paul's instruction in the way of spreading the Word about the living God.

The women began to edge away, their expressions a mixture of apprehension and outrage. A passionate man who was also a prophet was one thing, but neither a man nor a prophet should seriously expect them to renounce anything, or at least nothing more than their virtue.

Paul took my hand. "Greetings, Nathaniel. How is your father?"

I replied that he was well. Paul eyed me closely. "Something tells me you are here for more than trade."

"That is true." He showed no curiosity, but I felt I had to tell him about Julia. It was as if his personality acted as a vacuum, which needed to be filled by one's confidences. I began by asking him if he knew what had happened to Pontius.

"So far as I know Pilate underwent the same fate he meted out to our Lord and many others—he was crucified by Tiberius on the Appian Way. The avenue to Rome is paved with bones and in the morning the dew glistens red with the blood of our martyrs, and those who have offended Rome's emperors in other ways." He ushered me into a nearby tavern next to the city's famous amphitheatre, built fifty years previously, which had room for nearly four thousand spectators. It was devoted more to theatre than to circuses, and had a small stage, behind which rose a great wall of scenery, dwarfing it.

"The time will come when I shall need a place as big as this to hold my converts, Nathaniel. The oppressed of Rome will turn to their salvation through Jesus Christ." The light in Paul's eyes glowed with the madness of the fanatic. "And you also will become a Believer," he went on, "and give up all you have to follow the Way." He looked at me challengingly.

"Your oratory is impressive, Paul, but like my father I would never give up the pleasures of the secular world, which I can touch by reaching out my hand, for those of the spiritual world, which cannot even be defined."

Paul shook his head. "You are too young to appreciate the notion of renouncing the ways of the secular world. In time though you will become sated with what is at present new to you, with carnal pleasure and silks and perfumes, and then you will seek fulfilment through the things of the spirit."

"I want to speak with you about fulfilment of the longings of the flesh as well as the spirit, Paul. I love someone, and I would be grateful for your help in attaining her."

He smiled grimly, and I wondered if confiding in him about my love for Julia would be more like confessing a sin than speaking of a joy he could not understand. However, I needed his advice.

We took our goblets to a rough-hewn bench near the door, and peered from the gloom of the tap-room into the dusty sunlight outside. The street was alive with traffic; the affluent in their sedan chairs carried by slaves, the big four-wheeled *carrucas* on their way to the docks to deliver merchandise for Rome, the nimble, two wheeled *cisia* which were the taxis of the day. Paul's henchman had settled on other benches and I could hear them discussing the public reaction to Paul's speech that morning.

"Do you want to tell me about your – aspiration?" Paul asked.

"She is a Roman, Paul. Pontius Pilate was her uncle."

"What did you say? You love the niece of Pontius Pilate?" He began to quiver, the light in his eyes reddening. His fury as he took it upon himself to judge us enraged me, and we glared at each other like stags in the rutting season, about to lock antlers.

"I think, Paul, you are too quick to condemn." I managed to speak calmly. "She and her brother are the children of a senator, who did not have time to bring them up, so they stayed with their uncle in Judea. They became the principal friends of my childhood. Lucullus joined a legion and was sent to Britain, Julia could be dead, but I prefer to believe she is alive, and in Rome. I do not seek your condemnation, but your counsel."

I had managed to control my anger, and he seemed to succeed in quelling his. He nodded, and his eyes lost their fury. "Very well."

"You told my father and me that you were a citizen of Rome as well as being a Jew," I went on. "Do you think that, if Julia and I discover that we still love each other, it would be possible for us to marry? My father's brother says the laws of Rome are strict, and that as a Jew I would never be permitted to marry a Roman, especially the daughter of a Senator. As Jewish laws are strict too, to wed a Roman I would probably have to fight the Sanhedrin. "

Paul's face did not soften, as I had hoped it would. Romantic enough to risk his life daily for an ideal, he seemed unable to appreciate that romance took other forms, and that to a normal man there was infinitely more comfort in a woman than in a cherubim, or a Being without shape or substance. Or, for that matter, that to the lover, earthly love transcended earthly law.

"Roman laws change frequently, but marriage is governed not by law but by custom. For instance, in law a freedman may marry the daughter of a Senator, but that might arouse so much hostility within her family such a marriage could be impossible."

He had evidently decided to change tactics; instead of outrage his tone took on the persuasiveness of the proselytiser, quiet, reasonable, but nevertheless implacable.

"However much you find you love each other, are you sure you could forget she was the niece of the man who condemned God on Earth to death?"

"She was innocent of Pilate's action. Why do you persist in trying to cloak her in his guilt?"

"She is of his blood!" In spite of his apparent calmness, I could see how hard it was for him to discard his prejudices. There was saliva at the corners of his mouth; he was beyond reason. I decided to leave, and stood up.

"It is obvious that you, one of the principal voices of the new religion, are as biased and bigoted as any Pharisee. I have entirely misunderstood you, Paul. I have credited you with qualities you do not possess. I had also thought you a friend!"

"And now you think I am not a friend?"

"I think the coldness of your own loins denies you understanding of what I feel."

"They are not cold, Nathaniel. If they were, that would prove nothing. A man without lust is not a man, because lust is part of the human condition which begged for the redemption that Jesus Christ through his death and resurrection gave it. I understand that, because I am a man. If I were not, do you suppose that I could have the slightest knowledge of the meaning of redemption?

"If my loins were really cold, I could not understand the gift, the infinitely precious gift, of salvation! Do you suppose salvation can compare with any other gift? Do you think it comparable with a jewel, a flask of perfume, a vial of elixir? How could I be redeemed, as Jesus redeemed me, if I were not a sinner? And how can a man who can't feel passion, acquire virtue through resisting desire?

"I am simply a man, Nathaniel, a passionate man who directs his love towards God, the God who smiled on him, the God who died for him!" He put his arm round me. "Do you really think I would deny you the help of a friend, simply because I could not understand any longer how a lover felt, do you think I am such a Spartan as to equate godliness with frigidity?

"Self-denial can claim some credit, Nathaniel, for its strengthening influence on character, its example of setting aside luxury in the face of poverty, but in itself it has no intrinsic value. A Parable is not a Commandment, and should not be interpreted as such. Poverty is an imposition, not a virtue, and if wealth did not exist, it could not be renounced to prove the point of its sacrifice. Similarly, if desire did not exist, one could not overcome it in oneself, the better to understand it in others." Paul's set mouth eased into a smile.

"I am aware of what you feel, Nathaniel. I am fully aware of the value of love, without which our beings cannot be irrigated. I can understand your determination to overcome any challenge, but it is essential for you to understand what that challenge consists of."

I sat down again and he went to buy two more goblets of wine, putting them in front of us and leaning towards me. "I apologise, Nathaniel. Believe me, I have a very real and personal concern for your wellbeing. It is not only the danger you could face from the reaction of Julia's family towards you if you persisted in trying to marry, and possibly too from those Jews who do not wish any good for a Jew who loves a Roman."

"What other danger could I face, Paul?"

His expression was sombre. "That from the Emperor."

"The Emperor? I had thought of asking his help in finding and marrying Julia. If we acted under his auspices—"

"If you acted under his auspices you would be killed at his leisure.

"The Emperor is the State. The Emperor is a Blasphemer, claiming to be God. The Emperor's mind is rotten with cruelty.

"Until the legions can be persuaded to overthrow him, Caligula will continue to impose his madness on the people. In fact, he shows even more signs of being unbalanced than Tiberius."

"Rome fears attacks by barbarians but its own culture is itself barbarous in many ways. Central heating and crucifixion, philosophical discourse and bears ravaging a Christian in chains. The love of one individual for another has no more significance to Caligula than the mating of a pair of frogs.

"Caligula is evil, and love and evil of course are foes, something which love, because it seeks to look kindly on people, often fails to recognise till it's too late.

"Tell me, Nathaniel, what is the name of Julia's father?"

"Gaius Lucius Octavius. Paul, I am prepared to go to the Senate—"

"No!" Leaning towards me, Paul grasped my wrist. "You will go to the Senate only if you want to die! Nothing happens at the Senate that Caligula will not find out about; he has a thousand spies and toadies infesting the Senate and every other public body.

"If you go seeking a senator's daughter at the Senate, Caligula's interest will be aroused, and Caligula always selects his women for the night from the noblewomen who have to attend him for dinner, with their husbands. It amuses him, and in any case he thinks it is a privilege for them to see their wives dragged into his bedchamber. "

"I would kill him," I said brashly.

"Undoubtedly somebody will, but I don't think it will be you, my boy." Paul stood up.

"Be discreet, find out where Julia's father lives and go to his house. You are a merchant, go as one. And remember that Lucius Octavius is bound by the customs of Rome and will invoke them to dismiss any inappropriate relationship."

Again, he put his hand on my shoulder. "When I speak in praise of God, I cannot afford to be discreet, no matter how great the risk to myself and my converts. Discretion would destroy the dissemination of my teachings. Earthly love, on the other hand, especially when it is illicit, demands discretion. There is no point in your becoming the martyr to a worldly passion if you don't live to enjoy it.

"That is the risk you run with the niece of Pontius Pilate." He moved to rejoin his retinue, taking the warmth of the day with him. I felt a chill like that of the desert at moonrise, and for a moment had a cowardly hope, instantly banished, that when Julia and I met I would discover that my love, with all its dangers and complications, was dead.

Chapter 15

A pig garlanded for sacrifice to the Goddess Demeter was being dragged squealing past the Temple of Mars The Avenger in the Forum. The Forum was the centre of political life in the Empire, and contained also some of Rome's most notable architecture.

In the morning sun the recently completed Arch of Augustus gleamed blindingly, and I was thankful to rest briefly in the coolness of the Temple of Venus. It was vast, and I reflected how puny even Paul and his beliefs seemed compared with the might of the Forum and its hallowed gods.

It seemed ludicrous to try to overthrow Venus, as well as Mars and the rest of the Graeco-Roman gods, in the name of a bloody, skinny man hanging on a cross and shouting at a storm to forgive his tormentors.

After resting I continued past other temples, built to honour Saturn and Castor, and the Basilica Julia. The building's name seemed to whisper encouragement. A wedding procession nearby was also an encouraging omen, and I stopped to cheer, like many other passers-by, as musicians feted the couple being carried abreast in their palanquins, burly slaves driving a way for them as the litter-bearers panted through the heat.

The *sistrum* players raised their bronze rattles and chanted in time with the rhythm, tambourines and cymbals clashed, and a dwarf blew melody from crossed pipes almost as big as himself.

I fought to continue my way to the Senate; I wanted at least to try to catch a glimpse of Julia's father, but I was being pushed backwards by the crowd. Their armpits reeked, it was like being herded among goats.

The sound of horses whinnying in panic soared over the noise of people now swearing and arguing as, being forced off-course like myself, they began to rage and in some cases, to panic.

The horses, now shrieking, were pulling a *carpentum*, a four-wheeled conveyance shaped rather like a curtained double-bed. Each horse had a rider, striving to control the increasingly terrified animals, and four hefty, sweating slaves tried to counter the others making way for the wedding party.

A battle between the two groups of slaves seemed inevitable, with the crowd being caught up in the melee, but a white-haired man, wearing the purple-striped toga of a senator, stood up in the swaying *carpentum* and, in the loud, almost stately voice of authority, demanded order. Sitting next to him, staring proudly ahead, I could make out the profile of a woman. She turned, and I saw that it was Julia.

I yelled her name, but my cry was lost in the clamour. Ignoring the weight and smell of the people surrounding me, I tried to fight my way forward, but the bow wave of stumbling plebeians being forced aside by the slaves was being channelled into a relentless, increasingly terrified human cascade, and it was impossible to move against such a torrent of garlic-breathed, sweat-soaked, cursing citizens.

The *carpentum* was now free of the mass, and I stared after it in despair. I was no longer in doubt that I loved Julia as much as ever, my glance at her proud and, it seemed at that moment, unattainable profile, convinced me that this was not simply a romantic dream deriving from our childhood together but a fierce mixture of passion and determination to let nothing thwart me.

All that I could see of Julia in the distance was the blue ribbon securing her hair, as highly arched as a cock's tail. At least I had an idea of the direction she had taken; I would follow it later.

Enraged and frustrated, covered in dust and smelling of the crowd's sweat and my own, I entered a wine shop and gulped a small amphora of white wine from the south, crisp and chill.

I followed it with several more, until I became convinced that I could overcome any obstacle, was a young god, irresistible in my strength and purpose. I could swoop like an eagle and soar like Phaeton in his chariot. I was as much a bull as Zeus had been in his pursuit of Europa; I was invincible.

I emptied my goblet and went home to the small house I had rented on the Oppian Hill, not far from the wall screening it from the Forum. Lying on a divan I plotted my movements for the next day. Go to a stables early, hire a horse, ride it to the Senate and wait for Julia's father to come out. Follow him to his house, and his daughter.

Ask for her hand in marriage.

Chapter 16

I was able to observe the Senator much more closely than on the previous day. He emerged from the impressively colonnaded portals of the building and stood for a short time, speared by the sun almost directly overhead, before his slaves appeared with the *carpentum* and stood respectfully beside it.

Before bothering to notice them, Gaius Lucius Octavius yawned as he gazed over the hurrying mass, pausing by the vehicle's step. He was a tall, slender man with a high-bridged nose and sandy hair cut short, making him round-headed in the Roman fashion. He said something to one of the slaves, and climbed into the *carpentum;* the door shut as the slaves mounted the horses, and the vehicle creaked into movement, clumsy as a barge moving into mid-river.

I urged my horse to follow through the stinking dust, the high roof of the *carpentum* looming just in front of us.

Languid as he seemed, Gaius Octavius Lucius had, I knew, been a soldier, probably with a distinguished record, as unlike his brother-in-law Pontius Pilate he had survived Tiberius' purge following the Sejanus affair.

Noise and dust swirled everywhere but according to the ostler, my horse had belonged when young to the Legions, and did not seem fazed by it. Even the flies swarming round its eyes didn't seem to worry it much; occasionally it shook its head and a gob of froth hit my cheek or spattered my tunic.

We left the centre of Rome well behind and headed from the Palantine Hill along the Appian Way towards the Via Latina, turning off just past an olive grove into a pleasant, sylvan district whose large villas reminded me of that of Pontius in Judea. The road we were on was straight and flanked by cypresses, so I dropped a long way behind the senator, in order to avoid attracting his attention.

After a few minutes the *carpentium* turned off the road and continued down a long, straight stone-paved drive leading to a large villa whose portico's lines were picked out in gold. I dismounted, hitched my horse to a tree and lay on the ground, watching.

Waving away assistance from slaves, the senator stepped down; a watchman appeared and saluted him smartly as he entered, and the senator disappeared into the atrium. The door closed, and the *carpentum* rumbled round to the stable block, whose red tiled roof gleamed through the trees.

I left the horse tethered to the tree and walked towards the house. It would have been more discreet to have returned to Rome, and come back here tomorrow morning, when Julia's father might be at the Senate. I was in no mood to be discreet, though. Impatience to see Julia drew me irresistibly towards the building. It was almost moonrise, when the Roman dinner started and often went on till midnight; I could not wait.

I forgot that Julia might not reciprocate my feelings, that she might have mentally discarded me. My longing for her, especially after catching a glimpse of her after so long, was too powerful.

As I approached the portico I was conscious of the smell of jasmine, which reminded me of Golgotha, and blending with it the scent of orange blossom.

The watchman emerged from his portico and held out an arm. "Who are you and what is your business here?" I was sure he had been a centurion.

"My name is Nathaniel ben Ezra."

"Who?" A cry of disbelief as a woman hurried towards us. A gold circlet in her hair set off the vivid whiteness of her tunic. She stood on top of the two steps in front of me, arms stretched out, not in welcome but as if to repel me. The watchman looked from one to the other of us.

"Julia, darling, it—"

"Go away!" she demanded, in a voice so low it was almost a whisper. I was shocked by the fear in her eyes. The watchman tensed, ready to enforce her command, when another figure joined us. Eyes hooded, he had the expression of a rapacious bird of prey. It was the senator.

"Who is this, Julia?" His voice was quiet, resonant, and cold.

"We knew each other as children, when we lived with Uncle Pontius in Judea." I was unsettled by her lack of assurance, her voice almost quavering.

"He is a Jew?" the senator asked in the same tone.

"I am," I answered for her. "I haven't been in Rome long—"

"I noticed you outside the Senate this morning, astride a pitiful horse. Did you follow me?"

"I did. I do not wish to interrupt your meal—"

"Do you carry a weapon?"

"I do not, Sir. I came here as a friend". I felt I had nothing to lose by being direct. "I love your daughter and came here to ask for her hand." Julia closed her eyes and clung to the senator's arm. Her colour matched her tunic.

"So you want to marry my daughter, Julia?"

"I love her, Sir. I think she loves me." Julia gasped, and fainted. I hurried to help the senator support her, but the watchman grabbed my arm.

"Come inside, Nathaniel." The Senator pronounced my name with a faint but obvious sneer, and almost dragged Julia through the atrium into an inner chamber. He placed her on a couch and nodded to the watchman, who released me. I sat on a divan as a female slave came in carrying an amphora of wine and some silver goblets.

"Wine, Nathaniel?"

"Thank you, Sir." The slave poured wine and handed it to me; the senator held a second goblet to Julia's mouth. She choked, and opened her eyes. As she tried to speak, the senator cowed her with the look of a spider on a rock.

"So, you think I am Gaius Lucius Octavus, Julia's father?"

I went cold. "Are you not?"

"I am Marcellus Servius Portus." He glared at me. "Gaius died on the Gemonian steps as one of the accomplices of Sejanus. He was strangled and then dragged down the steps with hooks before being thrown into the Tiber. His brother Pontius was accused of being involved in the same plot and crucified.

"Having grown up alongside Caligula in the Army, after his father Germanicus died –shall we say, too early?—I, as a close and loyal friend of the Emperor

Caligula, persuaded him that Julia and Lucullus might be spared the death sentence for the crime.

"Being merciful"—the same scorn in his voice as when he had spoken my name—"the Emperor gave Julia to me as my wife, and arranged a generalship in the Army for Lucullus, who is currently serving beyond the Pillars of Hercules, in the province of Britannia, which is, I believe, as unruly as it is damp. He will probably die of congestion of the lung, if he survives the depredations of the blue woad wearers.

"Julia is more fortunate, she has my name and therefore my protection."

I could think of nothing to say. Not only was Julia married to someone else, I had in effect betrayed her. At the very least I had dishonoured her, and put her at the mercy of a man who had quelled her pride and substituted fear of him in its place.

As I stood up to go, he went to the doorway and clapped his hands, and a pair of huge Nubian slaves padded in, reminding me of Pontius' slave Sarda.

"Take him a good way from here, and cut his throat."

"No!" Julia cried out. She stood up. "You have no reason to kill him!"

"But he has the impertinence to love you. He even gives the impression of thinking you love him. How can you therefore imagine that I would let him live?"

He went on quietly, while a slave pinioned my arms with hands strong as grappling irons. "I am your husband and protector. Without me you would have followed your father to the Steps, or your uncle to the Cross. One hundred and sixty thousand people have been immolated to the glory of Caligula since he became Emperor—do you think the death of a solitary Jew has any more significance than a horse's turd?" He smiled at her.

"I am prepared to make one concession." He turned to the slaves. "It would be perhaps more discreet to break his neck instead of cutting his throat. Go, and hide his body by the wayside after you have despatched him."

Julia cried out as I was rushed outside into the night air. The white cotton tunics of the slaves smelled freshly laundered as they half carried, half dragged me up the drive at a trot, loping like leopards as we turned into the main driveway. We swung off the road into the olive grove I had noticed as I followed the *carpentum* earlier in the day.

We were still moving when a huge hand came up under my chin and wrenched it sideways. There was a crack like lightning striking a tree and my legs folded.

The slaves loped away as I fell to the ground, where I lay helplessly amongst a few fallen olives. I could not move, my head rolled loosely until my nose was resting against a tuft of grass, which tickled. I sneezed, and movement began to return.

My neck became firm on top of my spine again, I coughed a couple of times to clear my twisted throat, and shortly after that was able to raise my head. Climbing to my feet, I swore vengeance on Marcellus. I had been brought up to believe in the old philosophy of vengeance, an eye for an eye and a tooth for a tooth. A life for a life.

I found my way back to my sleeping horse, and woke and mounted it. The villa was in darkness, apart from the night watchman's lantern. Inside I could hear wailing. I was sure that Marcellus would not forgive

Julia for my love for her, but as she was a patrician, he could not for the time being kill her legally. First he had to fulfil the requirements of the constantly changing, but strict procedures of Roman law.

Buoyed up by thoughts of love and vengeance I started back for Rome, alert for robbers. It was only when I was safely home that reaction set in, and I started to shake.

For the second time in my life I had somehow overcome death, and had no explanation for it.

Chapter 17

My slumber was deep, but not easy. Death, dressed as a yellow and black harlequin, danced round me, moving like a dervish, a fanged grin under its mask. It seized my hand with a grip of ice, and fastened it to another's, and I saw that Death was presiding over a *caracola* with Julia. Her throat had been cut, and her head flopped against my shoulder as her blood ran down my tunic. I woke up screaming.

I looked out of the window; a pallid light spread across an anaemic sky. My bed creaked shrilly as I left it to fling cold water into my face, after which I changed into a fresh tunic and gnawed half a loaf of bread, which was stale. I was ravenous, and the thought of hot, steaming bread made me burp. I went outside.

The horse was peacefully cropping grass, its coat shining with dew; I felt guilty for not having unsaddled it. I mounted and set out for breakfast: fresh bread and eggs were my favourite then as they are now.

The baker was a big man with an encouragingly villainous face. I bought a loaf and, acting on instinct, took a gold *sesterce* from my purse. "I have no change." The baker eyed the coin greedily.

"You strike me as a man who would like to keep this coin without having to give change."

He gave me a flash of sparse yellow teeth, and remained silent as an old woman arrived, dallied before making a small purchase, and finally left, grumbling about the price.

The baker still said nothing, and eyed me enquiringly.

"There are many men in Rome who would like to earn a gold sesterce," I said.

"That is true."

"Do you know any who would participate in a venture for gold, perhaps much more than a sesterce?" He put my coin and the old woman's into his cash box and turned its heavy bronze key.

"I have an enemy," I went on.

"We cannot love everybody."

"My enemy is dangerous."

"Most enemies are, especially if they know they are your enemy. Does yours?"

"He thinks I am dead."

The baker raised a thick eyebrow above an eye now glowing with greed.

"He thinks he has had me killed," I went on.

"In such a case a man has a right to avenge himself." I did not think the baker would have cared much as to whether or not rights and wrongs were involved, so long as gold was.

"I think so too. I would pay generously, but the matter would have to be dealt with subtly. My enemy is a man of some importance."

The baker nodded. "Be here at sundown," he told me.

I spent the day restlessly, fighting the urge to return to Marcellus' villa to try to rescue Julia. I remembered her crying, but I remembered too the military-looking watchman and the Nubians. I was a merchant, not a swordsman, and although I was strong I had no illusions about overcoming the household slaves and Marcellus if I went back by myself. To fail would be tantamount to killing Julia; I had no doubt that Marcellus would hesitate no longer to bury a dagger in her throat.

At last it was time to return to the bakery. I rode down the narrow, stinking street, its open-fronted shops and laundries billowing steam, and took a deep breath as I dismounted outside the bakery; the smell of newly baked bread overcame the general reek of turds and urine making their casual way down the open sewer.

Our meeting took place in a small room in the depths of the place. The smell of bread was joined by a combination of sweat and garlic, as by the light of an oil lamp I inspected my band of prospective assassins. There were half a dozen, all of various degrees of repulsion, and taut as wolves on the trail of prey.

"Now, Sir, tell us what you want." It was the baker who had spoken.

"I want someone killed." The words still contained a sense of enormity in my ears, but evidently not in those of my listeners. "I want the death to look like an accident," I added.

"Everyone wants an assassination to look like an accident," commented a man with one eye. A greenish patch covered the other, like a dirty eyelid. The others chuckled. "Sometimes it's easy to fake an accident, sometimes not. Who is the citizen we're to dispose of?"

"Marcellus Servius Portus."

Indrawn breath. "The Senator?" demanded the baker.

"That'll cost a lot more than an ordinary citizen," chimed in a tall young man with the body of a tight-bum, a species of youth much favoured for carnal purposes by Tiberius. He had a youngish face and old eyes, remote and bleak. A butcher's knife hung from his broad leather belt. "How do you want us to kill him?"

"Bring him here and bake him," suggested a short, pock-marked man with grey hair to his shoulders and three teeth equally spaced at the front of his mouth like distance markers. Several men chuckled.

"Though senators die as quick or as slow as anyone else," the pock-marked man went on.

"I just want him dead. As quickly as possible, and as I said, apparently as the result of an accident."

"Probably have to be on the road, then. Dangerous places, roads. Accidents all the time," said a wizened, thin monkey-like man with astonishingly long arms folded across his chest. "Does he use a sedan-chair, horseback, or maybe a chariot, to get from his home to the Senate and back?"

"I've seen him leaving the Senate in a *carpentum*. He had two slaves in attendance and a coachman. I think four more went ahead to force a way through the traffic."

"I'm not croaking a senator," said the tight-bum. The others murmured in agreement—no matter how villainous they were, the punishment for murdering a senator of being crucified upside down and set on fire evidently didn't seem worth any number of gold sesterces.

Only the baker was silent, his mouth set in a rictus of avarice. "Anyone who wants out can quit now," he said softly, when the others had finished speaking. "I'm still in, Sir, if we can agree a price, which I don't doubt."

I gave each of the others a coin to keep him sweet, and they went out, leaving the baker and me to agree terms.

"First, I get a ten sesterce bonus for each slave, freedman, or anyone else who gets in the way," said the baker. I agreed, and the rictus became a smile, so that he looked almost cordial.

"Do you know where the Senator lives?"

"Off the Appian Way."

"My terms for killing the Senator are twenty-five gold sesterces in advance, and the same again after the job's done."

"Agreed."

"I usually prefer doing things outside," the baker told me. "Gives me more space and a chance to see in advance how many citizens we're going to have to deal with. And of course it's much easier to have a fatal accident in the open."

"I suppose it is," I answered, remembering the huge hand almost caressing my face before seizing my jaw and twisting it.

I took out my heavy purse and filled the baker's large grasping palms with sesterces.

"Be here at the same hour tomorrow," he commanded, as if I was his subordinate. "Can you arrange a mule or a horse for me?"

I told him I could.

"Good—save me the trouble," he said. I left. The stench of the street was numbing, but I was content.

Chapter 18

The baker's name was Lars. He mounted the mule, which was quite small, and framed it with long, heavily-muscled legs whose feet were almost brushing the ground. I rode the same animal as previously. Lars looked more physically formidable than all the others I had met in the bakery put together, with his battered bald head and legionnaire's shoulders.

Setting off through the gloaming, we splashed into the squalid alley.

The majesty of Imperial Rome was certainly tainted by its smells, but then the same obtained wherever I had been. Stench was the lowest common denominator linking the cities of the world as music and art, the highest common denominators, were to link them later.

As the street grew narrower, I went on ahead. I was at Lars's mercy, if he wanted to stab me with knife or dagger, but felt I could trust him, if only so that he could collect the balance of his fee when Marcellus was dead. Also I seemed to be proof against death.

We entered open country, and Lars came alongside me. I began to feel easier away from the city. There was no moon but our eyes had got used to the dark and we could see a fair way ahead.

"It's not my business, and I shan't take offence if you don't want to answer me," Lars said after we had ridden in silence for a while, "but any man has a right to be curious. Why do you want this senator killed?"

"Because he tried to kill me."

"That seems a fair enough reason, but why would he want you killed?"

"A family matter."

"Family matter? I had you down for a Jew."

"You had me down correctly."

Lars could see I was irritated, but could not stay silent. "So how come a Jew is involved in a family matter with a Roman senator?"

I decided that it would be more politic to keep my temper than tell him to shut up. "Jews and Romans can love each other, Lars. I am in love with a member of the senator's family."

"I understand. His daughter?"

I didn't answer. "That certainly wouldn't make him happy," Lars said. "A Jew entering a senator's family via marriage." He chuckled. "No wonder he wanted to put you in your place—under the ground, he'd say it was." He chuckled again.

His curiosity was now at full gallop. "How did he try to kill you, if I may ask? I'm always interested in method. Not that I'm a violent man at heart, you understand.

"I've done my share of killing, mostly in Britain, on active service in the legions. Savage sons of bitches, the natives of Britannia —must be the weather that makes them so difficult. If you can survive a winter there, you can survive anywhere. It's worse than any military attack, which you can beat back with your weapons—there's no weapon can repel the weather you get beyond the Pillars of Hercules."

As I had not answered his question about the senator's attempt to kill me he asked me again.

"He tried to have me strangled."

"He *tried* to have you strangled?"

"Yes, by two Nubians," I added incautiously. His face was turned towards me, but I could hear the new respect in his voice, rather than see it in his expression. "You got away from two Nubians? How, Sir?"

I did not answer.

"Takes a lot of doing, to overcome two Nubians,." the baker murmured to himself.

Still I made no comment, and tried not to think about my experience as we came abreast of the olive grove in which my attempted murder had taken place. The clouds parted and a moon the colour of sour cream hovered over watery clouds. A few dusty stars shone disheartedly from the attic of the Stygian sky.

We approached Marcellus' villa silently.

"Wait here," the butcher murmured, nearly pulling the mule over as he dismounted, "I'm going to do a recce." He moved forward in a half-crouch, the moon refracting from his bald head. There was no frantic barking of a guard dog, no geese fluttering and squawking in alarm. They had saved Rome from an incautious invader, but there were none here to warn Marcellus.

Then Lars appeared at my side, filling my nostrils with garlic and sweat. "There are gardens on all sides, with doors leading into the house," he breathed, as I forced myself not to turn my head away.

I did not want Julia to be frightened. "You said you preferred to attack in the open," I reminded him.

"That is true. But you said you wanted the job done as soon as possible."

90

The nearness of Julia, excitement, and the longing for vengeance, were making me incautious. I moved forward.

"What in the name of Jove are you doing?" the baker whispered, putting a hand as big as the Nubians' on my arm.

"I agree—we can do it ourselves."

"Yes, but first we need to know how many people there are inside. Do you have any weapons?"

"Hatred and surprise," I hissed at him. I felt a strange, abnormal ecstasy at the thought of attacking Marcellus and his Nubians. "The senator and the slaves who tried to kill me at his orders believe I'm dead. When they see me they'll think I'm a ghost."

He removed his hand from my arm, looking at me intently, summing me up. He nodded. "Hatred and surprise, eh? Used right, it's true they can be as efficient as any sword. "We'll go in now—I'll lead."

"There's just one thing," I whispered. "I don't want anyone killed who doesn't have to be."

"If a man's on the wrong side, he dies," Lars replied with typical Roman callousness. I decided not to argue, and we crept forward.

Lars' army training had taken him over, and I could sense he was back in the legions, taut-backed, every sense alert, a man with the present of death. A glimmer of light as the feeble moon caught the blade of his dagger before disappearing again behind cloud.

"No watchman," he whispered, pausing.

"There was one before."

"If there is one, I'll lure him out. Lie down." He pressed down on my wrist, and I obeyed, lying on the newly damp grass. Lars dropped down beside me, raised his head, and made a sound like an owl hooting. He hooted softly at first, increasing the volume until inside the villa it must have sounded as if the owl was perched on the threshold, trying to get in.

The door of the portico opened, and a new watchman, not the one who had been on duty at my first visit, peered cautiously out. This one was old and I remembered seeing him replenish the oil in the lamps inside the house. He was a house slave or an old freedman, evidently without military training or experience; he held an oil lamp above his head, and his voice quavered.

"I can't see anything," he called to someone behind him.

"Well go outside, you oaf. Your place is in the portico, whether there are owls about or not." The door banged angrily. I had no idea whose voice it was, certainly not that of Marcellus.

The night was so quiet we could hear the watchman sigh with resentment. Lars made another sound; this time he screeched, not so much like an owl as its victim's, something furry and small and helpless, being torn apart.

The watchman swung his lamp like a censer, and stood straining his eyes into the darkness, which owing to the reappearance of thick cloud was now absolute. I felt Lars' leather tunic hard against the linen sleeve of mine. He was poised, slightly raised on his hands. The wretched watchman left the doorway behind him and came slowly towards us. I did not want Lars to kill him, but knew I must not break the hunter's concentration. Lars did not move.

"Who's there?" The watchman was obviously wary of whatever might be in front of him, but he was also afraid of whoever had been standing behind him.

Cautiously he descended another step, and was almost on top of us. Lars leaped to his feet and had his hands round his throat before he could cry out. He lifted him into the air, and the pale moon reappearing showed the man's eyes bulging with terror. He let go of the oil lamp, which lay guttering on the ground.

"If you want to die, make a sound," Lars whispered. "Just answer our questions. How many are there inside?"

"Fifteen, including the Lady Julia and two concubines," gasped the watchman. "The cook Serena, her five helpers—all slaves, Gracchus, a freedman."

"Is the Senator there?"

The watchman's eyes almost came out of their sockets as Lars again squeezed his throat. "No, he left for Rome early this morning."

"He comes back this evening?"

"So far as I know."

Lars looked at me. "And which slaves did he take?" I demanded.

"The two Nubians Felix and Marsa, and two others."

"So the Lady Julia is inside?" I could hardly breathe.

"She's a prisoner in her room, —under guard. She's forbidden to leave it till the Master says she may." He was staring at me. "I know you from somewhere, Sir —"

"Now we'll have to kill him," said Lars, "he's recognised you."

"No, no, I beg you —the man I thought I recognised is dead!" The watchman cringed.

Lars looked at him with contempt, his huge hand creeping like a tarantula round the man's throat.

"What makes you think so?" he whispered.

"He—the man I thought he was—was carried away by the Nubians to be —" he was beginning to choke.

"To be?" prompted Lars softly.

"I heard they had been told by the Master to kill him. The Lady Julia was distraught. The Senator had her taken to her chamber and locked in—I've not seen her at all today."

"Did he harm her?" I demanded, so loudly that Lars shushed me.

"We were instructed not to go near her. She was to have no food or water." I was enraged. "I do not think she has eaten or drunk since she was confined," added the watchman. I felt like strangling him there and then.

"Are you armed?" Lars demanded.

"I have only this dagger," answered the watchman, and handed it over.

Lars passed it on to me; it was small, but at least it was a weapon.

"Where in Hades are you, Articus?" A man with the build of a gladiator appeared in the doorway of the portico. It was his voice that had forced the watchman out of doors.

Lars threw the watchman aside and rushed forwards, his bald head lowered as he head-butted the other man, who fell backwards. His head hit the step and there was the sound of his skull fracturing. Lars swung round and grabbed the watchman, swinging him into the air as he leaped over the fallen man's body. I ran after him, into the house.

We halted in the atrium; the usual dolphins wrapped round the customary oil lamps sputtering in golden sconces, the distant hum of voices in the kitchen quarters.

"Where is the Lady Julia being held?" I demanded, as Lars held the watchman by the throat again.

The watchman didn't answer. Instead, he looked at me in horror. "In the name of Jove—it is you, but you're dead," he whimpered.

"The Lady Julia's room!" I slapped his face. "That will show you how dead I am!"

"The Master will kill me—"

"He will be too late, because we shall kill you, if you don't take us to her room this instant!" I raised my hand again, and the watchman flinched.

"I'll show you," he gasped. "It's up those steps, along the rotunda."

"Who's guarding her?"

"The eunuch, Mezra."

"Fetch him." Lars held the point of his dagger against the watchman's throat, and put his large mouth to his ear. "If you'd rather I slit your throat now—"

"No, I'll fetch him," the man gasped. Lars let him go, and he led us up a flight of marble steps to a pillared rotunda, stopping at the top.

"Mezra, it's Articus," he called. "There is someone here to see you."

We heard the eunuch padding towards us, as we waited just out of sight; he rounded a pillar. He was as big as Lars, his black, round polished head was decorated with a crescent-shaped scar running across his entire scalp. Fat rippled all over his epicene body, and he exuded a faint smell of musk. He carried a scimitar.

He stopped abruptly. "Mezra?" I called softly.

His lips parted to show brilliant white teeth. Without answering, he raised the scimitar, the musk accentuated by his bare armpit.

Still smiling, he feinted with the scimitar as I danced just out of reach, holding my dagger. The watchman was standing with his back against a column, his mouth open. The eunuch shrieked, as Lars struck from behind; as he swung round, Lars struck again, sliding his dagger up to the hilt into Mezra's colossal belly and bringing it up in a wicked slicing motion which disembowelled him.

Mezra's intestines tumbled out with a soft, slithering sound, amidst a rumble of foul-smelling visceral gases, and he folded slowly downwards, like a camel settling. He dropped a large bronze key.

I grabbed the key and ran round the rotunda, stopping at a pair of blue doors limned with gold. As I inserted the key there was a woman's cry of alarm on the other side, and I flung the doors open. Julia stood in front of me.

I reached for her. "There's no time to talk now, darling, we have to leave at once."

"Nathaniel, I thought you were dead," she gasped, as I hurried her past Mezra's corpse.

"I should be. I'll tell you everything later."

At the foot of the steps Lars crouched like a mastiff; he was covered in blood, as if he had just butchered an ox. His face glistened with sweat and triumph.

"Pity we can't take that," nodding at a handsome ivory lily held by a girl sensuously carved in ebony, standing on a small gold table. "Maybe we could come back when the job's done."

We ran through the portico into the garden and the watchman ran with us. As we reached our mounts he began to speak quickly. "I can't stay here, Sirs. Please take me with you, otherwise the Master will kill me. "

"You'll have to look after yourself, friend," answered Lars. "We only have two mounts."

"Let him come," Julia said. "He's right—when Marcellus finds me gone and Mezra dead, he'll have Articus torn to pieces."

"He can ride with us till we've taken care of our business," I told Lars, who looked disgusted. Julia mounted, and clung to my waist as I sat in front of her.

"If Marcellus arrives now—"

"You mustn't worry about Marcellus," I murmured as we set off. "He tried to have me killed, and now it's his turn."

"You're going to kill him?"

"If we don't, he'll rip Rome apart until he finds you, darling. After that you'll either live like a prisoner, or be killed."

I felt Julia against me shiver, but she said nothing.

"No more talk," commanded Lars, and we fell silent, only the hooves of our mounts making a faint drumming sound on the grass.

We had just reached the outskirts of the olive grove when Lars hissed under his breath and reined in. Straining our ears, we heard a voice on the road, some distance ahead. Our eyes were once more used to the darkness, and with the faint light of pale clouds we were able to see a sedan chair borne by two slaves, with two more acting as escort.

Lars turned in the saddle and lifted the watchman by the scruff of his neck, dropping him to the ground. I helped Julia to descend, and she stood beside the watchmen as the baker and I braced ourselves for the charge. Marcellus and his escort were almost level with us when Lars whispered: "Now!"

He gave the mule a mighty slap on the rump, and our two animals flung themselves forward, galloping straight at the chair and the slaves bearing it. Marcellus swore as I broadsided into him, knocking the chair to the ground. My horse reared up and plunged a hoof on to his face as he lay on his back; there was a cracking and tearing as the mule completed the demolition of the chair and a scream from a slave as Lars raised his dagger and brought it fiercely down.

One of the Nubians recognised me and I could see his expression of terror and disbelief. He cried out and began to flee but Lars went after him, the mule almost close enough to knock him over. Lars' arm moved and the Nubian crashed to the ground, a dagger in his back.

Jerking it out the baker turned on the other Nubian, who also seemed paralysed by terror at the sight of me. Lars cut his throat.

Surrounded by dead men, Marcellus was still alive, lying in the wreckage of the chair. "So my slaves disobeyed my instructions, you Jewish upstart!" he snarled.

"No, Senator, they carried them out." We glared at each other. Lars was beside me, dagger held in front of him, ready to give Marcellus the coup de grace.

"You jest."

"No, Senator, I do not jest. They broke my neck, just as you instructed."

"Are you, then, claiming to be a god?"

"No, I am not."

"Then how—" His eyes shifted to Julia, who had come to stand beside me. "Julia!" He tried to rise, but Lars stood over him, the dagger at his throat. Marcellus' lips folded back, like those of a wild animal about to attack. "Julia, you are a specialist in betrayal. You betrayed me with this –this Jewish lover, and you betrayed me with this—this thing that cannot wait to slit my throat!"

"You are right, I am an impatient man, Senator." Lars brought the dagger down and across; a fountain sprayed upwards in the moonlight and fell lazily back into Marcellus' face. His heels drummed briefly against the ground before his eyes turned upwards behind their lids. Lars gave me a grin.

"We've got some clearing up to do, Sir." He heaved Marcellus from the splintered remains of the sedan chair and slung him over his shoulder, and I struggled to do the same with one of the Nubians.

99

Much later, the road was clear; and all the evidence of life and death at that spot had been washed away, as though Marcellus and his slaves had never been.

Chapter 19

Fortunately for Julia and myself, and for most of Rome for that matter, Caligula was Emperor for less than four years before being himself murdered. According to rumour, he died the sort of bloody death he so much enjoyed administering to others; apparently a number of senators had been involved in plotting his assassination, which had been led by one Chaerea.

Some said Chaerea had played Brutus, attacking the emperor from behind and slicing deeply into his neck with his sword, whilst another assassin called Sabinus stabbed him in the chest. It was said too that Caligula's genitals had been sliced off, and that altogether he had received thirty wounds. His German guards came dashing to the scene behind Caligula's litter-bearers, who used their poles to bludgeon several of the attackers, but Caligula was dead.

My father had welcomed Julia and forgiven me for marrying a Roman, but Julia never felt completely at ease in Judea. She could not rid herself of the memory of being escorted out of her home by the cataphracts, and she hated the slight of not being wholly accepted by either Roman or Jewish society.

To please my father and great-uncles, Julia agreed to convert to Judaism and undergo rabbinical instruction but I knew at heart she believed more strongly in her own gods than I could in the God of Israel.

I therefore set a room aside for her, to which only she had the key, and which she furnished with representations of her *lares* and *penates*, whom she could worship in private. I don't know what she prayed for or whether her prayers were answered, but our love remained strong and we had, so far as I can recall, four children, though I have had so many since I can't remember all their names.

On our return to Rome we built a house on the Quirinal Hill, and I also constructed warehouses at Ostia and in the Roman dock area to facilitate our trading.

Helped of course by Julia's connections, and because of the Roman love of exotic jewellery, spices, amber and ivory, I found that, like my father in Judea, I gained access to the most aristocratic households. There was even talk—but not I think much—of the new emperor, Claudius, making me a senator. He was a friend of a cousin of Julia, but to be Rome's first Jewish senator would have ensured the forfeit of the privacy I had always cherished, and given me dangerous prominence and celebrity; it might even have caused a public outcry, given that envy is an efficient assassin, whether in blood or ink.

We had been married for twenty years before Julia, for the first time, looked at me with unexpected hostility. We were sitting beside the carp lake at our villa in Capri; to swim naked among the fish gave us an extra touch of sensuous pleasure as their slippery bodies brushed ours.

"Why are you so unchanged, Nathaniel?" Her voice was resentful.

"Unchanged?"

"I looked into the mirror this morning, and noticed shadows under my eyes. I noticed too that I had some grey hairs."

"I see no grey hairs, darling."

"Look, then." She bent her head towards me, and I saw indeed that her hair, which had always been black

102

as the wing of a raven, contained a few filaments of grey.

I made a stupid mistake. "We must all grow old, darling."

"Must we?" she responded angrily. "*You* have no grey hairs, and no lines on your face. You have not changed at all; your body too is as supple and strong as it was when we were married. I need youth more than you do! " she added.

"Do you?"

"Of course!" She spat with impatience. "Older men look distinguished, whereas older women simply look—old. If things go on as they are, I shall become as bent and grey as a cypress without water, whereas you will continue to resemble a sapling!" She was pouting with genuine resentment, and there was something else there too: I realised with astonishment that she was afraid. "You are not like other men, Nathaniel."

I made another mistake. "I shall always love you, even if you do become bent and grey," I told her light-heartedly.

"And is that supposed to console me?" She glared at me. "You will still be young when our children are old."

"How can you say such a thing?"

"I can say it because it is the truth."

She leaped up and strode towards the house. I started to hurry after her; and stopped. To reach out to her at this moment would be like trying to reach out to an angry cat. I returned to the pool, and contemplated the serene, slowly-swimming carp. I stared at my reflection in the pool, not out of vanity but to check that Julia was not mistaken: was there really no sign of mortality, no hint that I would soon wake up one morning, creased and crumpled and rheumily smiling at the wrinkled face beside mine?

Was that what I really wanted anyway, to take my place beside Julia on the final shore, offering her my overdue senility as my ultimate gift? Were we perhaps destined to consummate our mortality together in a last spasm of passion, a febrile imitation of our youthful intimacies, determined to gulp the last sour draught as the skeletal Charon came rowing across the Styx for us?

If that didn't happen, if my continuing youth placed me on one bank of the Styx and mortality ferried Julia and later my children to the other side, would I prefer to go on living without them or follow them?

I can no longer remember the answers I gave myself, but I am pretty sure that life would have won over love.

With the erosion of her physical beauty, Julia lost her magnanimity. She became increasingly unforgiving of my continuing youthfulness, bitterness perversely accelerating her decline. She seemed subsumed by a sort of cosmic resentment, as if my unchanging youth and good health were some form of sickness offending against the normal, sad course of human frailty. I suppose they were.

Why had youth and beauty decided to renounce her, leaving me untouched? Our children too were now falling under age's shadow, having lingered briefly at the summit of youth's bright mountain.

As they began their forced descent, unable to deflect any longer the cold and chill of old age, would I be with them, or still miraculously out of reach, all of us unable to accept that they and I inhabited different planes?

There was cruelty here even more refined than his worshippers attributed to God, except of course that they construed it as God's will and turned it into a philosophy of acceptance.

Chapter 20

I remember the day of Julia's death with a unique clarity. After all, hers was a virgin death, its hurt pristine and agonisingly poignant. She died with an expression of disbelief, still baffled by her advance into old age whilst I remained unblemished by it.

She lay as white as the marble stand her bier rested on, her eyelids still open on reproachful eyes. How could I remain when she was gone? How wake up to a new dawn, when she had to take her permanent leave of me the previous twilight? My tears were real, my emotions heartfelt; it was only when I could look back much later on a score of dead wives that my feelings became landlocked, and the flood of tears turned to drought.

Trying to evaluate that first chilly deprivation, I don't doubt the sincerity of my love for Julia. However, as she sank deeper beyond the horizon of history, so the truth of her diminished, and someone I might have taken to bed for one night could have assumed a greater reality.

Did I really love Julia so overwhelmingly, and was the death of those early generations of my children as devastating as I remember it? Or were my many bereavements simply the product of an all-powerful imagination?

Surely not, I had been left genuinely distraught with grief: how could it have been otherwise? The world's raw new emptiness was visceral.

Julia had been my first love, my deepest love, the children had been our creation together, and their children too were close to us. I sensed, though, that they had come to regard me with something of their mother's fear, if not her envy of my unchanging youth, as they began to wither with the years and descend into what these days is known as body crumble.

They died, and mourning metamorphosed once more into a matter of wooing and winning. Grief became routine, and routine bestowed its own comfort.

So Julia is buried alone, my place beside her in her marble mausoleum still unfilled. She lies in the grounds of what was our villa in Capri, above her an angel. At least, visitors have thought for centuries it was an angel or even a winged madonna, but it is in fact a representation of Venus.

Julia would not have rested in peace under the protection of any but her Roman gods.

Chapter 21

Shortly after Julia's outburst beside the pool, she accompanied me to Caesaria on business. A few months previously Nero had made his mark on the calendar by murdering his mother Agrippina. Even by the standards of Imperial Rome this was a fairly drastic act and caused a huge scandal, although maternal dominance and its consequent emasculation of male descendants has so often had the effect of causing an uncontrollable act of hatred by the filial victim. Nero had reached that state of exasperation and resentment of his mother which demanded revenge.

I knew that Paul was a man beyond fear, and had ignored the enormous dangers of proselytising in the name of Jesus. He was not one of those, numbered probably in thousands, who was afraid of insane Roman emperors, and had continued to preach in the name of Jesus until he was arrested in Jerusalem, shortly after our arrival in Caesarea.

He was brought before Felix, the Roman procurator of Judea. Before Felix could do more than put Paul in irons, he himself was recalled to Rome and succeeded by a timorous man called Festus, who bypassed his responsibility by deciding to consign Paul for judgement in Rome. I was outraged at his cowardice.

"Nathaniel, I don't want you to interfere," Julia told me. "It is not your business."

"I can't let Paul rot, Julia," I retorted, and went to intercede with Festus for the apostle. After a heated argument, it was agreed between Festus and myself that Paul reside in our house, under my guarantee that he would not escape, until the seasonal winds had subsided and it would be more or less safe for him to be escorted to Rome.

Julia was out when Paul arrived for the beginning of what turned out to be a short period of house arrest. I had him bathed and put into clean clothes by a pair of my house slaves, efficient and plain barbarian women of middle age, so that Paul could not accuse me of offering temptation.

After we had eaten, Julia went out and left us to talk, Paul sitting upright on his divan, myself reclining.

"You told me when we first met that you had given Our Lord a goblet of orange juice whilst he was hanging on the Cross, Nathaniel." Paul's eyes were as intense as usual.

"Yes."

"Did anything happen whilst you were with him?"

I thought. "Only that the ladder slipped. I had to grab the first thing I could, which was the crown of thorns."

"And then?" Paul was leaning tensely forwards.

"Nothing. I sucked my fingers."

"Was there any of Our Lord's blood on your fingers? Blood that mingled with yours?"

"I suppose so."

"If there was, that was when you received the Gift." Paul could hardly contain his excitement.

"What gift?"

"The Gift of Eternal Life, Nathaniel!"

"Eternal Life? I don't believe there is such a thing."

"Do you have a better, a more logical explanation for your appearance?"

"I have no explanation at all, perhaps it is simply a question of destiny."

"The Gift is not simply a question of destiny! It is destiny's answer, and only God can give that answer, because he is the Creator of our destinies."

"Paul, it is far too soon to talk of gifts of Eternal Life. The incident happened less than thirty years ago."

"It happened, that is the important thing. It was your action that has started you on your voyage through immortality."

We were warm with the afterglow of good food and wine, but Paul's phrase made me shiver. A voyage through immortality sounded too much like a curse.

I heard subsequently, after Paul had been consigned to Rome, that he had again proved himself against a storm at sea, and saved the lives of his guards and himself when they were shipwrecked off the coast of Malta. When they did finally arrive for his trial, Paul had time to write a number of books, including his Epistle to the Ephesians and Philemon and Colossians, before his trial.

Incredibly, he was acquitted and released. I can only believe that Nero showed Paul mercy at that time, instead of more characteristically having him fed to the lions, simply to spite those who urged so keenly that Paul be punished.

After the Great Fire of Rome, Nero reverted to type, hoping to distract attention from the allegations against him that he was responsible for the fire and neglected it. Persecuting Christians with vicious rigour, the Emperor had Paul arrested as soon as he returned from a journey to Macedonia, and flung into prison.

I saw him twice more, before he was executed in the summer of AD 68, a few weeks after Nero himself had been forced to commit suicide as an alternative to the senatorial decree that he suffer execution by 'ancestral custom', which meant being sentenced to have his head jammed into an instrument like a fork after he had been stripped naked and flogged to death.

When I went to see Paul for the last time, he seemed in a state of exaltation at the approach of what he conceived of as martyrdom, his eyes lighting up the cell with his ardour, his smile grim as usual. "Greetings, Nathaniel."

"Greetings, Paul. I am sorry to have failed to contest the judgement against you successfully."

"I told you, my death has been predestined, just as your eternal life has been." As it had before, the phrase made me feel accursed, and I shivered. Paul of course did not notice, having concentrated on preparing himself for the joys of a martyr's death.

"Thank you for trying to save me, my son. My soul is already saved." He made the statement as a natter of fact, not with any hint of self-congratulation, simply a fact beyond doubt. The guards, whom I had bribed to stay outside, came back into Paul's cell.

Turning to me, he raised his heavily chained arms in a final blessing, and I left.

Chapter 22

Through the centuries after Julia's death I continued to marry, procreate, and weep at the funerals of my wives and children. The Roman Empire, mighty and unassailable, had gradually imploded, impaled on the glittering shards of its decadence.

Hannibal had almost succeeded in breaching it a couple of hundred years before the birth of Christ; it took the Goth, Hun, and Visigoth barbarians, from the third to the fifth century, to complete the work of devastating Rome and the rest of Europe.

The barbarians were hardy and tough, and able to endure the cold of their lands of origin, whereas the Mediterranean peoples on the southern perimeter of the Empire had become conditioned by temperatures hot enough to encourage indolence as an essential part of their character and culture, and were nowadays dangerously soft.

So the City of Rome, still intact in its marble glory, became surrounded by a land that was depopulated and impoverished, its peoples, mostly from provincial backgrounds, having been leaders in the fighting against the invaders.

As they were subjugated, Rome's predominance subsided into a nostalgic dream-world.

To my surprise, the eloquence of Paul, expressed in his writings and those of his fellow apostles, grew so successful in displacing the Romans' beliefs in the old gods that Jesus and not Jove now presided over the religious landscape.

In fact, so powerfully had these teachings permeated even the minds of kings and caliphs that it was often non-Christians who faced persecution.

All religions cherished their intolerance of each other, and no matter how much lip-service was paid to them, mankind's natural instinct for defending his territory, coupled with his innate love of aggrandisement, frustrated the unwontedly gentle aspects of Christian belief and psychology. Renunciation of wealth, honouring the poor, weak, and humble, and turning the other cheek, no longer made much of a mark on what Christianity's founder had once taught.

Inevitably Christian priests came to learn that their flocks' fear of death offered huge profits, and became corrupted; absolution had its price like anything else in the market.

The sale of indulgences became an important part of the Church's economy, so that the highways and byways of the Christian world became infested with sacerdotal salesmen, the footpads of religion, who would waylay and rob anyone in whom they could arouse a sense of guilt for having transgressed, and the desperate need to be shriven.

If there was one thing calculated to enrage a Pope and his Court living in power and luxury, it was the self-denying practices of the sects, such as the *Humiliatii*, who did their best to follow Jesus' way. How dare they pose as preferring sackcloth and ashes to fine silks, and even if they did, so blatantly to parade their consciences?

Although I travelled widely, I spent a good deal of time in Caesaria, and when the Emperor Constantine flexed his Christian muscles and decided to move his capital eastward to Byzantium, was in a position to take full advantage of the resultant increase in trade and transport.

I did not, however, lose sight of the west, and had built large fleets of river boats, which plied up and down its great complex of waterways: the Rhone in the south-east, the Garonne and Loire to the west and centre of Gaul, the Seine, Rhine and Danube to the north.

My Dolphin fleet also traded beyond the Pillars of Hercules with Britain, often with armed escorts, because I did not accept easily the murder of my crews and pillaging of my cargoes by barbarians and pirates.

I built warehouses and homes in several of the great Italian seaports, and was as much at home in Genoa, Venice and Pisa, as in Rome and Jerusalem.

Quite often I would find an opportunity to visit Antioch; though Saphira, like everyone else I had known in her day, had long ago become dust. I had never forgotten my inauguration by her into the sensual arts; Antioch was still, I was glad to see, a city of grace and elegant iniquity.

Even there, however, my unchanging looks began to generate suspicion that there was something strange about me; some people addressed me as Messiah and others as Prophet, but many considered me rather as a magician of ill intent.

My own sense of myself was clear-cut: life was life and death was death. Living was as natural as any other habit, when I walked out of a mausoleum—of which I had built many—I did not feel that it was uncomfortable or unnatural for me to leave the dead behind the closed gates. They had died; I was alive.

As I grew accustomed to permanent survival, I took it for granted. Occasionally I wondered what the reason was for that survival, but it ceased to be significant. In fact, it had taken me a century to be sure that my life was uniquely different from everyone else's. My strength and energy were still those of a healthy young man; it was my knowledge, and beyond that my wisdom, which had developed beyond the reach of a young man's mind.

My sentience too was beyond the emotions of a young man; accepting permanent youth as an unchanging, and therefore normal condition, would in the long run—so far as I was concerned, there was no other sort—erode my emotions and substitute boredom for almost all of them.

That might have been a gift to a saint or a philosopher, but to me it gave a hint of alarm. Emotion was such an integral part of living, how could I conceive of physical life linked forever to emotional death?

It was not for several hundred years that that particular thought began to assail me. In the meantime, there were others who, hating what they couldn't understand, tried to vent their frustration by removing the problem.

Once, as I emerged late at night from one of my favourite seraglios, I was set upon by a number of acquaintances with daggers. They were camel drivers and porters who often worked for me, but their curiosity had got the better of discipline, and they were also drunk.

"We were young men when we first knew you, and you seemed the same age as us, but now we're old but you haven't changed. What sort of man is it who isn't affected by age any more than a rock by the tide?

115

Even a rock becomes eroded eventually, but you're not eroded, you've no line, no wrinkle, and you don't have to have your food mashed to a pulp because you no longer have teeth to eat it."

They crouched round me in the shadows made by their torches, their hostility growing by the minute.

"Maybe we should smash you to a pulp, to see what you're made of," said a tall, thin man menacingly hefting a stone.

"You would find me made of flesh and blood, just like yourselves," I told them. I looked at them, braced for attack.

"Show us then!" demanded a camel-tender He handed me his dagger. "Cut your arm for us, here." He put a thick finger on my right bicep. I gritted my teeth and cut myself; blood sprayed from the wound, but the pain only lasted a moment.

"Not like that!" He snatched back his dagger, raised it, and plunged it deeply into my arm, savagely tearing the flexus muscle.

I let out a howl and bent over, clasping the wound as if in agony; the men laughed.

"The poor bastard's like us after all," proclaimed the camel-tender. "Sorry we had to find out by cutting your arm, friend. We owe you a flagon of wine."

They made off, still laughing, and so did not know that I was bent over a wound that had already healed.

In order to try to reduce similar suspicions I took to dusting my hair with powder or wearing a grey wig, but the cosmetics of the times were too unsophisticated to be relied on to aid disguise.

However, there was nothing I could do to avoid outliving my families, and they died frequently in fear of me, as Julia had done.

My burnished young face had peered down on too many death beds, and I suspected that, no matter how poignant my grief, my words sounded no more sincere than the pretended interest of a priest absolving someone he neither cared about nor even knew.

Now and then, travelling to places where I was well-known, I pretended to be my own descendant. I became skilled at thanking people for their eulogies, and accustomed to hearing myself referred to in the past tense.

Every day became in some way an obituary.

Chapter 23

Stephen Scott-Harmon was Executive Vice-President, New Clients, in my PR firm, Dolphin Lateral Corporation. Dolphin Hierarchical might have been a more accurate name for the company, as status was on a basis as perpendicular as the building itself.

Stephen was well aware of his seniority as, in effect, he was the leader of a team of global scouts looking for potential clients, corporate or individual. He had a good ear and a keen nose and was as polished as an apple. Treacle-coloured hair lay silkily backwards along his head, and the effete impression he gave overall was satisfactorily misleading. In fact he was like what used to be called a Q Ship during World War Two, a seemingly unarmed merchantman which turned out before a foe could react to be extremely well gunned.

A prospective client, lulled into thinking that Stephen was not on the ball, could find himself signing a contract which he had intended to leave for another day, or sign with another company.

The large white teeth, like ivory headstones, flashed at me as I came into the board room.

"Good morning, Stephen."

"That it is, Nathaniel." He was drinking coffee, peering at a computer screen, and trying not to look too self-satisfied. He rang to ask his secretary for another cup and offered me a chocolate cookie.

"Congratulations on the new televangelist account."

I could almost hear him purring. "Thank you. The Church of the Loaves and Fishes: Pastor and Founder, the Reverend Francis Foxglove. He's already big down south and we've arranged TV time for him on CBS, although of course the internet's full of CLF invitations to click on and be saved. The Reverend doesn't like anagrams—he prefers the Church to be called by its full name.

"What sort of billing is the Church likely to commit to?"

"Initially ten million dollars a year. CBS's percentage should keep them happy about the extra five seconds' air time per show, which is what we reckon not using the anagram will take."

"I expect we're paying for those seconds on a gross basis," I said drily. "Try to mention Foxglove more than his Church on the scripts, because those seconds are going to mount up to minutes pretty damn quickly. Unless CBS really is going to make us a present of them."

Stephen chuckled. "OK, Nathaniel, I can arrange that."

"What do you reckon the exponential increase will be for a successful campaign?"

"Foxglove's talking about an extra ten million on his advertising and PR budget within two years."

"Well, evangelism's always been a good business, Stephen." Except, of course, for the founder of Christianity and its various sects which are evangelism's inspiration, apart from the dollar. Indeed, Jesus has always seemed to me to have had much in common with van Gough and all the other talented artists, writers, sculptors, musicians and inventors who have only attained acceptance and renown posthumously.

119

Wryly, I had long ago realised that one of the advantages of eternal life was that there was no posterity beyond which to be recognised.

Chapter 24

So far as I was concerned, it was as dangerous to be ostentatiously rich in those post Roman Empire days —as indeed it is now—as it was to be perpetually young. Europe teemed with predatory tribes and treasure-hungry kings and chieftains. The appetite for other people's riches grew keener as inadvertently the undefended western ports of the Frankish Empire serenaded the Swedish corsairs who had already honed their raiding skills to the south east, as far as the Baltic and Constantinople, ready to colonise the surrounding Slavs and in due course create the Russian state.

The Swedes favoured approaching the Frankish ports as merchants rather than brigands; the Danes and Norsemen, on the other hand, enjoyed savagery for its own sake. They had even begun to chasten the Barbary pirates, who like themselves often raided as far west as the Irish littoral, murdering, kidnapping, and slaving before returning with their terrified prisoners to their coastal lairs near Rabat.

Moslem brigand armies from the East infiltrated untidily but dangerously westward, ravaging Sicily and each side of the Alps, penetrating northwards as far as the Teutonic province of Swabia.

To protect my riches I had to launder them, in modern parlance, as discreetly as possible by investing them in goods, vessels, and property. And, of course, in influence. I built a noble palace in Venice, one of the greatest centres of seafaring, which was eventually to become sufficiently powerful to drive out the various invaders in a series of sea battles. It was thanks to the Venetian fleet that Bari was narrowly saved from Byzantine capture at the turn of the new millennium,

1002, and three years later other invaders from the east were defeated by the Pisan navy at the Battle of Reggio. In both instances I was responsible for financing a sizeable percentage of the Italian ships.

It was not until more than a century had gone by that I became involved in the Fourth Crusade, which became, not so much by coincidence but design the bloodiest, as well as the most profitable, of them all.

Through an alliance of riches and marriage to his niece Corinda, I became friendly with the Chief Magistrate of Venice and Genoa, the Doge Enrico Dandolo. Dandolo was an excessively cunning man who was to embarrass me, after we became business partners, by revealing a quite extraordinary capacity for wickedness.

Even as a youth he had no look of innocence. His eyes were black and flat and fast-moving, engaging with someone else's, flickering elsewhere, reengaging. They were like a pair of insects in his head.

In middle-age Dandolo was to become as round as a puff-ball, and later as skeletal as a holy eremite living inside a cave-mouth. He also lost his sight, and although his insect eyes still seemed the same, was totally blind. He travelled a great deal, and made many enemies; it was rumoured that it was on one of his expeditions that he was deliberately blinded by the Byzantines.

It was also alleged that he lost his sight through a heavy blow to the back of the head, or a fall, but he never spoke of it. Dandolo's principal characteristic was his blood lust, which was almost as powerful as his avarice and like his avarice did not dwindle at all with age.

Being a Jew I could do little to counter it, because no matter how successful I might be I would always be vulnerable to Christian malice, and dependent on the good will of those who owed suzerainty to the Pope. Certainly nobody would thank me for trying to control a doge, but I have never enjoyed the infliction of terror as a means of conquest, whereas it was a major weapon in Dandolo's armoury. It seemed to me that old age had not simply thinned the Doge's blood, but had dried it up altogether, or at least cooled it below freezing point.

Seemingly a devout follower of the teachings of Jesus, not that Jesus would have recognised them as such, Dandolo's basic belief was that Christ's teachings couldn't do too much harm so long as you had the Pope on your side, or at least in your pocket. In Innocent III, however, we had a Pope who had most of us in *his* pocket, being a skilled statesman with an inflexible will.

In fact, Innocent needed a new Crusade. The previous ones had proved an excellent way of stuffing western treasuries with gold because Christian armies, no matter how near to God they thought they were, needed money more than His blessing.

Saracen blood was like Holy Water, every heathen throat cut in the name of the Prince of Peace part of Holy Communion, and no amount of rape or butchery justified in the eyes of God unless it was done beneath flying pennants adorned with silken crucifixes. Thus the Prince of Peace spent an inordinate amount of time in combat.

One of Dandolo's worries, as yet peripheral but becoming tedious, was the rumour of a new self-proclaimed Son of God. Such had appeared at intervals, of course, ever since the original appearance a thousand years ago of the Jesus considered by an increasing number of followers to be the real thing: the Jesus to whom I had offered the orange juice.

I had myself come across at least half a dozen performers able to put on a passable display of godhead, although none of them seemed to have more than the haziest idea of how to redeem mankind's sins. They tended to speak and behave as if such redemption were an everyday event, instead of an unimaginable occasion to have to rise to. To become the Redeemer, they seemed to believe, one simply placed a couple of commodious metaphysical panniers on each side of a metaphysical ass, loaded them with examples of human misdeeds and carted them off to a metaphysical town dump.

"I have even heard it said that this religious mendicant speaks with the authority of a Son of God!" Dandolo grumbled indignantly, slashing a pomagranate with a silver knife and tasting it as it oozed red juice, as if wounded, in the winter light. "It is said that he does not approve of our fighting the Saracen in His name. How perverse are we supposed to believe Christ to be? Do kings practise treason, princes sack their own estates, and dukes raze their castles? Why then should this self-proclaimed Son of God blaspheme?

"Because he is self-proclaimed, Dandolo." The pomagranate juice speckled his lips, and he spat.

"We cannot have any discouragement of such a great and noble enterprise as a Crusade," he went on. "This particular Pretender to the Celestial Throne apparently preaches that the best interpretation the zealous Christian can apply to His teachings is to desist from chastising the ungodly physically, and persuade them instead through rhetoric and example, like an Athenian of the School of Socrates." He threw the remains of the fruit on to his plate. "What a doctrine of contradiction! How can anyone suppose that God would insult himself?" he shouted.

"I have not come across many prophets who were convincing," I told him.

He favoured me with a smile like the edge of a sword-blade.

"If he wants us to take pity on the Caliph and his armies, perhaps he regards it as desirable too that we should spare the Barbary pirates chastisement."

I said I doubted it: Dandolo had joined me in maintaining a fleet of light, fast warships especially to combat the pests who were after so long still such a canker in the western Mediterranean. As our action against them benefitted every shipowner and merchant in the region, we levied tribute throughout the Mediterranean ports to defray our expenses. In other words, we turned a massive profit.

It was now our intention to ignore any pretence that there was anything religious about the impending Fourth Crusade, and to concentrate entirely on the vast commercial potential offered by its secular glory.

It was, I recall, a group of nobles from northern France who began the impetus for this Crusade, towards the end of 1199. Pope Innocent III had already demanded a fortieth of clerical incomes from his clergy, and set papal heralds to work, preaching the Gospel Militant.

At the same time, the Jesus claimant was intensifying his Second Comeback, extending the number and range of his own heralds and teaching and preaching along the Adriatic littoral much as his namesake had once concentrated in the vicinity of Lake Galilee.

Innocent was beginning to be as concerned as Dandolo, and thinking aloud of dispensing with the troublesome prophet as soon as possible, but one could hardly claim to be Christ's Vicar on Earth and at the same time insist that someone calling himself Jesus Christ was without any doubt whatsoever a lying impostor who should at once be put to death for heresy.

More than a year passed; because of my religion and the problems it would present dealing with crusaders, Dandolo represented us both in bargaining with the negotiators for the Fourth Crusade. They agreed to our demand for the huge sum of 85,000 silver marks, to be paid in advance, before we would hand over the ships and supplies needed. We also contracted for fifty per cent of the booty of all future conquests, thereupon acquiring much influence in the direction of the Crusade.

"Our lusty young knights want to take ship for the Holy Land and rush to the battlefield as soon as they get there," Dandolo told me after a day's determined bargaining. "Of course, that doesn't accord with the desires of a number of their masters, who want instead to attack and conquer Egypt, on the grounds that it's not only immensely rich but also a major Moslem power and the principal source for the reconquest of Palestine."

"We can hardly agree to forfeit the obligations we've just agreed with the Egyptians, though, can we?"

"Everything has to be considered."

I wasn't sure that such a breach of faith could in any way be justified, but knew that no moral argument would carry any weight with Dandolo. "Do you believe going to war against Egypt with the Crusaders would be any more lucrative than our present arrangements?" I asked him.

Dandolo chuckled. "We shall not, I think, have to make up our minds whom to favour just yet. The

Crusaders cannot sail without our ships, and the Egyptians will pay us an extra tariff to ensure that our young knights and their praiseworthy passion for battle in the name of the true God, be constrained."

"What about the Pope?"

"I would say we have the Pope where we want him, although that may not be exactly where he wants to be himself. When you become as involved as he is, the net's likely to fall over your own head whilst you find yourself suffering an anal fistula from impalement on your own trident." The Doge's thin lips stretched into an extortioner's grin."I may not be able to see, Nathaniel, but there is nothing wrong with my sense of smell, and my nostrils are full of the rich perfume of profit."

Chapter 25

I recall it was an intensely humid August night in 1202 that the negotiators arrived to complete arrangements for transport to Constantinople. The trouble was that they hadn't managed to raise the agreed price.

Dandolo was furious. He arrived at my house in a golden gondola, escorted by a number of lesser vessels, greeted me with his usual mixture of warmth, suspicion and envy of my continuing youth, embraced his greatnieces and nephews, and handed Corinda the gift of a jewelled box in anticipation of an excellent dinner.

"What do you suggest we do about our knightly friends?" he asked, when we had finished and were sitting by ourselves in one of the salons. It was quiet, the water lapped gently below, and the smell of sewage wafted soothingly, rather than offensively, through the open window." My old bones can't stand the chill," he added, "kindly send for the windows to be shut."

Given what I suspected about his blood I did not argue; the windows were closed on the comfortless evening by a sweating footman.

"Perhaps we should drop our demand to, say, 80000 marks," I suggested, as a way of still making a vast profit without having to kidnap an army.

"Certainly not!" snapped Dandolo. "We shall intern them until they find the money we agreed on."

"You intend to intern an *army*?"

"The islands in the lagoon are ideal for the purpose. A few weeks of this chill and I am sure they will keep to the arrangements agreed upon."

"Enrico, there it is no chill."

"You have uncommonly hot blood, Nathaniel." He glared at me, eyes screwed up like a mole's.

"And I swear on Corinda's heart I would exchange every one of the 85,000 marks for the gift of your eternal youth," he added peevishly. "Already my niece stoops with age and yet you still carry yourself like a young stallion." He ran his hand over my shoulders.

"That's because I have lived a life of flawless virtue, Enrico."

He cackled. "I must go.Whatever you say about the temperature, this house is confounded cold."

I saw him into the vestibule, where a servant helped him on with a bearskin cape held together by a pair of diamond claws.

"It is time to get rid of our friend who aspires to godhead," he added, as footmen held the front door open and the gondoliers of his household stood ready to help him on to the jetty.

"No. I do not think that is an enterprise we should consider."

"His voice is getting louder and nearer. I do not desire it to fill the ears of a stranded army."

"And I do not want to have an innocent man's death on my conscience, whether or not he is who he claims to be."

"Innocent? Innocent of what?" Dandolo's black eyes stared quizzically in my direction. "For whatever virtue we may claim innocence, there is a vice of which we are guilty. Even the Pope, who has given himself the title of Innocent, has inevitably mocked the word by doing so."

"Enrico, of what sin are you accusing the Pope of being guilty?"

"He does not have to be specifically guilty of anything. It is enough for him to carry responsibility." He cackled again and gave me a quick kiss on the cheek.

"If you would prefer it, I shall take the sole responsibility, embrace the guilt, for this fellow Jesus' death. A fair trade for my redemption, don't you think?"

His watermen helped him into the gondola and settled him round with cushions.

Corinda waved from an upper window and a dog fell into the canal in the excitement, paddled vigorously off course after a big rat and, getting caught up in some weed, resentfully drowned.

I had to make up my mind whether to allow the murder to go ahead, or, as he would regard it, betray Enrico. Venice was like a huge ear, into which every whisper penetrated, sooner or later, and I knew he would find out about my perfidy towards him.

I wondered if my apparent immortality would be proof against a dagger.

Chapter 26

The would-be crusaders greeted Dandolo's proposal to hold them captive on an island in the lagoon with the indignation and rage which we expected, but whereas I was apprehensive and expected them to turn against us, Dandolo was unperturbed. He sat in his throne room, and received Count Theobald, the leader of the expedition, and his deputy Boniface, Marquis of Monserrat, with contemptuous dignity, so that they found themselves almost apologising for not having sufficient funds, instead of behaving as if it was ourselves at fault for demanding too high a figure.

Theobald, who came from Champagne, was a tall man who had evidently until recently been burly and in good health; now he seemed to have imploded, his flesh slack and an eerie grey colour, as if the spirit had already died in him. That probably accounted for his fairly passive acceptance of our conditions.

Boniface was furious, but could not show his anger and so discredit his commander. He was aggressive in personality, a frowning, hard-eyed warrior who would have daunted most opponents but had no effect on Dandolo at all.

He and Theobald were invited aboard one of our ships, and rowed briskly to the island where tents and provisions had already been put at the army's disposal; the knights, squires, armourers, quartermaster's staff and the rest of the army were all ferried across in their wake, each group in ships whose crews were comfortably outnumbered by Venetian sailors and soldiers.

The horses, farriers, blacksmiths and grooms were taken to a separate island. Further discussions were

131

scheduled to take place the following day, but soon after going into his tent Theobald was taken ill with a remorseless fever, which didn't leave him for several hours, until he died.

Boniface was already entwined in the affairs of the East; his brother Conrad had been King of Jerusalem and William, another brother, Regent. A third brother, Renier, had married a Byzantine princess. Boniface was therefore not only accustomed to power, but addicted to it, and thus ruthless in the quest for it.

"I think Theobald's death will be to our great advantage," Dandolo said thoughtfully, a few days after the crusader's leader had undergone the ceremonial pieties of departure.

"Surely he was more malleable than Boniface is likely to be. He won't be constrained by us for long."

"If he agrees to a scheme I have in mind he won't need to be." Dandolo's grin was chilling.

"What scheme, Dandolo?"

"I will discuss it further with you when I have mentioned it to Boniface and obtained some sense of what he makes of it. If he agrees, God will smile and our treasuries will burst. First, though, I must deal with this perverse nuisance who claims to be the born-again Son of God, Jesus Christ."

The claimant had arrived with a crowd of disciples and followers at what was to become the Lido. I was curious to hear him speak, and see if there was anything about him that would remind me of the other Jesus whom I had so briefly but poignantly encountered more than a thousand years before.

It was evening, and Jesus was addressing his congregation from a boat, by torchlight. Dressed unobtrusively, and accompanied by only one servant, Adolfo, I joined the throng who stood either holding torches, or under sconces flaring on poles driven into the soft ground.

This Jesus was taller and stronger than the one I remembered, but I had not seen him before his tormentors turned him into a bloodied wreck. This one was as yet unhurt.

His eyes were black under scimitar-shaped brows; thick dark hair fell beyond his shoulders. He had the dialect of Naples and was possibly a Magyar. He raised a white-sleeved arm and the murmur of the crowd faded into silence.

"I have come here to bring you the Word of God, my Father. How shall I tell it to you? Shall I say to you: "I have proof that I am the Son of God? Shall I roll back the sleeve of this garment to show you a Sign?"

There was a shiver of excitement among his listeners. "How would a Sign bring you faith, though? A sign would say: I am proof.

"Therefore to accept that God is my Father, you would need no faith in face of proof, no eyes to see, no ears to hear the Word. You would need no belief, no feeling, no joy, no doubt, no inspiration. You would need neither mind nor soul.

"Why? Because to believe in God you *must* have faith; to hear God's voice you *must* trust in words that cannot be heard and visions that cannot be seen. You must accept the challenges of faith rather than the assurances of man or of the Sign you would have me show you." He paused and inspected his congregation.

"Now there are men," he went on, "who wish to make war in my name. The war they call a Crusade.

They have already slaughtered many they accuse of heresy against the Word they proclaim as being mine.

"They lie. Their word is not mine. We do not speak with the same tongue, for I do not speak through the sword, but through Faith.

"The cock does not crow at dawn to spread the Word of God, it crows to proclaim its strength to the farmyard, so that the hens will offer it obedience and respect. In the same way those who call themselves Crusaders do not in truth fight for the Cross which they claim as mine, but for their own glory, pride and profit." He raised his arm again.

"They have no power to impose any sort of salvation, and they have no power to deny it."

There was a rumble of anger from his listeners.

"It is as cocks at dawn that they challenge the sun as it rises, and as cocks at eventide that they are mute as the sun leaves the sky without having acknowledged them."

"What shall we do, Master?" a man shouted, "about these men who offend you by falsely claiming to fight in your name?"

"They shall be given the opportunity to listen to reason and change their intention."

"And if they do not, Master?"

"I shall, when they have repented, redeem them."

There was a furious growl from Boniface. His men joined in until every man we had brought to the islands was baying like a wolf. I thought Boniface was ready to leap into the lagoon and strike out for Jesus' boat in order to rock it so that everyone in it fell into the water.

Whereupon Boniface could seize Jesus by the beard, pull him underwater and drown him.

Aware of his peril, Jesus was rowed clear and brought to shore, where I tried to speak with him, but he was surrounded by retainers. Some were big men, obviously guards and protectors. None was armed, however, and I didn't give much for the claimant's chances of survival if Dandolo decided on his death.

Chapter 27

The next morning, the waters of Venice were crowded with small boats and, to my surprise, an ornate scarlet gondola which was part of the Doge's fleet. One of his servants had been sent to escort me aboard it, and we set off, the half dozen oarsmen each side plying their oars with powerful, almost sensuous elegance.

Wrapped in a cloak and sitting on cushions as usual, Dandolo welcomed me with the smile that I had never entirely trusted. I knew my wife was probably the only person he really cared for and trusted and that he tolerated me as his business partner only because he needed me. There was no real personal warmth in our relationship any more than there is between a pair of scissors and a stone, because my trust of him was similar with his for me. However, our needs too balanced each other.

"Nathaniel, I thought we would enjoy this performance together. I received heralds this morning from the self–proclaimed Son of God, requesting an audience of me. Perhaps he has decided not to renounce the Holy War we are about to wage in His name; in any event he wishes to discuss the matter further with me, in front of his rabble."

"I told him that he would do better to debate the matter with the leader of the Crusade, who would certainly not call it off unless convinced that he would indeed be acting on the orders of Jesus Christ." He cackled. "Do you think that is what will happen, Nathaniel?"

"I cannot see how he will convince Boniface of his identity without proof."

"And what proof could he possibly provide?" asked the Doge silkily, as we sped through the damp heat across the sparkling wavelets, towards the island where Boniface and his impotent army waited. A smell of rancid sweat from the stranded warriors tainted the breeze.

Jesus and his supporters and followers were in an armada of small vessels, all of us heading for the island. We shipped oars and stopped near a small jetty, on to which strode a bull of a man wearing a sword in a jewelled scabbard slung over a frilly silk shirt, and black velvet pantalons over blue silk hose.

As he had been last evening, Jesus was in a white robe. His boat lay gently rocking a hundred metres or so from the jetty.

Boniface said nothing for a moment, scrutinising Jesus' face, before roaring: "Is it true you claim to be Jesus Christ, the Son of God?"

"That is who I am." Jesus spoke quietly but with an orator's ability to cast his voice so that even those listening in the quite distant outer ring of boats, could hear it distinctly.

"Prove it!" shouted Boniface. "And don't ask me to have faith! I want proof!"

There was an extraordinary tension right across the lagoon and the crowded island, men standing quite still amidst their early-morning tents, whose sides now and then gently quivered, as if awakening and taking their first breath of the day.

"Yes, give us proof!" Boniface's army shouted in support. Jesus slowly stood up in the thwarts of the small boat, two oarsmen holding it as steady as possible, and maintained his dignity as he drew himself up to his full height, which was considerable.

"Who are you, to demand proof of God?"

"And who are you to claim to be the Son of God *without* proof ?" bellowed Boniface. "How dare you demand that we abandon the Crusade we have dedicated to you and your cause?"

"I detest the very name Crusade," Jesus said quietly. "Do you think the vision of the Cross and all it stands for, the cruelty of which mankind is capable, and the pleasure mankind takes in it, is pleasing to me? Do you believe that I would want to make it a condition of life for so-called infidels to believe in me at the point of a *sword*?

"It is love that I offer men, and love embraces reason, not violence. What comfort would it give me or my Father in Heaven, to drive sinners to repentance by twisting their arms behind their backs or grappling them to salvation with chains?"

Boniface glared across at him from the jetty. "You have shown me no proof of who you claim you are. You are a coward and a blasphemer, an Unbeliever daring to try to masquerade as Him in whose Name we go forth to fight the Fourth Crusade!" Boniface crouched at the jetty's edge. "Come here and fight, let us all see the colour of your blood! I'll warrant it isn't red, or purple! In fact, I believe you to be a bloodless charlatan!"

Jesus turned to scan the intently listening flotilla, before again confronting Boniface, who was almost drooling with rage.

"If I accept your challenge to combat, what will the death of either of us prove?" he asked quietly.

"I seek to rid the world of a blasphemer, not to prove anything!"

"And suppose that you were in fact to kill Jesus Christ, the Son of God?"

Boniface gave a savage laugh. "Well then you would offer me redemption, would you not? I would be forgiven."

"If you killed me, it is my Father who would decide whether or not you deserved to be redeemed."

Very slowly, Boniface placed his hand on the pommel of his sword, and very slowly drew it from its scabbard, his eyes never leaving those of Jesus. "So be it, Blasphemer. We shall see who dies. But I shall not claim to be the Son of God when you perish on the point of my sword," he almost whispered, "I shall simply be avenging Him against one who has taken His Name in vain."

Dandolo raised a hand. "Enough! We do not want either a dead claimant to the throne of the Son of God, or a dead army commander. I am persuaded, therefore, that our Prophet should depart with those who believe in him, but that we should reconsider whether to continue with the Fourth Crusade."

There was utter silence, but Dandolo was obviously concealing something. Boniface, I think, had the same thought, because he uttered no protest, simply slipped the sword back into its scabbard.

It was too early for me to be relieved that the claimant was still alive; he would not be entirely safe, I thought, until he was well away from Venice. Every boat turned about and headed away from the island. "What do you have in mind?" I asked Dandolo.

"The Fourth Crusade will not be abandoned, of course, no matter how fervently our Jesus renounces it," Dandolo said with a chuckle. "It will just be – not quite as we originally envisaged it. I have, I think, resolved the difficulty of choosing between Constantinople and Egypt. There need be no further delay."

"Without Boniface needing to find the balance of the funds, Enrico?"

"There is a way in which we can forgive him the outstanding sum, I think."

"The only way you would consider forgiving him a single silver mark would be if our generosity led to our making two silver marks for each one we forgave."

Dandolo laughed and allowed an attendant to help him up as we grated gently against the Doge's Jetty. "Precisely, Nathaniel. I have invited Corinda to join us – no doubt she is waiting for us indoors."

By the time I discovered the deal Enrico had arranged with Boniface enabling him to 'forgive' the balance of the monies originally agreed between us, it was far too late for me, or anybody else, to try to stop him.

As a consequence, furious and betrayed, the Pope took the unprecedented step of excommunicating everyone, including His Excellency the Doge Dandolfo of Venice, and his commander Boniface, for betraying the true faith, and for committing what today would be termed Crimes Against Humanity.

Chapter 28

Dandolo gave no hint of his plans, merely announcing, to the considerable surprise of Corinda and myself: "I have decided to accompany the Crusade." He looked as if the limit of his endurance would be to hobble the length of his palace terrace before having to take a prolonged rest.

"It is for the sake of my immortal soul and, of course, the coffers so dear to you and me, Nathaniel, that I intend to ride under the banner of Holy Church against the heathen. Not a privilege, alas, available to yourself," he added slyly.

Whether the presence of the claimant in Venice had anything to do with the Doge's plot, I am not sure; a few days after the confrontation seemingly every boat in the Venetian fleet sailed to the two islands to collect the Crusaders and their horses and supplies, and carried them back to the mainland, whence in military formation they started marching eastward.

There was no sign of Jesus or his acolytes; I have no idea whether or not there was any real justification for his claim, but not surprisingly came across no evidence for it. However, Venice's canals had plenty of room for bodies, and the rats were hungry and left no indiscreet traces.

What the Fourth Crusade under Dandolo's guidance achieved, was not to gain booty and riches through the sacking of Saracen cities but by marching on an affluent Christian one.

Zara, in Dalmatia, was stormed by the Boniface and the Fourth Crusade in November 1202, thoroughly looted and sacked, and almost every member of the population butchered. After stripping it of everything worth carrying, the Crusade resumed course for Byzantium, heading initially for Corfu and planning a side-swipe at the Greeks in order to force them to reunite the Greek Church with Rome. Innocent formally forbade the action, but having demonstrated that he had lost the power to control events, did not risk further humiliation by attempting to regain it.

I offered my share of the profit from the sack of Zara to the Ascetics, who were establishing monasteries and friaries run under spartan and self-denying disciplines entailing vows of poverty. They refused it.

Chapter 29

Christoforo Colombo was a young Genoese seafarer whose large dark eyes were luminous with ambition.

Determined to find a new sea route to China and the East Indies via the Atlantic, he had written for financial backing to King Ferdinand of Spain. Ferdinand, however, was intent on unifying Spain and expelling or converting to Catholicism the Moors who had been entrenched in Granada and whom he had at last driven out of the Alhambra. He therefore passed Colombo's letter to his Queen, Isabella of Castille, who combined excessive piety with a love of power.

Whereas Ferdinand was ruthless and cunning, Isabella was intelligent, single-minded, and dangerously self-righteous, one of those who tolerates enthusiasts but is much keener on zealots. She therefore brought to power some of the cruellest zealots ever to have stained the pages of history, including the sadistic Archbishop Ximenez Cisnero, whose asceticism ironically brought him more into line with the self-denying, Manichean sects murdered a couple of centuries previously in South West France for trying to follow Jesus' example of renunciation of worldly goods, such as the Cafards and *Humiliatii*, than with the lovers of wealth, such as the Catholic Church, which had been responsible for their persecution.

Also, as Russia's Czarina Alexandra was fatally to do five hundred years later in submitting so much of her power to her personal priest Rasputin, Isabella permitted her chaplain Thomas Torquemada to acquire immense influence over her and the religious life of her country. This enabled Ferdinand and herself to feast on each other's bigotry and virtually hand Torquemada, a man infested with his own demons, control of the administration of the Inquisition.

As Inquisitor-General, he was able to douse the sunshine and flower-scented air of Spain in the smoke and stink of torched 'heretics' as the country fell victim to merciless hypocrites masquerading as Christians but determined to have nothing to do with the gentleness of shepherds and their metaphorical lambs.

After several months of waiting, Colombo gave up hope of ever getting a reply to his letter from Ferdinand, and came to me with his proposal for the expedition. He wanted to outfit three vessels, and marched up and down my office with a seaman's slightly swaying gait, emphasising his certainty that the Atlantic route to China would result in trade routes developing far more quickly and cheaply than was possible along the tortuous land route to China via Central Asia that had been used by Marco Polo at the time of the papal ravishing of south western France.

Polo had returned to Venice by sea through the Persian Gulf, only to find that Venice and Genoa were at war. He was taken prisoner at the Battle of Curjola and imprisoned for some eighteen months, which he used to write his memoirs, including an extensive and illuminating account of his travels.

"Marco Polo spent eighteen years in China in the service of Kublai Khan!" Colombo was almost shouting in his excitement. "My intention is to introduce myself to the present ruler and obtain the sole right to trade with China. The sea route would be so much quicker I estimate trade could increase tenfold over what it is now."

"If the sea route exists," I said gently.

"It exists, Sir. I *know* it exists." The young man quivered with self-confidence and excitement.

"Perhaps. However, I do not want to have to wait eighteen years before I am reimbursed."

"I have no wish to remain with the Khan, Sir. Only to be the only foreigner he deals with."

I was quite excited at the prospect myself, but of course expressed doubt rather than interest in order to strike a better bargain with him. "To raise money to try to reach China by sea is more of a gamble than an investment," I went on, with, I hope, the right mix of hesitation and encouragement. "I appreciate that nothing worthwhile has been accomplished without some element of gambling, but I would need to be convinced that any venture had at least a chance of success for me to back it."

"Back me, have faith in me!" Colombos' eyes were glowing much as the claimant's had glowed, demanding our faith as he balanced in his tilting boat on the Venetian lagoon. I had no idea what became of him, any more than I knew where the destiny of the young sailor standing in front of me would lead him or any investment I might make in his enterprise.

Colombo came round my table to stand over me. "Have faith in me, Sir!" he repeated."You will only be gambling money, whereas I shall be gambling my life."

"I would not separate them entirely," I said drily, as he fidgeted and tried to hone his will on mine. "How many ships would you need?"

"At least three. Robust vessels with plenty of room for the cargoes I shall bring back!"

He leaned forward again, willing me to finance him.

145

"What do you expect to find?" I asked, thinking of my father, keen-eyed, adventurous and brave, and the places which few men, at least non-easterners, had trodden before him. I recalled too the objects of his travels, emerald peacocks and lapis lazuli frogs with ruby eyes which made the eyes of the most sophisticated Romans shine as brightly with greed, and the emeralds and ivories he had brought back along the narrow mountain passes perched on the crumbling lip of disaster, like the one I had fallen over.

Colombo went on: "Because of the Mongols and their wars the old land routes have, as you know, been unusable for years—there has never been a time like the present to seek a new sea route!"

I did not need convincing: Tamerlane's fearsome depredations, and the resultant fall of China's Mongol Yuan dynasty, which had shown itself intellectually enlightened and freethinking in contrast to many western rulers, had been followed by incessant, undisciplined fighting between lesser warlords.

The result was that, over the succeeding years, inland trade across Asia had suffered almost complete shut-down.

"And there are no warlords in the Atlantic Ocean, Signor Nathaniel. We—"

"There is the weather," I interrupted. "The Mediterranean can be treacherous enough, but—"

"I am a first class sailor and navigator, Signor Nathaniel!" he interrupted in his turn. "I have experienced many storms and I can handle a ship in any weather. I am willing to gamble my life. I can take those ships across the Atlantic to China with empty holds and bring them back bursting with treasure!"

I looked at him, summing him up. Enthusiasm was no substitute for skill, responsibility and experience, but without it those worthy qualities lost most of their value. Besides, how could he acquire those qualities without actually pitting himself against the ocean?

He was staring at me ardently, and I knew I was going to back him. If I had not had a business to run I would have joined him, instead of having to do so vicariously. He was shivering with expectation.

"I want a half of whatever profit there may be. If you come back, I shall transfer ownership of the vessels to you, and we shall be partners in a new merchant fleet."

Colombo vaulted over my table and kissed my cheeks. "I shall come back, Signor Nathaniel! I shall come back in triumph."

I picked up my quill and wrote him my note for one thousand marks. "Here is my commitment to your seamanship skills. Come back at the same time tomorrow and we will discuss details."

Impulsively he hugged and kissed me again, and sprinting to the tall, ornate doors of the room, flung them open; I heard him shout for joy as he dashed down the stairs to the street and watched from the window as he rushed exuberantly along the quayside.

The response, from Isabella of Castille, Queen of Spain, finally arrived a week later.

Chapter 30

Cristoforo Colombo came into my office looking subdued, almost afraid. His expression, devoid of joyousness, was doleful, and he couldn't look me in the eye.

"What has happened, Colombo?"

He shuffled on his feet like an embarrassed child, almost crying.

"I have just received the letter I had been waiting for, before you and I agreed a partnership, Signor Nathaniel. The letter from Queen Isabella of Castille."

"And?"

"Signor, she wishes me to go to Castille to tell her personally about my plans. If she approves, Spain will offer to back my venture."

"*Our* venture, Colombo."

He looked utterly wretched, but I was so angry I felt it difficult to pity him in his predicament. I was the one who had agreed to take the risk of backing him, I had agreed to buy the ships he needed, and I was the one who would suffer personal loss if he failed.

Now the Spanish Queen was casually taking over. I regarded it as a misuse of privilege, and my anger stifled any natural magnanimity I might have possessed.

"And if the Queen turns you down, what then? Will you still regard us as being committed to our joint enterprise, Colombo?"

He continued to shuffle his feet. "Signor Nathaniel, I dare not offend Her Catholic Majesty."

"Is it then, easier to offend me?" I glared at him. What enraged me as much as anything else was the fact that, no matter how rich and powerful I might be, I was still a subject and not a sovereign; there was also the Inquisition. Its arm was long, its avarice infinite. Nobody regarded by it as an offender, was safe. It was a devil's wastebasket which, before destroying those physically whom it chose to regard as ungodly, tried to derange them mentally with its casuistry. Specious argument combined with hot irons and inventive torture meant that black was irrevocably white, and white black, if the interrogating friar so decreed.

"And my thousand marks?" I held out my hand.

"I have already used most of it to buy timber and hire shipwrights, Signor Nathaniel." In his shame, he was whispering.

"In that case, it is I who shall have the privilege of being the partner of the Queen of Spain."

Columbo went grey. "She will take no partner, Signor. Even to speak of such a thing—" at this point, I pitied him in his distress, although not enough to relent entirely.

"Signor Nathaniel," he went on, "I will return your money. I swear it. As soon as I receive my Spanish backing—"

"And if there is no Spanish backing?"

He looked at me despairingly. "I beg you, Signor Nathaniel, understand that for me to lose my life at sea would be one thing, something I could accept, but to lose it at the stake—"

"What does trade have to do with heresy, Colombo? Are the Dominicans traders in souls? Tell me, which spice would you attribute to a soul?

149

Cardomon, turmeric, cinnamon perhaps?" My anger flared again. "Are you telling me that your business partner, Queen Isabella of Seville, will hand you over to the Friars of the Inquisition if she discovers you have become impatient with her, and that you contracted to take a Jew as partner instead, because he could make up his mind without delay?"

"Heresy by its nature can be discovered wherever it is sought," whispered Columbo. "Especially for a Jew."

I looked at him a while longer, before putting my arm round his shoulder and offering him the absolution of forgiveness. "Go to Castille and repay my money from the treasure I am sure you will find, Colombo," I told him.

He stared at me through his tears. "Signor Nathaniel, I am in your debt for far more than money. I am desolate at what has happened." He took my hand and kissed it before opening the tall doors and going sadly down the stairs.

The Inquisition arrested me anyway, not long before Columbo and his small fleet set sail from the port of Pallo. A half-dozen soldiers brusquely invaded my home and ordered me into their gondola, and there was no Dandolo to intercede. The Bridge of Sighs glided overhead, and I thought of Pilate and Julia and their family being escorted from their home by the cataphracts on the first stage of their journey to Rome.

I, however, was bound not for Rome but for the Inquisition's headquarters in Seville.

Chapter 31

Everything about the Inquisition was black. Its friars, the 'questioners', wore black cowls and in silhouette looked like illustrations of death, except that of course none carried a scythe; working the land and helping feed his neighbours was not the role of those appointed to root out heresy.

Most of the interrogators were perhaps not so much happy in the infliction of pain on others as suffering from lack of imagination and intellectual protein, being allowed only to partake of religious orthodoxy. They were, however, implacable and skilful verbal duellists, experts in casuistry and playing by no rules. Words to them were like wet clay, blank and devoid of any meaning or sincerity until the verbal arabesques began.

Some of those determined to save the souls of heretics by purging their bodies with fire, such as Francisco Cisneros, Archbishop of Toledo, became so obsessed with the joys of persecution and the overseeing of macabre and dreadful punishments, that the infliction of pain came to mean more to them than the bringing of salvation or, for that matter, the sin requiring it.

However, even the ardour of the Archbishop was generally judged to be excelled by that of Torquemada, whose reputation for cruelty was as black as death itself.

When we arrived at Seville the soldiers who had arrested me and transported me from Venice handed me over to a trio of Dominicans, first chaining my hands behind me. Nobody spoke; the soldiers were evidently used to the friars' silence.

Rush lights, giving far less illumination than the oil lamps of Imperial Rome more than a millennium and a half before, guttered in sconces weeping moisture, a structural lament for all those who had been dragged along these passages to face the questions whose eventual answer was fire.

I was pushed into a dungeon and chained to a wall, after which my jailers left me to stand or try to sit on a few mushy stalks of filthy, urine-soaked straw. Stained and crumpled by my journey, my clothes already seemed impregnated by the reek of the place, and what had been finery was now rags.

After what could have been minutes or hours, there was a faint swishing sound outside the dungeon door, as someone wearing a long garment came along the passage towards me.

Through the grating in the massive door I saw a turnkey bend and thrust a heavy key into the lock, which screeched as the key turned. Slowly, it swung open, and someone entered. The turnkey placed a rushlight in a sconce, and went out, returning a few moments later with a chair, which he set down. After that, he went outside and waited.

My visitor was a scrawny friar, a short man dressed to look as tall as his brooding shadow on the wall.

"Now, my son, what language shall we speak?" the friar asked hoarsely. Decayed teeth appeared between full lips, garlic-scented saliva glistening in the dim light. I suggested Greek, hoping he didn't speak it.

"Very well, although I would have thought Latin more appropriate to your heresies against Christ and his Church."

"I do not follow your reasoning, Friar. Jesus was a Jew, and spoke Aramaic. It was the man who condemned him to die whose natural tongue was Latin."

"Yet another heresy, my son." The language of paternity sounded chillingly false in that mouth amidst the dim, twitching light that seemed alternately to beckon and rebuff the shadows. The friar hawked and spat into the straw near my feet.

"Jesus was the Founder of Christianity, and thus to be regarded as a Christian." The friar's tone was placid, but I suspected his apparent serenity was only a ploy to lull me into a false sense of security, so that I might carelessly incriminate myself as the questioning became more intensive, the casuistry more sophistic. If I made a mistake, those eyes, sunk deep into their sockets, would come fanatically alive.

"Christ was a Jew," I repeated.

"I repeat," in his hoarse whisper, "He was the Founder of Christianity, which transcends all. It is the man who does not believe in the Truth of Christ, the Sanctity of the Holy Virgin who was the Mother of Christ, God the Father of Christ—"

"Christ was a Jew," I said yet again.

The friar seemed not to have heard. "It is the sinner who refuses to recant, the heretic who refuses to acknowledge his fault, who will linger for Eternity outside the gates of Heaven unless in its mercy the Holy Mother Church purges his sins by fire."

"Is that what Jesus preached, that the key to entering Heaven was to be burnt alive? If that is true, what was the point of his bothering to come here as God's son in order to redeem us, when all the Church had to do was set fire to those to whom it offered salvation?"

The friar still retained his serenity, but the rushlight showed eyes glittering with annoyance.

"Are you suggesting that if Jesus Christ had not existed, there would still be His Church and the religion he preached?"

"Of course not, although the religion he preached and your interpretation of it are absolute opposites. He offered redemption through love, whereas you offer it through fire." I added: "And of course, he believed in such qualities as humility and meekness, not greed and arrogance. How many people do you accuse of heresy, so that you can confiscate their property for yourselves? Why did you decide to exterminate the Albigense? And, of course, the Manicheans? Was it not because they lived by Jesus Christ and through Jesus Christ, and therefore shamed the Church and its aggrandisement?"

The friar's whisper was like the rustle of paper. "You are compounding your heresy by making such accusations against the Church."

"Are they not true?" I persisted. "Persecution is never gentle, or just." I eased myself against the damp wall as the weight of my fetters increased the pressure on my swollen ankles. There was no pain, but the discomfort was becoming tedious.

"Persecution?" The friar leaned forward, fully directing at me his expression of false concern. "Is that what you call helping heretics towards enlightenment, my son?" He contrived to sound hurt, marinated as he was in the uniquely savage hypocrisy of his sacerdotal trade.

"You do not recognise the mercy the Church has already shown you. Take the Plague, for example, that which is known as the Black Death. You Jews—"

"Are you accusing the Jews of causing the Plague?" I interrupted. Even by the standards of the Inquisition, this was an extreme accusation.

"You are merchants, and the Black Death has followed your sea routes." The Dominican fondled the broad leather belt round his skinny waist and nodded in self-congratulation. "Your trade started in the East and has spread westward, a curse that has condemned to death a third or more of humanity." He glared at me.

"Our country is now joining the rest of civilisation in becoming a cemetery, its dead proliferating like grain in a good season."

"Are you not attributing too much power to men, *Father*," I sneered, "in accusing us Jews of bringing the Plague with us? Is not the Plague, like those of Egypt, not rather an Act of God?" I was sick of his prejudice and complacency; it was time to get at the savagery beneath. Embers glowed in the depths of his eye sockets.

"An Act of God?" he whispered. He was unmoving and malignant. "It is for us in the Church to interpret God's actions, and to condemn yours! It is a wicked corruption of our acceptance of God's will to attribute to him that which is ungodly."

Slowly he levered himself to his feet, his eyes never leaving mine. "Your heresy will be extirpated," he hissed caressingly, as the guard pulled the door open for him, and he went out, taking the rush light with him, and leaving me in the damp blackness.

Talk of the Black Death brought to mind the image of my last wife, Francesca, a Princess of Parma, and one of the most beautiful women I have ever seen.

One morning, I awoke to notice a tiny black blemish on her jaw. I blinked, and the blemish hopped off her face and disappeared under the sheet. I did not realise at the time that what I had seen was to be the cause of Francesca's death, a rat flea.

Within a day or two her impeccable beauty had become disfigured by scarlet pustules, which like miniature volcanoes had erupted under her arms and between her glossy thighs. She died gasping for breath and writhing in feverish pain like a chopped-up worm.

The friar was at least right in suspecting that the Black Death followed the major maritime trade routes; it was not the Jews, of course, or for that matter the Arabs and Phoenicians, who were responsible for the disease, but the enterprising insects who lived off the rodents which infested our ships. These gorged themselves on anything they found – grain, wheat, spices, silks, dates, figs, the wood of casks and the wine inside; drunken rats were as common aboard our vessels as drunken sailors.

I had come across the prejudice before, that it was the Jews who spread the plague, because they traded in money as well as merchandise, and falsely accusing a Jew of heresy gave the debtor a chance to clear his debt without having to repay it, still an objective of slander and betrayal today.

False witness continuously added to the numbers of cords of blazing faggots to which the Inquisition applied its doctrinal bellows in complete contradiction to its proclamation of the mercy of God.

I had no idea whether it was night or day when I next heard footsteps at the end of the passage. They stopped outside, and there was a pause before the heavy key began its rusty copulation with the lock.

The door creaked open, one of the guards held a rushlight aloft, and a man was flung on to the floor, sending a spray of cockroaches skittering frantically for cover.

The turnkey withdrew the rushlight and heaved the door shut, but not before I had time to note the extraordinary Spanish beauty of the latest captive's features, although his face was caked with blood. Perhaps because they had had the pleasure of beating him up, the guards had not bothered to chain him to the wall.

I welcomed him, and he answered with more the litanical cadence of a priest than the roughness of a peasant.

"What are you accused of—heresy?" I asked. I could hear him climbing slowly to his feet.

"I am accused of claiming to be Jesus Christ, the Son of God." I felt the hair rising on the nape of my neck.

"And are you?"

"I am." His confidence was apparently untroubled by having to address me in the thick darkness, which erased the faces on which we could have seen each other's expressions; our voices were all we had to offer each other in the way of identity.

He was committing suicide, of course: proof of his claim would shortly be demanded, and he would be unable to give it. "If I claimed to be the Son of God and wasn't, then indeed I would be committing heresy," he went on.

"And you would then deserve the punishment the Church would inflict on you in your own name?" I asked. I could feel his breath on my cheek as he moved to stand beside me.

"I have never demanded punishment for anyone. Repentance, of course, for the evil deeds that humanity seems unable to deny itself, but not punishment for heresy, for refusal to believe in me. Redemption at the stake is no creed of mine."

There was, it seemed to me, a smile in his voice as he added: "If I cannot convince men that I am the Son of God, I, not they, am to blame for their lack of faith."

"Does that apply to the people who have dragged you here?"

"Yes," he answered simply. "Why are you here?"

"I am a Jew, Nathaniel ben Ezra. And you are Jesus Christ?"

"Yes." he said again. Although Jesus was not an uncommon first name in Spain, including those parts that had been under the suzerainty of the Moors, the Greek Cristos was not a common family name. My companion had said it with casual certainty.

I had a strange desire to see if he remembered our meeting long ago, in that garden perfumed with blood and jasmine, but it was claimed for Jesus that he had been resurrected, not reincarnated, and this claimant was not the Jesus I had encountered on the cross., any more than the Venetian claimant had been.

The darkness seemed to have weight as well as depth, and became suffocatingly heavy. He didn't answer my next question, and I fell asleep.

We were left in the dungeon for a long time, expecting to hear at any moment the footsteps which would lead to the next stage in our pointless interrogation, for I was sure now that whatever we said would be irrelevant, and would end at the stake.

"If you're Jesus," I said, "these Inquisition swine aren't exactly following your teaching." We were both awake, although the darkness was as heavy and intense as before.

"That is why I have been reborn."

"But what's the point? You're only going to be put to death all over again. What will that accomplish?"

"That is in my Father's hands." At that moment I hated his father, not the peon who had actually sired him but the Great Abstract who had deluded himself, and those who believed in him, that humanity was salvageable through the sacrifice of his own son, inevitably in the most painful way possible, towards which mankind had directed so much of its perfidious inventiveness.

"And you can simply accept that, the application to you of evil, and forgive it?"

"What else is there to forgive?"

"The incurable disease," I said bitterly. "If you accept it, how can you fight it?"

"By absorbing and purifying it. You will see. I am not being simply weak."

"Good. Believe me, there is no strength through weakness."

"I have never believed that there was."

"I could hear the smile in his voice, and in spite of its blackness the dungeon became momentarily a place of light.

159

"So how will you conquer the Inquisition? How will you persuade it to give up torture and follow your teachings?" I spoke as if I believed him when he claimed to be the Son of God, and perhaps deep in my mind was the hope that he was. One thing I was sure of was that he would not overcome the specific horror of the Inquisition's cruelty with generalised philosophic vapourings; one would need all one's philosophy to endure the speciality of death as inflicted by the Inquisition. He was giving me an answer.

"By example. There is no other way. These people are too self-righteous and too immersed in the arts of casuistry to be convinced by argument."

"What about meeting fire with fire ? I recall that"— the words stuck in my throat – "your Father did not hesitate to use physical force when he thought it necessary – the Old Testament is full of examples of his warrior spirit."

"There is a huge difference between being God and being His Son, Nathaniel. If I sent lightning from the heavens to blast the Inquisition and its tormentors, it would be a matter of vengeance, not of teaching. I am not a warrior, but a messiah."

"Your spirit is too generous," I said, and was silent. The footfalls we had been waiting for were coming towards us.

They stopped; the screech of the lock, the entrance of a guard, followed by another. We were dragged to our feet and ushered along wet stone flags between guttering rushlights until we arrived at a torture chamber.

The friar who had first questioned me sat at a small table. Behind him, ominous against the wall, hung the chains of the *strappado*, drooping over a rusty pulley set in the ceiling. Jesus and I were pushed against the wall, and the guards attached the chains to the shackles already locking together Jesus' wrists.

"So you did not listen to me before, but you will listen today." The hoarse voice within the cowl was directed at me. "You will be privileged to learn from your fellow blasphemer's suffering that you have no choice but to recant. Or die, of course." He turned to Jesus. "Recant now, and you will have that gift from Mother Church too, acting mercifully in the name of God."

"Yes, in our benevolence." A tall, thin man stood in the doorway, and the friar rose hastily to his feet. Another chair was brought in, after which the heavy door closed, leaving Jesus and me with the two guards and the Dominicans.

"What, no response to our offer of mercy?" The newcomer's eyes were glittering with anticipation.

"Does the Son of God not wish to take this chance to acquit himself of his heresy?" he continued.

Jesus pointed to the large golden cross hanging across the front of the man's robe. "Men mocked me before, and after scourging me nailed me to that," he said. "Today it is the *strappado* and the stake. I asked my Father to forgive men before for what they did, and I shall ask forgiveness for them this time. For you, Inquisitor General," he added.

"So you know who I am, Heretic?"

"I do not have to know. I sense the devil in you. That is why you so desperately need forgiveness."

Torquemada leaped to his feet and I thought he was going to strike Jesus. "You dare to ask forgiveness for me?"

"You stand on the brink of the pit. You have perverted my teachings into a travesty of their intent, you have tortured and burned thousands in my name, and now you are about to burn as a heretic Him whose divinity you pretend to worship."

Torquemada's voice was almost a whisper. "Do you still claim to be the Son of God?"

"I do not claim. I state a fact."

The friar looked at Torquemada for permission to speak before holding up a crumpled document. "This says that your father is an Argonese peon, Jose Pascal, working on the land of Don Arturo Iglesias, near Tarragon."

"He is my earthly father, just as Joseph was before him."

"And which one of your fathers, the holy or the secular, has taught you to speak perfect Latin?" interpolated Torquemada sarcastically. He screamed: "You are an impostor, a fraud, a heretic! Your hypocrisy sickens me! Raise him!" he commanded. The chains tautened as the *strappado* took up the slack, until Jesus was standing on tiptoe.

"Well?" Torquemada's voice was silky. "Behold our benevolence – you have a last chance to speak before your arms are dislocated. "Do you recant?"

Jesus looked straight into Torquemada's expectant eyes. "I forgive you," he whispered.

"You forgive – *me*?" Torquemada leaped to his feet. "Raise him!" he screamed.

Jesus was hoisted slowly upwards, until his head was almost pressing against the pulley, itself seeming to creak and squeal in pain as the chains passed over it. Torquemada made a gesture with his hand and the guard

162

let go the handle from its ratchet, releasing the chains and almost at once recapturing them, so that Jesus was brought abruptly to a halt. He did not cry out, but the blood ran from the lip he had bitten.

"So, Son of God, do you still forgive me?" whispered Torquemada.

"I – forgive you," barely able to speak.

"You will curse me, my son. And at that moment, when your masquerade comes to its end, I shall know you are on the way to salvation." He glanced at the guard, almost unable to look away from Jesus' tormented face.

"Raise him a little, then drop him further." Sweating with the effort, the guard obeyed the order, and I could hear faintly Jesus' shoulder muscles tearing.

"Father forgive them," Jesus murmured, "for – " and fainted.

Back in the dungeon, the guard put Jesus on the floor gently, and stood for a moment, looking down at him. I couldn't see his expression, but the act that he hadn't dropped Jesus like a sack indicated pity, if not belief. Also, he left us with the burning rushlight.

Whilst Jesus remained unconscious, I managed to force his dislocated arms and shoulders back into their sockets. I was surprised that Torquemada had not immediately subjected me to the torture, but it was often the way of the Inquisition to delay its torments, in order to magnify the terror instilled by apprehension.

When he came to, Jesus massaged his arms and managed to smile at me. "My arms do not hurt as much as they did. Did you attend me?"

"I put them back, a trick I learned as a child from an Arab physician."

"Thank you; you have my blessing. I hope you don't think my blessing is devalued because I bestowed it also on our tormentors."

"It is not a blessing but a curse that Torquemada longs to hear from you."

"He shall not have it. If ever a man needed Redemption, it is the Chief Inquisitor." He managed to smile at me, and I thought there would probably never be a better time to speak to him of my encounter with his namesake in Golgotha, but my mind could not encompass the possibility that I had met this handsome young Spaniard in the guise of a Jew from Bethlehem in a previous incarnation.

I had to have proof before I could accept him as who he claimed to be, just as I had needed it in order to be convinced of Jesus' godhead by the eloquence of the passionate and highly articulate apostle, Paul. Yet proof was the thing he could not offer, and he would soon die because it was impossible for him to inspire belief through faith alone.

"Do you remember anything of being on Earth before?"

"Nothing. All I know of it is what I have read, and what my Celestial Father has told me."

"What is your Celestial Father like?"

"He is like everything," Jesus answered simply. "He is in everything, so he can resemble everything. He is in me, and His voice speaks in my mind. It is of course not a human voice, but – elemental. It has the power of thunder and lightning, and the gentle music of a stream. Its rhythms are as insistent as those of a waterfall. Its tones and cadences are profound, in anger and in joy, as they are in love. I know that I am His sacrifice to Redemption, and for that he loves and esteems me."

I could not help being brutal. "Redemption hasn't worked though, has it? Fifteen hundred years ago, according to his disciples, the Son of God died in order to redeem mankind from its sins, and since then there has been an ocean of cruelty, just as there was before."

"If one sinner comes to repentance," he murmured, and gave me a flash of white teeth through his black, blood-stained beard.

"That isn't true – Paul, for example, could bring sinners to repentance with words."

"In the end men killed him for those words, and for his belief in them and his desire to implant that belief in others. How could I have expected Paul and all those others who have believed in me, to die, without myself dying?" Sombrely: "Now it is time to die again. I hope that you are spared."

"I shan't be."

"Then you will die with my love, and that of my Father in Heaven."

We looked at each other with the affection of brothers, as the footsteps once more slithered towards us.

Chapter 32

Now it was our turn to follow so many so-called heretics to the fire. We stood side by side on a platform of dry wood, our hands chained behind us to stakes. I had been spared the *strappado*; I was a Jew, but rich, and there was an inborn obeisance towards the rich in the Inquisition, which was thoroughly corrupt. Also, at the last moment a deal might be done; for payment of a few thousand marks or ducats, I might purchase death by hanging instead of by fire. I might even lose my nerve and reward the Inquisition by recanting, a sinner brought to salvation through repentance, albeit a repentance that had been forcible.

"Wait!" Torquemada approached our pyres, his black robes greenish in the garish sunlight. The secular arm was represented by a detachment of troops wilting beneath heavy metal helmets. Six drums had been set on stands at an equal distance from each other, and the drummers stood, sticks in hand, to serenade our deaths with a heavy roll as soon as our executioners had been given the order to apply their lighted torches to the bone-dry faggots.

"I have not yet received your curse, heretic!" Torquemada glared at Jesus, who was barely alive, having been repeatedly subjected to the drop and then severely whipped. Jesus managed to raise his head and look into his tormentor's sable eyes.

"I forgive you your sins," he pronounced, somehow managing to speak loudly and clearly so that his voice was audible across the square where our *auto da fe* was taking place. "I forgive you your sins," he repeated, "and beg my Father in Heaven to show you the road to benevolence."

"Burn him!" screamed Torquemada, his spittle crackling on the torch held by a terrified monk. "Burn them both at once!"

The executioners swooped forwards as the drums began to roll. Through the shimmering haze of the flames erupting round me I stared at the crazed Inquisitor General.

Everything began to melt into darkness. Before the flames had sunk into embers my body started to reconstitute itself. Torquemada had turned his back to us; now, something made him swing round. Jesus' remains smouldered, unrecognisable as having been human.

Pennants of burning flesh still hanging from my arms, I stepped over the embers and walked slowly towards Torquemada. A cry ran round the square from the spectators, and one of the drummers dropped his sticks and fled. The soldiers moved together protectively.

"You! It is you who is the Son of God!" Face convulsed, Torquemada fell to his knees on the hot cobbles. "God forgive me."

"He did," I told him. "You have just killed him, and he refused to curse you or take back his blessing."

"But it is you who have survived, you who have performed this miracle to prove that you are the Son of God.!" I looked at him with all the contempt I could muster, and raised my head to address the crowd.

"Do you know so little of God that you believe he needs to perform miracles to prove Himself?" I pushed Torquemada with my foot, smearing him with ash. I was determined to avenge Jesus, and was so furious that for a brief while I actually believed in my fellow victim's claim. I bent and removed the large golden cross Torquemada wore, and held it aloft.

"This man and the organisation he leads have profaned the teachings of God!" I announced. The crowd rustled uneasily. "Any of you who support the Inquisition and its ungodly cruelty is guilty of offending against the words and teachings of God," I continued, with Pauline severity.

"Furthermore it is corrupt to purchase absolution for your sins from a priest, and blasphemy to suppose that these creatures here"—I flicked a hand at Torquemada and the cowering friars—"would be chosen by God as His representatives on Earth.

"These are miserable, venial men who have lost any chance of salvation, and are guilty of leading you too to damnation!"

By this time the crowd, groaning, had prostrated itself, as had the soldiers, and apart from myself all that remained on its feet was a donkey loaded with a couple of panniers of faggots, in case the fires died before their victims.

"I do not speak to you in my name," I went on, "because I am an ordinary man whom God has spared from the fire. I speak to you in the name of the God whom Torquemada and his Inquisitors have violated!

"I do not believe in the forgiveness preached by Jesus, I regard it as weakness to turn the other cheek, just as this filth does," grinding my foot on Torquemada's head and pressing it into a pile of manure. "My God is the God of the Hebrews, who are now being so cruelly persecuted because they believe in the One God, the vengeful God who believes in an eye for an eye and a tooth for a tooth. I pray Him to smite wickedness wherever he finds it. Especially the wickedness of the Inquisition!"

I beckoned the hoarse-voiced friar and two of the executioners. "Drive in a stake and chain him to it!" I commanded, pointing down at Torquemada.

"He is a sorcerer!" cried the Inquisitor General, as I ordered faggots to be heaped round him. "A sorcerer is a heretic and must pay the price of heresy!"

"Just now you were telling me I was the Son of God." I turned to an executioner. "Light a torch."

Torquemada began to tremble, convulsing as far as the chain would permit. I flung an arm out at the drummers, who scrambled to their feet, their uniforms soiled by the detritus on the ground. Like clockwork soldiers being wound up they began the death roll.

"I wish to confess my sins!" cried Torquemada, at last believing he was about to die.

"There is not enough time for that between now and the end of the world," I told him. In spite of his terror he gave me a glare of pulverising hatred.

The mortal tableau stood motionless except for the drummers' arms. The friar with the torch crouching to light Torquemada's pyre, the patient donkey still on its feet, the crowd prostrate on the baking and filthy cobbles, the guards in their heavy glittering helmets. Above all there was the tall, thin body of Torquemada standing on his lethal dais of faggots, taut against the stake. He had soiled himself, and the stink of him was heavy in the heat. His eyes burned like the pyres themselves.

"I would have watched you burn as gladly as you watched me," I announced, "but the other man you have just burned insisted on forgiving you. You scorned his generosity, but I shall extend it to you as he would have wished. Whether or not he was the son of God, as he claimed, he showed you a compassion I would never have done. It is therefore in his name, that of Jesus Christ, that I shall show you the mercy you have always denied to others." I signalled to the stooping friar not to set fire to the wood round the stake, and to free Torquemada.

"To the dungeons with him!" I ordered. I stopped deliberately in front of the chamber where Jesus had been tortured on the *strappado*,and Torquemada flinched. I had him chained to the wall. "He is not to be fed or visited until the day after tomorrow. Neither is he to receive water. Is that understood ?" I demanded.

The friars mumbled assent, none daring to look at their chief's contorted face.

"Swear that you will obey in Christ's name."

I waited as they mumbled again, holding their crosses, then helped myself to Tomas Torquemada's fine dappled grey and rode out of Seville unmolested, regretting, as indeed I do still, that I had not commanded his execution to go ahead.

Chapter 33

The sad and frantic resonance of cows unmilked echoed across a soulless landscape. Most had already died for lack of tending and lay, bloated hummocks, among the human corpses. Great clouds of flies seethed among them, giving the impression that they still lived and were writhing in agony on the ground.

Most people I met, when they dared to talk to a stranger instead of fleeing from possible contagion, blamed themselves for the Black Death. It was an Act of God, of course, and they wondered what sin they could have committed which merited such dreadful punishment. Most of them, who had lived their quiet, limited lives without doing anything other than working and procreating, were hard put to it to find anything to feel guilty about. With all the fight knocked out of them, starving and in despair, they died wondering.

At the same time as the plague and the Inquisition flourished and slaughtered, the marvellous irony of the Renaissance began to spread across Europe from Italy. The Pope might be in Rome but it was from Seville that the inhumanities perpetrated in the name of Jesus and Mary meek and mild emanated.

Although I owned a trading empire, it was much safer in those days to be associated with art than trade, given the suspicion about mercantile traders being responsible for the Plague.

Artists were colonising Chartres, Amiens and Rheims, and joining their creative aspirations with those of Sienna, Florence and Padua. Art would provide too the change I needed from commerce; my body had always been well fed, now it was my spirit that needed nurturing.

Near Rheims I was attacked by a group of starving peasants not so much interested in robbing me as in devouring my horse; they were armed with sickles but no longer had the strength to raise them, and I had no difficulty in eluding them. Apart from that my ride was sombre but uneventful, a voyage through a sea of the dead.

The great cathedral of Rheims reared up over the horizon; I was almost level with it when the setting sun acted as a touchstone to a broadside of bats, which rocketed out of the cathedral's eaves in their thousands and vanished into the dusk. The horse reared and nearly threw me into a heap of sewage and detritus, an al fresco mausoleum of decaying and stinking bodies.

I spent the night at a tavern which was almost empty, because of peoples' fear of being in contact with one another. Apart from the landlord, wizened and skeletal, the only other man present was a jovial fellow who lurched heavily when he walked. "Let me introduce myself, Sir. Rene Casson, known to all as Le Boite, because people like to name us for our frailties." He laughed and limped towards me, bowing. "I shall not kiss your cheeks, in case one of us carries the poisonous vapours of affliction."

We had a glass of wine together, and he told me how he had received a ball in the thigh during one of the interminable wars between the French and the Burgundians. These days he preferred the company of artists to that of soldiers; artists knew how to enjoy themselves even in these dark times and he met girls at their parties who did not spurn him.

"After all, when I'm lying down I'm as good as any man!" he exclaimed. I told him I was looking for a house to rent.

"No need to rent – there's a fine house by the cathedral but there's nobody left alive to take your money. Reckon the bishop and his clergy were so loved by the Almighty He couldn't wait to call 'em to Him early." He chuckled.

If they were still alive, I reflected, I would probably have been unable to sleep because of the proximity of the bells; as it was, I took Rene's advice and moved in.

Rheims was as stricken by the plague as most other cities, and there was an air of fatalistic merriment among its artists, who were determined to enjoy what was left of their lives. The likelihood of imminent death seemed to inspire rather than quench their talent; they drank a great deal of wine, and frequently toasted posterity.

"After the Black Death has passed, and ourselves with it, we shall be acknowledged as geniuses by future generations – if there are any!" cried an artist called Andree at one party. "Meanwhile there are only two ways to live – as if tomorrow will never come, or as if today will never end!"

Everyone cheered and flagons were drunk to celebrate the long night which would help the postponement of tomorrow.

Andree was a flaxen-haired gamine, boisterous and hoydenish except when she was working, her pixie face set in concentration. We became friendly and she invited me to a party at her atelier the next evening. "If we're still here, of course."

I thought about her during the night. My emotional dehydration seemed to have undergone a change, I could sense that it was giving way to some sort of irrigation of the spirit.

In the morning I woke up thinking about her, an intense anticipation of the coming evening. When at last the light faded into dusk I followed Andree's directions, walking along a narrow street which was really an alley, hardly wide enough to accommodate a horse. There was the usual, all-encompassing reek of ordure and decay, and in due course I found myself outside a broken door.

I climbed a narrow, dark and creaking staircase to the atelier, and opened the door to colour and light. Candles cast lively shadows across the walls and ceiling, and a number of people sat on the floor and on two hard-backed chairs, talking and laughing, goblets of wine in their hands. Through Rene I had met most of them, and as I entered they greeted me as one of themselves. I went up to Andree and greeted her, looking round as she poured wine. "Where's Rene?"

"Oh, he woke up dead this morning." She told me light-heartedly. "His morning did come after all, but he lived as if it wouldn't. At least he was taken in his sleep, and still in his cups."

We toasted Rene and a sculptor called Colin, who had also died during the previous night. The air was thick with the smell of dirt and fusty, verminous gabardine. At the far end of the room was an easel, and nearby a worktable on which something lay, covered by a cloth.

"Be careful, Nathaniel," Andree called, as I went over to it. "It's very delicate, like me." She laughed; unlike most people she had a full set of white teeth. She came over to me and gently drew back the cloth, which

174

had been protecting parts of a stained glass window showing an idealised Jesus and Mary, both fair-skinned and blonde and wearing contemporary western clothes.

"They weren't like that, Andree." I spoke without thinking.

"Like what?" She looked puzzled.

"Jesus was dark-skinned, and wore a white caftan." She was frowning. "And Mary wasn't pale and her hair wasn't golden – she was as dark as Jesus and her hair was black," I went on.

"Why should your idea of them be more accurate than mine ? Have you seen a vision of them?"

I decided to shrug off what I had said, and in any case I did not want to offend her. "No, your faces are beautiful, and when I was in Judea I never saw any so fair. Of course Mary and Jesus would have been different. Tell me, how did you manage to make them so bright – you give them the luminous quality of jewels."

"It's a new technique,"she answered, reassured by my compliment. "I don't know who first started it, but what we do now is to fuse the colours in the glass as it's made, instead of applying them later. After that, as you see, we arrange the pieces of glass in this lead framework." She finished her wine and I fetched her some more. She continued with a proud artistic passion which contrasted strangely with her elfin features.

"Until the beginning of the century I wouldn't have been able to express myself, my personal feelings. I would have had to confine myself to medallions depicting stylised scenes and figures, there would have been little of my creative ardour in them. Also staining glass was so closely linked to illuminating manuscripts that in a way it was like one art being subservient to another.

"My interpretation of Jesus and the Virgin shows how *I* see them, which is different from the way *you* see them, Nathaniel," with a smile.

"But then, Andree, I am not an artist."

"You don't have to be," she conceded. "Everyone can have a personal conception of something. The artist part comes in depicting your vision. Now, what do you think of this?" She took me by the hand and almost danced over to another worktable, again pulling back a cover to display her work.

I was looking at an enamelled garden of roses that shone through a nimbus of emerald leaves. There were amethyst carnations and a lake that had the deep blue gleam of top quality aquamarine. The work was as small as it was exquisite – it would have taken a dozen or more to fill a normal-sized clerestory window, and I fell in love with the art before extending my emotion to the artist. I have that garden still.

Andree wanted us to get married, a gesture of permanence in a world whose existence was so erratic, but the caprice of life and death had left no priests to perform the ceremony. She moved in with me anyway and established her atelier at my house.

She never had a chance to suspect that I could not die, because she did not have a chance to grow old and sere herself; within a month the Black Death reached out for her, and left me once more alone.

Chapter 34

Late one afternoon, three months after my Dolphin Lateral Corporation had acquired our televangelist account, I was sitting on my penthouse terrace, enjoying a Bloody Mary. I stirred Worcester sauce and Tabasco with a stalk of celery and added a small amount extra of Stolichnaya.

I was happy for Stephen and the other individuals who had worked so hard to get the account; it meant little to me personally. It was pleasant to have accomplished something, but the snags of success would, I was certain, soon appear. Foxglove for a start was a difficult man to deal with.

My thoughts wandered to the alleged Creation, and I felt almost sorry for God. He had expended such a vast amount of ingenuity, imagination, and energy, only to discover how imperfect his creation was. Who could console him? What other Being of similar magnitude could assuage his discontent?

The need for comfort could sometimes call for sexual relief as much as lust, and a question came to mind. Had God created Eve for his own comfort, rather than Adam's, to console him for the mess he had made? Surely not; how could Eve fill a bill as big as that?

Idle reflection, and my glass was nearly empty. For a man as agnostically inclined as myself, I spent a remarkable amount of time thinking about God.

I was just about to get up and make myself another drink, when there was a knock on the glass door between apartment and terrace.

Stephen Scott-Harmon stepped out. He didn't exactly look flustered; his fine, pale blonde hair was spread as usual like butter over his scalp, and his clothes looked as if they had just been delivered from Gieves of Vigo Street in London. Yet he seemed panic-stricken.

"I'm sorry to interrupt you, Nathaniel, but I've just had a weird phone call. I don't quite know what to make of it."

"Tell me."

"The guy who rang gave his name as Mr. Christ. Jesus Christ."

"The world's full of nutters, claiming to be Christ, Napoleon, the King of Siam—"

"I know, Nathaniel, but this guy doesn't sound like a nutter. In fact, he sounds like a Harvard man."

As Stephen had himself attended that distinguished institution, I knew that he had just bestowed the highest compliment he could on the Jesus Christ caller; the interest I showed was therefore genuine. "What did he want, Stephen?"

"He said he was looking for a first class PR organisation with experience of handling religious accounts. He knew we represented the Church of the Loaves and Fishes."

"Did you set up a meeting with him?"

Stephen continued to look flustered and adjusted the handkerchief in his top pocket. I offered to get him a drink and he opted for an Arran malt with an eyedropper of water to bring out the flavour.

"I said we'd be pleased to meet him in person, and he answered that that would be fine and he'd reflect awhile before calling us back."

"Even Harvard graduates can be nutters," I said, "are you sure the call didn't come from Bellevue?"

Stephen took me seriously. "I checked; he was phoning from Central Park South.

"You know, Nathaniel," he continued, " his voice bugs me—it was the dignity, the music, the sheer authority of it—that could have belonged to a College dean or a President of the United States." He added: "Still, he's got to be a fake, of course, hasn't he?"

"Why should the sole onus of proof have to rest on him to prove that he is who he claims to be?" I said mischievously. "Why shouldn't the onus be on the rest of us to prove he's not? What would convince *you* that he was the Son of God, Stephen?"

He looked shocked, when he realised I wasn't joking. "I haven't the remotest idea. A miracle, maybe?"

"If he performed one, most people would probably compare him with Houdini, or David Copperfield. Making the Statue of Liberty disappear comes pretty high on the list of miracles, wouldn't you say?"

"Doesn't that count as an illusion rather than a miracle?"

"Of course it's an illusion." The telephone on the table beside me bleeped softly.

"Sir?"

"Good afternoon, Mia."

"I'm sorry to disturb you, Sir, but I have a caller for Mr. Scott-Harmon. He says he's Jesus Christ—he wouldn't give me his real name. He doesn't sound weird, though. I think he's the same person who called this morning."

"Mr. Scott-Harmon's with me, Mia. Put the call through, please." I mouthed the name of the caller at Stephen, who leaned forward.

179

"ben Ezra here. Mr. Christ ?"

"I am, yes." His voice was indeed unusual, so deep, musical and measured. I wondered if he was black; there was something of Paul Robeson or Willard White about its tone and cadence.

"I'll hand you over to Mr. Scott-Harmon," I said.

"Wait. Are you the owner of the Dolphin Group?"

"I am."

"Then you can help me. I asked for Mr. Scott-Harmon because he is listed as Executive Vice President, New Accounts, at Dolphin Lateral. I would like to discuss the possibilities of becoming a client."

"May I ask what your object in becoming our client would be, Mr. Christ?"

There was a brief pause. "My purpose in calling you is not to discuss my needs on the telephone, but to arrange a meeting with you, Mr. ben Ezra. If we think we can work together, we shall proceed from there."

"I need a hint of what you have in mind, in order to choose the people who will attend it, Mr. Christ."

"You and I will attend it, Mr. ben Ezra. We need nobody else at this stage."

I did not like being told how to proceed, but I could understand his caution, especially if religion was to be involved. Mia had said he wouldn't give his real name, but suppose it *was* real—how infuriating to have it doubted by everyone he met.

"Very well, Mr. Christ." We set a date and time for our meeting in my board-room, and disconnected. Stephen was looking at me curiously.

"He wants to meet me first to sound me out, Stephen. If he thinks we can help him, he's prepared to go further."

"It's not like you to waste time on someone like a guy calling himself Jesus Christ."

"I'm just intrigued, Stephen."

He didn't look reassured. "But why?"

"Why not? You seemed intrigued yourself."

"Well, up to a point."

"Maybe I am too. At least I'm prepared to give him a hearing."

"You don't normally see people until schedules are pretty well advanced."

"It isn't for me to come in till the groundwork's been laid. Even then I'm perfectly happy to leave it to you and those under you to do the business. In this particular instance, I have my own reasons for being interested."

I smiled at him to show him I wasn't crazy, and that he and I were partners in doubt, and he went back to his office. I finished my drink and went inside the penthouse.

So I would shortly be meeting another claimant. What was his point in claiming to be Jesus Christ? I assumed that was what he wanted to discuss at our meeting. Perhaps I was wrong, but my imagination wouldn't stretch to anything else. Maybe he wasn't mad, and yet still thought he was the Son of God.

However I doubted if any sane claimants could believe they possessed godhead, or that they would be allowed to survive. Christianity's history was rooted in a corpus of saints and martyrs and suffering, where virtue was hymned and at the same time invariably punished on the grounds that the virtuous were in fact sinners. The name of the Lord had been taken in vain, heresy had been committed, one way or another death must be invoked as punishment and purification.

If this new Jesus Christ was claiming divinity, I didn't give much for his life expectancy.

Chapter 35

As I waited in the boardroom for the arrival of Jesus Christ, I couldn't help thinking that if God were intending to donate his only son these days to the redemption of mankind, he was too late. Hitler had succeeded to a hideous degree in out-heroding Herod, and it was not God who had finally defeated Hitler but that cunning alternative practitioner of mass murder, Joseph Stalin.

With the ambition of such nations as North Korea and Iran to own an atom bomb, and the dangerous oxymoron of institutional anarchy posed by terrorism, surely I thought people would give anything for a Supreme Being to believe in.

There probably couldn't be a better time for an avatar to arrive on earth, but had that not always been the case? The only difference was the size of the world and thus the appropriate extent of the redemption. We were nowadays not simply a collection of parishes, but a planet. What we needed was not simply a number of religions, but one all-embracing religion, governed by an all-enveloping Holy Power.

This theocracy would embrace not only every great Abstract but every gender. From a Christian perspective there would be God the Father, God the Mother and—as a bonus—God the Offspring. This would play the part of the hitherto- named Holy Ghost or Spirit, their genderless and hermaphroditic child.

Behold them then, illumined in the dubious light of a cherubimic aurora borealis, the Incarnation of a Happy Holy Family, gentling the peoples of the world as if they were packs of mustangs being rounded up from prairies of eternal disbelief to graze together in the warm sunshine smiles of God the Uxorious husband/wife and their obedient loving son/daughter. Call him Jesus, call her Gertrude; the children's surname is God.

Through my musings I became aware of a susurration increasing in volume—Mr. Christ was approaching the boardroom. One of my PAs, Polly Wychwood, knocked at the open door which displayed me rising ready to extend a welcoming hand to my Redeemer.

Mr. Christ was tall, with a neat van Dyck beard and auburn hair worn long. His eyes were luminous green and his skin bronzed, and he wore a light camelhair coat which Polly took carefully and put on a hangar before installing it in my personal wardrobe.

When she had closed the door, Mr. Christ and I assessed each other. However he wanted to approach being a claimant to godhead, I guessed it wasn't going to be along the suffering route, or at least not yet. He didn't have a face or figure suited to pain and emaciation. His attractive warmth was undeniable but did not speak of holiness or omniscience, only of a sense of power and authority subtly constrained.

"How can I help you, Mr. Christ?" pulling out a chair for him.

"I have been examining details of a number of PR firms representing televangelists and other religious bodies, if we may call them that. You represent The Church of the Loaves and Fishes, one of the biggest at present. That must be an interesting client, though I'm not sure what it stands for."

"Apart from Christianity?"

His lips twitched. "I didn't know Christianity had anything to do with it."

"I must admit it can be a lucrative industry, Mr. Christ. From Father Divine to the Swaggarts and Bekkers and now Foxglove, Mammon and Christianity have shown they can make a pretty prosperous partnership. Many evangelical churches think lucre is itself worth standing for." I couldn't help wondering if I was merely explaining the obvious to someone who intended to cash in on congregational gullibility. I could imagine the man sitting with me at the boardroom table as a high class con man, but not as a martyr. He would have to take an intensive course in suffering first.

"Do you personally believe that there is a difference between religion and industry, Mr. ben Ezra?"

"They don't have a great deal in common, except when industry takes over religion," I answered. "When religion deals in meditation and wisdom, rather than allowing itself to become part of a national economy, I would say there is a huge difference between them."

"Buddhism was founded as a meditative religion more than five hundred years before Christianity, and I have a great deal of empathy with its theosophical intellect, but perhaps too much tranquillity is something we can't afford. What we have is after all a world that pulses with energy, almost as if it's undergoing a kind of endless puberty," Mr. Christ said thoughtfully.

"Would you rather have the natural uncertainty and aggression of puberty than the mature tranquillity of meditation, Mr. Christ?"

He frowned. "I don't think I'd necessarily include puberty in a list of ideals, or ideal states to be in. On the other hand, serenity can become boring, can't it, if it's not balanced by action?"

"Buddha maintained that 'existence is suffering', and was one of the four noble truths leading to enlightenment."

Mr. Christ smiled. "Two of the other noble truths were that suffering had a cause, and that the cause could be suppressed."

"By right thought, right speech, and so on." I returned his smile. "However, Mr. Christ, we are here, I believe, to discuss Christianity rather than Buddhism."

"We are here to discuss my Divinity as the Son of God, and how to propagate acceptance of that Divinity throughout the world. Once, the Church was virtually a cottage industry." He closed his eyes as though personally envisaging that world. "There wasn't much to help spread the Word of God, only the loyalty, faith and ardour of twelve men who believed. What is more, only four of them were born orators. That is why the spreading of the gospels was so slow."

"It was a slow world," I said. "Today we have the Internet."

"That offers speed, but scarcely profundity, Mr. ben Ezra."

"It is not the method which will convince, Mr. Christ, but the message. And above all, the person who brings it." I leaned towards him. "Tell me, what are you specifically looking for from me?"

"You own the most powerful PR firm in the world. You have experience of clients in the religious field and you know the language of the marketplace."

"That's our job, but will you be able to learn to speak the language of that marketplace?" I asked,

186

thinking of how profoundly the man on the cross had been able to communicate with other men. "You speak of the marketplace, your namesake on the cross spoke of mankind."

"My namesake?" Mr. Christ's eyes and voice had turned glacial.

"Indeed."

"You don't believe that it was myself on the Cross?"

It wouldn't help to offend him, but neither would lying to him. I thought his question offensive in itself, belittling my intelligence. If I told him I had actually witnessed the crucifixion of Jesus Christ at Golgotha, he would think I was belittling his own intelligence by telling him such a ridiculous lie. We would have to know and trust each other to an extent almost impossible to reach before that could happen. As it was, we had only just met.

"No, Mr. Christ, I don't." I answered. "I don't believe in the Resurrection on similar grounds. I don't believe the body of a dead man can leave his burial place and reappear to mortals, except perhaps as a ghost." I added: "Reincarnation is something else again."

"Reincarnation? Surely that is a non sequitur where Resurrection is concerned?"

"You may have lived once on earth, as an ordinary human being, and somehow the memory of that life, or a poignant period of it, has penetrated a second life. I don't disbelieve entirely in the claims of *déjà vu* we occasionally come across, that someone who in this life could not possibly have known or undergone a

187

particular experience, might have undergone something similar in a past life.

"Maybe you're a reincarnation of Jesus Christ, or the crucifixion may have dominated your thinking to such an extent when you were taught about it that it took over your imagination, and through the power of suggestion convinced you that it had been yourself who was crucified. Or perhaps there never was a crucifixion, merely an elaborate or distorted metaphor."

"And who was responsible for such a metaphor, if that is what it was?" The claimant's expression was still hostile.

"Somebody who was able to make a large number of people believe the whole incident of the crucifixion really happened."

"You think it was a hoax?"

I shook my head. "It wasn't a hoax."

"How come a man with your views sounds so sure?"

The untellable truth again, that I had encountered Jesus on the cross.

"My argument is with religion, not history, Mr. Christ. I believe that what you call the Crucifixion happened—it was an extreme form of punishment but permitted by Roman law. Jesus was not crucified for being the Son of God, but for *claiming* to be the Son of God."

"People began to believe that He was. That is what I need, people with faith."

"People with faith in *you*," I said gently. "You have a very long way to go before you can equate yourself with someone whose origins started two

188

thousand years ago. The Internet could certainly not be counted on for conviction, alongside the bible."

"So tell me, what would it take to make you believe that I *am* the Son of God?" Mr. Christ interrupted. The question repeated so often as to be a mantra.

I shrugged. "I have no idea." In fact I had a very clear idea, but again, I could not tell him what it was until we knew each other much more intimately, if that was what we were destined to do. "Certainly something beyond ordinary human understanding," I went on. "And that will apply to everyone else you try to convince. Have you ever met anyone who believed, without visible proof, that you are who you proclaim you are?"

Mr. Christ frowned. "No. But it's only quite recently that the power of a vocation has been welling up inside me. Now it's impelling me to proclaim who I'm sure I am, but I need help. I need a core of people to trust me and to endorse my claim to be the Son of God so that I won't be, so to speak, a voice in the wilderness."

"In other words, to give you moral support."

"To give me credence," he contradicted. "I know how hard it's going to be to get acceptance, but I have to fight, as I did two thousand years ago. I fought then in a different way, a way appropriate to that world. Now I have to fight in a way appropriate to this world."

"Men haven't changed intrinsically. They remain largely unredeemed," I said.

"I offered them redemption. Are you saying that they rejected it?"

"I don't know whether they rejected it or simply didn't accept it."

Mr. Christ sighed, and I wondered whether he could tolerate such ingratitude.

"Or simply thought I was some sort of avatar whose claims were without significance? A waste of time, perhaps?"

"I can't say that, because I have no idea what would have happened if you hadn't claimed to be the Son of God and founded a new religion in doing so," I told him.

"Buddhism or Confucianism might have become universal; after all, Christianity is based on the claim of Jesus Christ to be the Son of God, and one of the major tenets of Confucianism was its basis in filial piety. Even with the arrival of Communism two and a half millennia later, that survived."

Mr. Christ gave me a Titian-like smile. "There can surely be no greater expression of filial piety than to honour two fathers. I have to say that of the two, the human one has so far made more demands on me than the other."

"Tell me about your human father, Mr. Christ."

"If you believe that I am a reincarnation rather than resurrected, you don't believe that it was I on the Cross. You therefore don't believe that I was any part of what happened two thousand years ago, including that my father was a carpenter and that I was the product of a virgin birth. To answer your question, my current human father is a stockbroker."

"I don't see why that particular period when he was a carpenter should be the only one during which the Son of God could be born."

"Are you saying then that there is no reason why the Son of God couldn't be born today?"

"I don't see why a claimant to be the Son of God today needs to be born in any particular era. Nor do I see why he should be born with anything at all in common with the Jesus who was crucified. I don't see why he should have to have the same name, or even necessarily be Jewish. I don't see why his father has to be a carpenter, or what possible relevance his father's human occupation has to his son's divinity. And I don't see why the Creator of the Universe should have to restrict himself to only one son. For that matter, why shouldn't he have daughters as well? Who is to say that the Holy Family isn't tribal rather than simply a Trinity, a dynasty descended from the Creator?"

"I would be delighted to have holy siblings," Jesus said.

"Well, they could help share the burden of divinity."

"I am an only child. Solitude is a burden too."

"As an only child myself, I agree that it can be. Surely being the product of a Virgin Birth must be even more so?"

"The product of a Virgin Birth?" Mr. Christ spoke very slowly. His face was flushed as he slowly stood up. I wondered if, after so many words, the Son of God was after all going in for some lusty, old-fashioned violence. In any case I decided to risk it: I wanted to know the answer to my question:

"Must someone claiming today to be the Son of God acquiesce in the acceptance of the virgin birth, a biological impossibility, as a metaphor for purity?"

We stared at each other.

191

"Two thousand years," I said, "the history of the Christian Church does not belong to you. The Virgin Birth does not belong to you. The Resurrection does not belong to you. There is only one possible way you're going to obtain acceptance as the Son of God before you've had time to establish a history and that is at least to create your own legend and make people believe in it."

"I shall have to pray for guidance about that," said Mr. Christ slowly.

"If it is true that the Deity who was called Jesus Christ was resurrected, he must have become aware he was a legend. If not, he probably never thought in those terms. If something comes naturally to you, you aren't self-conscious about it because it's a part of you, just as God becomes part of a Believer.

"When the Believer observes himself he becomes aware of being under the spotlight, and that God's in the audience, watching. Stages require actors and actors require an audience.

"If Jesus had become self-aware," I continued, "he might have thought of himself as a legend, but I don't think he did. He was too passionate, too immediate."

"To be a martyr, don't you think you have to be?"

"Yes," I said. "That applies to you too, of course."

"It did." He spoke with complete conviction, his eyes focused on some limitless horizon and I knew that either he could be the Son of God to whom I had offered the goblet of orange juice all those years ago in Golgotha, about which I was irrevocably sceptical, or that he genuinely believed he was, which in a general context could be just as dangerous for him.

Of course it was possible he was merely a charlatan, but I didn't think so. Few people were prepared to be martyred for a conscious falsehood.

If I accepted him as a client I would, whatever my own beliefs, be making myself responsible for Mr. Christ's wellbeing. If I turned him down, and he was still determined to go ahead with his claim to be the Son of God and founder of a church currently in urgent need of salvation, he could well find himself quite alone, floating free of any sort of human gravity, and anchored only to the arctic chill of universal scorn.

I found that thought distressing.

Chapter 36

Mr. Christ stood up, and walked to the far end of the table and back. I thought he was going to hold his lapels like Abraham Lincoln, but instead he flung his arms wide in a gesture Moses might have used, that of a man uplifted after communing with God on top of a mountain. Or of a barker at a fair, peddling snake oil, came the unbidden whisper of the cynic.

"You say you don't see why a man claiming today to be the Son of God needs to be born with anything in common with the Jesus who was crucified two thousand years ago? The implication is of course that you don't believe I *was* that Jesus.

"I accept that I have to convince you of my true identity, just as I'm going to have to convince millions of others. To do that I believe I *do* need to have something in common with that Jesus. I need to have *everything* in common with that Jesus. I *am* that Jesus."

"Proclamation is not conviction, Mr. Christ."

"Of course it isn't, but you have to believe that the history of Jesus Christ is my history, and that I'm at one with it. Whether resurrected or reincarnated, I am Jesus Christ the Son of God and there is no alternative to that.

He went on: "My religion, the religion named for me, is breaking up. It's like a Beethoven symphony suddenly transformed into something by Schoenberg. Music can afford to be antiphonal; religions can't.

"What's more, Christianity's not foundering on the great rocks of disagreement that almost wrecked it so many times in the past—disputes over doctrine and interpretation of divinity—but about petty disagreements such as whether to ordain women priests

194

or homosexual bishops. Those are hardly appropriate causes for major discord within my Church, and as its Founder I have to lead it to harmony."

"There was some pretty ill-tempered argument in the past about how many angels could stand on the head of a pin, I seem to remember."

"True, but that wasn't petty within the context of its time," said Mr. Christ.

"You don't have to be the Son of God to unite your Church," I said. "A messiah could do it."

"Mr ben Ezra, I am not a messiah. I don't therefore have to suffer the constraints of being a messiah. " His eyes glowed like magma. "Far more than being able simply to teach and preach like a messiah, or for that matter to lead like a messiah, I have that holy relationship with God Himself—I am His Son!"

"Again, how are you going to prove it?" I persisted. "As a realist, you know that faith is not enough. People are too sceptical or too remote from a life of the spirit. These days, even seeing things with their own eyes probably isn't sufficient to convince them.

"Atheism is a religion in itself, unbelief a matter for passion. Miracles are regarded by such unbelievers as conjuring tricks or simply as fraud: tears shed by the alabaster statue of a virgin in a rural shrine somewhere in Donegal? Why, there's bound to be a piped water system connected to her eyes somewhere. Healing a leper? Not a leper at all, simply a cosmetic nose job and colouring, or sticking prosthetic fingers on to a damaged or mis-shapen hand.

"As for raising a man from the dead—of course, he was never even ill, probably just a professional Method actor.

"No, you don't need me to act as Devil's Advocate, Mr. Christ. You know that whatever you do or say, if you claim to be the Son of God nobody's going to attack you more fiercely than those who call themselves believers in Christian doctrine.

"They are the ones who are going to be far more dangerous to you than any unbeliever, because to them blasphemy is not a matter of offending God but of offending *them*. You'll be pulled down like an old caribou by wolves.

"There's no room for God or any Son of his in today's world, and my own view is that there probably never was."

Chapter 37

It was now, I thought, that Mr. Christ would leave —in fact he would probably flounce out. Instead, he sat down again and we looked at each other in silence.

"Are you saying there's no such thing as religion, Mr. ben Ezra?" Mr. Christ asked eventually. "Or are you saying there is no such thing as Christianity?"

"There's certainly Christianity, but as you say it's riddled with disharmony. Churches in that condition split into sects, just as the Israelites did long before there were any Christians.

"There are a great many sects, but I'm not sure if there is any religion, in the sense of a universal belief. Each sect is like an umbrella in a storm, offering very little shelter to anyone other than those holding them. Islam is disfigured by the ill feeling between Shia and Suni; Judaism has its own spectrum extending antipathy from Orthodox to Liberal via Reform; Hinduism is a state religion but its castes are as clearly defined as any political class and the Brahmin at the top of the tree is valued in a way unimaginable to the Untouchable at the bottom, whatever modern Hindu law may decree.

"The architecture of religion," I went on, "is like the architecture of mathematics—largely composed of fractions."

"Yes, but if we have any feeling at all for democracy in politics, we should also have it in religion. People should have the chance to follow me if I have the ability to arouse their faith in me. Not to be offered the chance to get close to God is the equivalent of being celestially disenfranchised."

"Surely the general idea of Christianity, and of most other religions, is that the nearness or remoteness people feel to God is the business of his intermediaries, the priests. You'd be usurping their jobs, including those at the top of the clerical hierarchy, the archbishops and the Pope, if you addressed them directly. You'd be regarded as an evangelist, a sheepdog to round up the flock, maybe an extremely articulate sheepdog, but a sheepdog nonetheless."

Mr. Christ unexpectedly smiled. "The fact that you make such a good devil's advocate inclines me towards you even more than the initial impression you made. I have no use for a yes-man." He smiled. "And you aren't as offensive as I thought you might be.

"Foxglove's an evangelist, and he's your client. I see he's holding what he calls a 'service' at Madison Square Garden tomorrow night. I thought I might attend, get an idea of what I'd be up against on the ground."

"And on the air. He's our leading media communicator in the religious field. You'd have to beat him—and his competitors—at their own game. And none of them claims to be Jesus Christ, only his servant. If you start to speak about being Jesus Christ and the Son of God you'll be denounced by the whole evangelical movement as a heretic and blasphemer. As a matter of interest, Mr.Christ, how far are you prepared to go with your claim?" I added.

"Until I can convince you, a cynic and non-believer, that I'm the Son of God."

"And what makes you believe you ever could?"

"Faith that the truth will win out."

"And if it doesn't?"

"I can't afford even to consider that. The truth is that I am the Son of God. Nothing can separate me from that truth."

I had lived too long and knew too much to believe that one man's truth was every man's truth, and I also knew that truth was often far from sacred. It was more often the eternal sacrificial victim of inconvenience, always ready to overpower it. The most important truths were those unsullied by being recognised. I sighed.

"I can't accept the responsibility of believing or disbelieving you or in you, Mr. Christ. I am prepared to accept you as a client, but if I ever accept you as the Son of God, it will be a matter of proof, not faith, as I have said from the beginning. And that is what you will, I am afraid, encounter everywhere."

He said nothing for some time. "Why would you accept me as a client?" he asked.

It was a question I wasn't sure I could answer. Partly perhaps it was because I liked him, and possibly it might have been a subconscious desire for insurance, just in case against all the odds he turned out who he claimed to be. I think my principal reason was because I was afraid for him. I was as sick of violence as I was of love, and if there was one tradesman the world could always willingly provide, it was the assassin. I gave him an answer which owed much to the politician's cowardice.

"It's impossible to find an answer to every question, Mr.Christ."

He nodded. "True. Nathaniel, I appreciate your friendship. Will you come with me to hear Foxglove tomorrow night?"

"All right, but you'd better not say anything to him about being the Son of God. He'd think you were making fun of him, and the Reverend Francis Foxglove doesn't have much of a sense of humour. Neither do his followers, Mr.Christ."

"Call me Jesus," he said.

Chapter 38

The Reverend Francis Foxglove had once been a Harlem Globetrotter. Seven feet tall, he frequently claimed that his height brought him closer to God. He had also run to fat, but his power over his enormous congregation was obvious.

Jesus and I had aisle seats near the back of the great hall, and were dressed in business suits. Many of the men in the congregation wore work clothes, and the women by and large did not seem to have dressed up for the occasion. Presumably everyone had somehow managed to find the $30 entrance fee.

A band, out of uniform and sounding as if it had been hired from the Salvation Army, opened the proceedings with a brass cannonade from its trumpets, abetted by a euphonium. Onward Christian Soldiers, a nice military hymn eagerly taken up by the congregation, bounced deafeningly off the walls of the auditorium, stoking the congregation's ardour.

When the singing had finished, Foxglove leaned on a rail in front of a speaking platform. He raised his hands in a papal-like blessing.

"We are here because we are Christians." He spoke quietly, with none of the brash, passionate fire I had expected, having heard him once or twice before. This was the voice of reason, not the raw fundamentalism he had used previously in person and on radio and television, the sort of tone and volume espoused by so many on the far right, politically and religiously.

"We are here because we are Christians," he repeated. "We believe in the love of God and his example of it in sending down his beloved Son to act on our behalf by redeeming us for our sins." He paused, looking slowly round the great hall, his eyes focusing on one sector of his congregation after another, the look of a sin diviner, whose nose for human frailty would lead him to those not worthy of redemption, as though God's act had been almost incomprehensible in its compassion, and ought to be contradicted. Matthew Parker, the witch-hunter, probably had a similar expression when he arrived in Salem.

"We are Christians and we are soldiers," he said a third time, nodding to himself as if to convince himself of the truth of the statement. Abruptly he screamed: "Why does a Christian soldier fight, and who is a Christian soldier's enemy?" We were plunged back into fire and brimstone.

"Let me tell you: a Christian soldier's enemy can be summed up in one word, one short but powerful word: a Christian soldier's enemy is EVIL! And what is evil, what do you see, what do you FEEL, when you hear that word evil? What I see when I hear that word, is a great dark threatening shape with horns and cloven feet. In front of it is a sack, and from that sack, like a perverted Saint Nicholas, it hands out unholy desires, it hands out envy, it hands out gluttony, it hands out covetousness, it hands out the temptations of the seven deadly sins. EVIL is the Devil without the D, EVIL is the Devil's spawn, out to steal your souls and get you to wreak his wicked will.

"The Devil and his EVIL are determined to turn you away from the teachings of God and to make you forgot your redemption by the Lord Jesus!

"The Devil wants to lash out and poison you with his sulphurous venom; you'll never find the Devil turning the other cheek or being meek. No Sir! You can't be meek if you're a soldier, you have to go forth and smite your enemies. Especially when you're a CHRISTIAN soldier and your enemy is the Devil !"

I took a quick sideways glance at Jesus. He was leaning slightly forward, frowning, nose aquiline, the profile of a hunter rather than a man of peace. I was reassured by his formidable aura; he was a fighter.

"Don't any of you be afraid to fight that fight!" exhorted the evangelist, as if reading my thoughts. "If you don't feel strong enough, gain strength from those who are. If you want to fight but are sick, come forward and I'll lay my hands on you in the name of the Lord and you'll be strong. Give me your faith, and the Lord will know of it immediately, give me your hearts and minds and strength and the Lord will bless you for it."

"Will He hell!" Jesus muttered. "All the Lord knows is that Foxglove worships himself in his own name; the Lord's got nothing to do with it."

A woman in front of Jesus swung round. "I heard that – that's like blaspheming!" she said indignantly.

"I've heard enough," Jesus told me, standing up as a dozen people made their way down the aisle towards the altar, in front of which Foxglove was now standing. "Now *I'm* going to address these people and tell them the truth about Christanity and Foxglove's fake version of it – "

"No, Jesus!" I held his arm. "If you do they'll defend Foxglove – they're mesmerised by him and although you might win them round eventually, you'd be in trouble which would be reported in the papers tomorrow, and any campaign to establish you as Jesus Christ by using the Southern Baptists, Born Again Christians and other fundamentalists would be blown!"

"I suppose you're right," agreed Jesus reluctantly, and we left the hall, running the gauntlet of aggressive stares as we did so. Evidently the scrutinisers thought us guilty of slighting the Reverend Foxglove by leaving in the middle of the service.

We took a cab to a bar I went to now and again when I felt life had become too overpowering. Ortega's Village Bar was comfortably gloomy and dark and there were never many customers. Ortega himself was a melancholy Puerto Rican, who passed his days polishing glasses, bawling at his ever-invisible wife upstairs and inhaling other people's smoke, much of it addictive.

This night there was a bartender on duty I hadn't seen before, a tall, drooping Rastafarian. In some ways he reminded me of the first Jesus I had encountered, his hair so unkempt it resembled the crown of thorns.

We ordered martinis, the bartender harrying the shaker with the desperation of St.Vitus. Having carefully poured the contents into glasses, he promptly dropped them.

"Jesus Christ, you fuckin' cretin!" shrieked Orlando, "can't you even pour a fuckin' drink?" He bustled to the foot of the stairs in a fury and bawled something at his wife.

Jesus scowled. "I still haven't got used to my name being one of the world's most popular epithets. Can you imagine how it feels, to have your name taken in vain all the time?"

"I suppose you have to get used to it."

"It's not easy," Jesus said "but then nothing is about being the Son of God." He lifted the newly charged glass which Ortega had placed in front of him, and tilted it back.

"Foxglove's version of Christianity doesn't have much in common with mine," he said a few minutes later, "so we'll be in competition. Do you mind giving me an idea of what his billing is worth to your firm?"

"Ten million dollars. Next year that will increase exponentially, and a team of maybe fifty people will be involved in spreading Foxglove's particular version of the gospels. Incidentally, I disagree with you. Foxglove's idea of Christianity isn't all that different from yours, only his style of presentation."

"It's not a style I can identify with," Jesus said.

"Maybe not, but I'd say St. Paul could have done."

Jesus looked at me in surprise. "Would you?"

"It's how I imagine him addressing his congregations. Plenty of passion and brimstone. "

Jesus frowned. "I wouldn't know," he said, "as I never heard him preach. I don't feel Foxglove and I have anything in common, so it seems there's a conflict of interest between us. I can't match Foxglove's marketing budget, at least until people begin to believe in me and support me. So to take me as a client you'd have to renounce several million dollars of billing?"

"If you can prove you're the Son of God, the question of the amount of our billing would hardly be relevant. But can you?"

"With your help—"

"We can't help you when it comes to proof, and I'm sure you don't expect us to. To prove you're the Son of God is something that only you can do. Or," I added, "fail to do.

"We can publicise your claim to be the Son of God, but we can't spread any gospel. It won't be our job to proselytise, even to act as if we endorse your claim.

"We can get people interested in coming to hear you preach, but we can't prevent them from calling you a fake and a blasphemer, if that's what they want to do.

"We can't provide bodyguards either, but we do have contacts which might come in useful if the National Guard has to be called out."

"You're pitching it pretty strong, Nathaniel."

"You said it yourself: Being the Son of God isn't easy."

Chapter 39

The R—standing for Redeemer—team sat in the Dolphin Lateral Corporation Boardroom. I was in the Chair. Leader of the team was Stephen Scott-Harmon, followed by Cassie Ross, V-P Client Development. She was a tall, slender girl in a white shantung dress, whose russet hair and upright posture reminded me of an altar candle.

Meg Bryant was a short, tough Account Executive from Chicago; George Hackforth, Client Liaison, came from New Orleans; Sam Collins was Press Liaison Officer on the account, and Horton James Political Liaison Officer.

Randall Premise, a one-time Bishop who had retired disillusioned from the Protestant Church, had been recruited as religious consultant. He would be official devil's advocate, combining a robust gift for argument and presentation with a wide knowledge of the darker aspirations of mankind. A perfect understudy for Lucifer.

"Mr. Christ won't be here for this meeting," I announced. There was a sigh of released tension and disappointment. "We're here to define the strategy the R—Team will follow. Stephen and I have discussed this and I shall therefore hand over to him at this point." I sat down and nodded to Scott-Harmon, who stood up.

"There are several ways we could play this," he began, "but it seems to me that two of them stand out. We can follow what might be called the Oligarch Route, starting at the top and working down, or alternatively we could do the exact opposite and go for the Bible Belt, which is what we believe is our client's preferred route." I nodded agreement.

"That would mean personal appearances combined with major Internet campaigns on various fronts, a proviso being that those campaigns would be conducted with dignity and respect."

"We're offering Jesus as the man who claims to be the Son of God. It's up to him how he does that. We do not try to convert on his behalf; we back him as our client but we do *not* proselytise. That is what Nathaniel has agreed with Mr. Christ, who has told us we may call him Jesus, by the way.

"The fact we've been permitted by him to do that does not mean we can be chummy with him. So far as we're concerned, the onus is on him to prove who he is, it's not for us to do that. However, we keep a distance between us, just as we do with any client.

"With the Oligarch Route, we'd go for the existing religious firepower and do our best to harness it. The oligarchs don't maybe shout as loudly as the Bible Belt fellows, but Rome's got the influence of history, it's got the power.

"The thing we have to ask ourselves is: would the Pope and his established international net of cardinals, archbishops, priests and so forth, accept a new Redeemer, whoever he was and however he was presented?

"We have to contend with the possibility, in fact I'd say probability, that there's nothing the Roman Catholic Church would loathe more—and I mean loathe —than the intrusion of someone claiming to be Jesus Christ.

"It's not just a question of erosion of power and money, but of influence.

"For centuries, the Pope's been top dog, the boss, Mr. Big, if you like. He's answered for God and some of us would say that in his own mind he's become God.

"Institutions become arthritic, they petrify and then they eventually become eroded, like every empire throughout history.

"The Catholic Church is the one empire that's so far survived, and the Pope is its Emperor. But it has a history of corruption, from the purchase of absolution throughout its history to the secret, baneful practice of pederasty whose extent is as vast as it is incalculable.

"The Pope rules to the point that Jesus is almost irrelevent, and however we approach it, The Vatican and its subjects aren't likely to want to go along with anyone claiming Son of God status. Chances are the Pope wouldn't even grant Mr. Christ an appointment.

"So it's the Bible Belt approach, Stephen?" Meg was looking at him avidly, hungry to get the preliminaries out of the way and start the serious business of selling the client.

"I'm not convinced about that yet, Meg. Everything's going to have to fall in behind what we recommend our client to do and his acceptance of it, whether we're talking about the politics of it, or the economy, or the approach to wealth and poverty. This is about the inclusiveness of humanity and the all-embracing philosophy behind our attitude."

She turned to me impatiently. "Well maybe, Nathaniel, you could give us some impressions of this Mr. Christ guy. Do you think he was kosher?"

"Maybe." I had committed myself enough so far, I thought, exchanging a lucrative and powerful client for an unknown who might just, given my experience through the ages, be who he claimed. If the onus was on him to prove it, it was on me and my company to treat him as if we accepted it, until we had a positive reason not to, such as his failure. He couldn't fail until we'd given him a chance to succeed.

"He had a voice on the phone like Paul Robeson's," said Cassie.

"Is he white or black?" asked Meg, "I wasn't around when he came in but if he looks like Paul Robeson did, I can live with that."

"He's white," I told her. She was looking at me, waiting for me to go on, but I was thinking of the Spaniard who had shared my cell and died with the same blessing on his lips as the Jesus on the Cross, and Torquemada's consequent fury.

Would the Aragonese Jesus Christ have insisted on blessing and forgiving one of our modern tyrants? Turn the other cheek and have your head knocked off? Not a good recipe for survival.

"His father's a stockbroker," I told her.

"A stockbroker?" She looked horrified. "How do we get a rich Jesus off the ground? Do we sell him to the rich and hope the poor join in? Or do we get him to go about in manger wear and launch a story that he was born in a hut on the Mississippi mud flats?"

"Manger wear?" Randall Premise pushed himself to his feet. He was a tall, ovoid man, who normally exuded benevolence. Meg's comment had offended him. "I am sure that no claimant to the title of the Son of God would ever deign not to be true to his origins. 'Manger wear'," he repeated under his breath, and I decided that, good as she was with the client relationships she handled, it would not be a good idea to let Meg anywhere near our latest client.

"Let us look first at the religious aspect of what we are considering," Premise continued.

"We cannot succeed in acting successfully for Mr. Christ unless we regard ourselves the way legal advocates do. Some insist on knowing the truth, of course, or at least a convincing version of it, in private. If their clients refuse to tell them the truth, they don't feel they're privileged, which wounds their professional pride.

"Others take the directly opposite view—they just don't want to know whether what the client attests to is true or false. If the client swears he's innocent of the crime he's charged with, especially if it's a horrific one, the advocate hopes he's telling the truth, because if the advocate can believe him, that makes him a mite easier to defend convincingly, and there's a chance the jury'll believe him too.

"At the same time, advocates have to maintain a sense of balance, which requires the sort of schizophrenic performance only the best lawyers can display, and they're the ones who insist on being told the truth. So the whole thing has something in common with a space walk—you've got to get used to a balancing act without having any sensation of gravity." He paused, looking round the table.

"It may very well be that we shall be acting for Mr. Christ without ever knowing for sure who he is. We may even *want* to be convinced he's the Son of God, but it's not utterly necessary, as long as we can muster enough belief in his divinity.

"That's where the Catholic Church will reach for its sword and its armour and declare war on our Mr. Christ. So, for that matter, will the Born Again Christians, the Anabaptists, the Plymouth Brethren and every half-arsed bigot in the Christian world. I've been to a sufficient number of religious conventions where, in the context of their declared belief, if you dare to utter a single original thought, the pack'll tear you apart." He leaned forward, knuckles on the table. "Believe me, the Christian Fundamentalist under a full head of steam isn't any more attractive than the Islamic or any other kind of Fundamentalist.

"That means it'll be Mr. Christ going to war on several fronts, with Dolphin Lateral Inc. right there with him among his Christian solders. I can assure you that claiming to be the Son of God, even if there's a chance you might be, ain't a safe way to make friends."

"Don't you think you're being a mite cynical, Randall?" George Hackworth was a big, blue-eyed black man from New Orleans, son of a Polish merchant seaman and a black school-teacher; he took his religion like his jazz, sweet and hot.

"I guess I'm being truthful, George."

"Do you honestly think so?"

"I do indeed, George."

George Hackforth gave a deep, angry sigh. "You've sure got a lot to say about Christianity, don't you? And I find it damned hard to go along with much of it."

"Then you're beginning to get an idea of what Mr. Christ'll be taking on when he's under attack on one count or another for just about everything he says." Premise looked up the table directly at me.

212

"The first major task for our client will have to be to restate and redefine the major constituents of Christianity, and to what ends those can be put. To extract the good and try to get rid of the evil. To persuade the Christian leaders of the world and their followers that he's their reason for being, that they work for him and pray to him. I've tried to give you an idea of how hard that's going to be."

"You'd have to be the Son of God to do it successfully," said Stephen without intended irony.

There was a pause, broken by Premise.

"I'm wondering whether it would be worth that fight even if Mr. Christ is for real."

"If he isn't, it would be blasphemy to present him as being the Son of God!" Hackforth stood up, fists clenched.

"You might have felt the same if you'd met Jesus Christ two thousand years ago," I said. "Look how long it took for him to become accepted, and look how many people have never accepted him. I feel like giving this claimant a chance."

Hackworth sank slowly back into his seat, looking at me in surprise. Others stared up the table with expressions of shock, but I persisted. "I'd give our claimant a better than fifty per cent benefit of the doubt," I went on "The fact that he's prepared to undergo what lies in wait for him whilst being under no illusion as to what that could be—and I know he's fully aware of what he's in for—is on his side."

"At least he's not likely to be crucified," said Premise.

Most people in the room continued to look disbelieving, but before Premise could carry on, Horton

213

James muttered: "Maybe we should be content with the Foxglove account."

"No!" Cassie snapped. She had been made Vice President at the age of twenty-five for her drive and intelligence, and for her fighting spirit; like Mr. Christ, I had no time for yes-people. "It's bad enough giving in when you've lost a fight, but to knuckle under before you've even started, that would be contemptible!" She glared round the table at us.

"And suppose he *is* the real Jesus Christ," she went on, "and we turned him away, how would we feel then? Whatever we say—and I'm sure you agree, Nathaniel—whatever odds we're prepared to put on Mr. Christ that he really *is* Jesus the Son of God—we have a feeling that it can't be true. It's not only the religious aspect, the faith aspect, we can't believe; it's the sheer enormity of the idea, the concept that God has chosen to speak, not from a burning bush or St. Patrick's Cathedral or St. Peter's in Rome, but in our own boardroom. As a client who just might be responsible for the existence of the Universe."

"What?" Randall Premise's mouth had opened slightly; he looked stupefied.

"Nathaniel just said he thinks we should give this Jesus a chance, and I don't see why we should disregard the opinion, the instinct, of the founder of this firm!

"I met Mr. Christ myself in the elevator when he came here to meet with you, Nathaniel, and I was impressed when you set up a second meeting with him to go hear Foxglove, and now some of you here are planning for his defeat already.

"When you, Nathaniel, obviously have time for the guy, you're not going to think it's a waste of that time to take him on. So how can we be simultaneously plotting to let him down before we've even begun to discuss a strategy?"

"If he *is* the real Jesus, surely he'd lick the competition easily," said Meg. "I mean, there just couldn't *be* any competition, could there?"

"I think we're straying from the subject of promotional strategy," I said. "Arguing about the merits and faults of religious and secular philosophy is irrelevant in the circumstances. We're in the business of selling someone whose aim it is to be accepted as the arbiter of what constitutes religion, or at least the Christian religion.

"So do we go the Fundamentalist route—Mormon, Baptist, Evangelical, Born Again Christian, Charismatic and so on, or the Catholic Oligarchal route— do we start at the bottom and work up, or at the top and work down?" demanded Meg.

Randall Premise stood up. He still looked shaken at what Cassie had said, but managed to smile at her, and at me. "We go the route that works," he said.

"I guess that to start at the bottom and work up would be the easier option, because we can gain access to the Bible Belt more easily than to the oligarchs. Besides, they usually scramble aboard once they're convinced the ship's not sinking."

"Yeah, they'll buy their way on board," Meg put in. "If Jesus really takes off, we can start shakin' the money tree. We could develop the sale of indulgences by staging Redemption Banquets. How's that for a notion?

"You pay a million dollars to touch Christ's robe —he'd wear a specially designed garment, more like the

Pope's robe than a suit—" she glanced round the table with more than a hint of triumph.

"This really is blasphemy!" George Hackforth interrupted fiercely, jumping up, fists clenched. "We may set up those kinds of deals for Presidents and visiting royalty, but for the Son of God—"

"It's reality!" argued Meg. "This is the secular age. Jesus Christ is no more immune to exploitation than King Kong was." Hackforth had gone the colour of a Homberg grape.

"Easy George," I said.

Sensing the atmosphere, Meg became defensive. "I was only saying it like it is."

Hackforth glanced from me to Meg and back, before unclenching his fists and slowly sitting down. Premise stood up in his place.

"As we all know, Rome has a history of combining cash and Christianity. If, against all the odds"—he looked at me—"our Mr. Christ turns out to be the real thing, the Vatican will indeed be leaping aboard his bandwagon and demanding a share of the power and cash at the same time. The Fundamentalists'll do their best to hold on to at least the cash, and we'll find ourselves, a Jewish firm, singing Onward Christian Soldiers and trying to hold the ring at the same time."

George Hackforth's mouth was working, but he didn't say anything more. I decided to put in a word.

"The two courses we are discussing aren't necessarily mutually exclusive, but they are at different levels. My own feeling is that, because of its structure and the power of its authority, the Roman Catholic Church would be simpler to canvass than the numbers of sects composing the fundamentalist practitioners of the Bible Belt.

"If we can convince one senior member of the Church, a cardinal or arch-bishop, that we represent the Son of God, we'll at least have a chance of an interview with the Pope. Then it will be up to Mr. Christ—as I think it's appropriate to continue to call our client unless he deems otherwise—to convince *him*."

"I can foresee another problem," put in Premise. "The Bible Belt people will automatically take against the Pope and all he stands for. If he endorses Mr. Christ as the Son of God, every zealot south of the Mason Dixon will spontaneously reject him, whereas the Vatican's far too pragmatic to risk missing out on something that could be to its benefit."

"I guess what we need to do is start the Bible Belt campaign first. That will at least give Mr. Christ a chance to cover the ground and maybe establish a reputation for himself in a comparatively short time. That could attract the attention of the Vatican.

"At the same time," Stephen continued, "we'll be able to establish style for Mr. Christ. He won't be ostentatious; what he'll be offering is dignity, low-key preaching or addressing, nothing flamboyant. We've got to distinguish between his style and that of the evangelists."

"I don't think there'll be any difficulty about that, Stephen," I put in. "Mr. Christ wasn't exactly sold on the way The Reverend Francis Foxglove held the Madison Square Gardens meeting he and I attended."

"Who's going to notify Foxglove that he's out and Mr. Christ's in?" asked Cassie.

217

"I shall," I announced. "I'll tell him that we reluctantly have to give up his Church's account, owing to a perceived conflict of interest that has just arisen. I think 'perceived' is the operative word here. He's going to demand to know what that conflict can be, and it's just possible I may be able to persuade him it my not be a conflict of interest after all, if he accepts that our new account is Jesus Christ himself."

"He won't," Premise declared flatly.

"Very probably not, but it's worth a try in order to keep his good will. I'm not sure yet what sort of friend he'll be, but I have no doubt he'd make a resolute enemy."

"Our contract with him still has eight months to run," Meg said.

"If Foxglove won't accept Mr. Christ as Jesus but thinks he's a fake we shan't have to wait eight months; the conflict will be immediate," I told her.

"Do you realise, Nathaniel, even if it's unintentional, you've started to proselytise for your Mr. Christ ?" asked Randall Premise.

"That's not a matter of religious belief, Randall, but of enthusiasm. This is essentially a sales organisation, and in order to sell successfully we have to be certain that the product we're presenting is the best; Jesus Christ rather than the Church of the Loaves and Fishes."

"Let's hope God is on our side," said Premise. "His relationship with his Son doesn't always seem to have been a happy one."

I could see that George Hackforth's anger was welling up again, and ended the meeting.

Premise turned to me when we were alone and his expression was bleak. "You're taking an even bigger risk than I thought, Nathaniel."

"Oh? What's that?"

"You're taking the risk of becoming a believer." he added: "I hope Mr. Christ appreciates your sacrifice." He got up and went slowly out.

Chapter 40

I called Foxglove and told him I wanted to see him urgently. When I explained why, he demanded an immediate meeting at his headquarters on the Upper West Side, just beyond the Natural History Museum. They were in a double brownstone building whose front door was laced with gold leaf. The name of the Church was in large gold neon-lit letters above an illuminated cross on top of a turret.

Inside, the threshold of the building was a white marble square on which was inscribed in large gold letters: Join Us For The First Step To Paradise.

Foxglove was wearing a black alpaca jacket over a purple waistcoat, and I could feel the heat of his anger as I entered the room. He waved me to a curved black-upholstered buttonback chair and threw himself into another.

"So you don't want my business!" he barked. "For months your—what's-his-name—Scott-Harmon was all over me, gave me lots of sales spiels and told me how delighted and privileged your company'd be to act for my Church! So what's happened to change your mind, ben Ezra? You owe me a fucking explanation and a hell of a lot more than that!"

"That's why I'm here, Reverend. Much as we appreciate acting for you and your Church, something has happened which we think might amount to a conflict of interest."

"There's going to be a conflict, you can bet your goddam life!" He jabbed a huge forefinger at me.

"As soon as you're out of here I'm going to instruct my lawyers to throw the book at you."

"Let's be original and settle this without litigation," I suggested. "We'll refund the amount you've already paid and we're prepared to make a generous contribution to your Church to compensate you for what's happened."

"Maybe you'd better tell me what *has* happened, ben Ezra." It had for a long time been Nathaniel.

"What would you do if a man came to you claiming to be Jesus Christ, the Son of God?"

"I'd slam the door in his face and damn him for an impostor!"

"Not a very charitable point of view."

"Charitable? I'm here to receive charity on behalf of my Church, not to give it! "

"Would you damn him for an impostor before hearing him out?"

"What the hell's this got to do with you going back on our contract, man?"

"That's why we've gone back on it, Reverend." I had never called him Francis, having never felt amiable enough towards him to want first name familiarity.

However, I still didn't know what had impelled me to incur all the trouble that breaking our contract would bring—I liked the man calling himself Jesus Christ but I certainly wasn't ready to believe he was anyone but a normal human being. On the other hand there was something special about him, and the strange feeling of protectiveness and responsibility for him I felt.

"Have you gone crazy? I don't understand what you're saying." He didn't take his glowing eyes off mine. "Are you seriously telling me you believe this—

this impostor, and that you've taken him on as a client instead of *me*?"

"Somebody claiming to be Jesus Christ the Son of God has asked us to take him on as a client."

He looked stunned. "And you believe him?" he asked eventually.

"Not necessarily. But I don't disbelieve him either."

"You *are* crazy. Has he given you any proof he's the Son of the Lord?"

"No. He does talk of faith in him, though."

Foxglove looked incredulous. "He wants you to have faith in him without giving you proof of what he claims?"

"Isn't that what faith is?"

"You're just playing with fucking words, ben Ezra. And I still don't understand why even if you want to give this freak a chance to prove something he can never prove, it means ditching our contract.

"I don't like it when someone thinks he can make a fool of me," he continued. "Now get out of here!" He screwed up his eyes. "Before you go, tell me what you'd call a generous contribution to my Church."

"Half a million dollars."

"You've got half a million dollars' worth of belief that this Jesus guy is really the Son of the Lord?"

I shrugged. "Maybe. Will you accept my offer?"

"There's some sense in saving money from the lawyers, I guess. In a way you'd be givin' up what you've got to follow the Lord, which is more than most of my Church members can do. They ain't got nothing to give up, but they follow the Lord anyway and hope one day He'll think it fitting to let them have something.

"I'll think about your offer, but I meant what I said about conflict, ben Ezra. What you've done is an insult, and insults are something I don't forgive." His anger briefly gave way to curiosity.

"What I don't understand at all," he said, "you're not even a believer. How come you have so much faith in this so-called Son of God? Ten million dollars' worth of faith, as things stand."

"Call it instinct, Reverend."

"Instinct." He nodded to himself. "I'm a man has no trouble getting folks to follow him. I'm in the mood, I can be a surefire Pied Piper. You've seen me preaching, you've seen and heard my congregations' reaction.

"I reckon core membership of my Church is around three hundred thousand, and growing. The annual membership fee for anyone over eighteen is ten bucks. We have folks showing their faith in us with donations, bequests, annuities and land. We're given stock in businesses and sometimes the businesses themselves.

"Why do you think that is, ben Ezra? Is that instinct, maybe? I don't claim to be Jesus the Son of God, but I do God's work. I know He holds me in high esteem. I hear him, I hear His praise, just as He hears mine."

"In that case, you would probably be able to tell me whether my new client is the genuine Son of God or not."

"And if I tell you, as I guess I surely will: no, he's not the Son of God, he's an ordinary man except he's a liar and a charlatan, what then? Are you saying you'd take any notice of what I said? Of course you wouldn't, not unless your faith wasn't real, not unless you realised you'd been conned or were trying to con other people." He blinked his heavy lids angrily.

"I'd listen to you," I said.

"You'd hear me, but you wouldn't listen, ben Ezra. And if you did, would you renounce this new client of yours? Would you apologise to me for insulting me?"

"And if he convinced you he was really the Son of God would you accept him and devote your Church to him?" I countered.

Foxglove shook his big head. "I'd want a sign. I could never believe without a sign. I just don't get it, ben Ezra." He turned away, not getting up, and I saw myself out.

Perhaps I *was* crazy, but that could be part of being a victim of eternity.

Chapter 41

When I returned, Mia had a message for me. Jesus Christ's father, Morris Christo, wanted to see me as soon as possible.

"I hope I did right, Mr. ben Ezra. He said he wanted to see you in absolute privacy, rather than in your office. I checked your diary and you had a free half-hour at six o'clock before going out to dinner with the Mayor so I booked him in."

"That's fine, Mia. When he arrives, send him straight in, please."

"Yes, Sir." She hurried out in her curiously self-effacing way, and I showered and changed and wondered about Jesus' father.

He arrived punctually at six, a sharp man who was all edges. His nose was like an adze and he had a chin to match, with a narrow mouth. The cut of his expensive suit didn't conceal the narrowness of his shoulders, and their narrowness was matched by his cold blue eyes. The physical difference between him and his son was so great I couldn't help wondering if, God apart, he really was Jesus' father.

He sat opposite me on the terrace and accepted a white wine spritza.

"I understand you've taken on my son as a client," he said. "Are you really going to promote him as the Son of God?"

"We've been hired by him to handle his public relations, Mr. Christo. We're not proselytising for him.

"My company is representing him as a commercial client. We couldn't do that honestly unless we believed his claim contained an element of possibility."

Christo's thin neck shot forward like a mamba's. "He's *my* son!" he hissed. "MY son." He leaped to his feet and began to pace up and down the better to emphasise what he regarded as the tragedy that had befallen him.

"I have no idea where my boy got this shitty idea he's the Son of God! Living in a dream world's OK if you don't make fools of your family, but Jesus is doing just that! He's claiming his mother was unfaithful to me, a virtuous and loving wife who'd never screw anyone else, not even the Almighty! And he's slandering *me*!"

He stopped pacing to glare at me, but there was more desperation than hostility in his expression. "Look, I'm not a cuckold and my wife was a virgin till our wedding night. Can you begin to understand the hell we're going through! Do you think we should maybe be flattered by Jesus' claim to be only half human, which is what a son of God is? Hell no, it's a fucking insult!

"Our son can imagine he's Jesus Christ, but he hasn't got the imagination—or just doesn't care—to see that what he's really doing is insulting his mother and by implication at least telling the entire world I'm impotent! How can a man who's not impotent beget a son from a wife who's a virgin? It might be OK as a biblical fairytale but its utter crap in the context of today.

"It's destroying his mother and me; he's our only child and we love him! So he thinks anyone could love him more than we do, even God, if there is one?" He blinked back tears.

"When did he start claiming to be the Son of God?" I asked.

226

"When he was about twelve years old. He was preparing for his *barmitzvah* and the rabbi told me he showed an unusual intellectual curiosity about God. I wanted him to join me on Wall Street, but if he chose to be a rabbi, there's nothing wrong with that. But being surnamed Christo with the first name Jesus somehow became this crazy illusion."

"Why did you call him Jesus?" I asked.

He shrugged. "Our roots are Sephardic. During the time of the Inquisition some members of our family recanted rather than be burned alive. Their descendants reverted to Judaism a long time later, but they'd used the name Jesus for so long the tradition persisted. You'll find men called Jesus in any country that's had a Spanish connection." He stood in front of me.

"Mr. ben Ezra, my wife and I don't want you to go on with this. It's all wrong. We're Jews, not Christians and don't tell me Christ was a Jew. I know that. My son was born and bred in New York City. He's from Manhattan, not Bethlehem or Jerusalem!"

"So why does he insist on carrying on, knowing how strongly you disapprove?"

He shrugged his narrow shoulders. "Who knows —maybe one of those sects has got at him, the Moonies or something. I'd have thought he was too strong-minded to succumb to something like that. Mr. ben Ezra, you obviously have some influence with him. Will you convince him to give up on this crap? His mother and I want our boy back."

"I don't think I have that much influence with him, Mr. Christo. And if I tell him I'm no longer acting for him because you've asked me not to, he'll resent your interference and simply find another PR company. We've talked, I pointed out the pitfalls and dangers he could face, and he still decided to go ahead. I can't refuse to drop him as a client now."

Christo sighed in the New York Jewish two-toned way, partly acceptance, partly resignation. "OK You won't refuse you won't refuse. Do you have kids, Mr. ben Ezra?"

I could not of course tell him of my dynasties, of the generations which had predeceased me. "Yes" was the only answer I was prepared to give.

"And if those kids were in danger because of the actions of someone else, you wouldn't go to that someone and tell him how you felt and expect him to put business to one side and listen to you, the father of those kids?"

I stood up in my turn, wishing I had the antidote to his despair.

"I really do understand the pain of your predicament, Mr. Christo. I understand your feeling that you and your wife have been dishonoured by your son's claim. But supposing the virgin birth was, like so much else in the bible, a metaphor?

Surely it was simply trying to find an explanation for the inexplicable."

"Metaphor? It doesn't sound like anything metaphorical when my son talks about it. To him it's the literal truth." We stood beside the carp pool, watching the big, whiskery fish swimming lazily in the warm water.

"You won't change your mind?" Christo asked after a minute or two.

"Correct, Mr. Christo. I'm sorry, but I've explained why."

"I'm not a vengeful man," said Morris Christo, "but if anything happens to my son because of this, God help you."

I saw him into the elevator and he didn't look at me, or say another word.

Chapter 42

Our campaign began as planned: a whisper in the cotton fields, an echo in the hamlets, addresses in churches and small halls across the Bible belt. We put out low-key announcements on the Internet to arouse people's curiosity: a real holy man is among us, a man who intends to recreate and revitalise the Christian religion. We did our best also to avoid claims that Jesus Christ was going to perform miracles.

Jesus decided to have as few of us in attendance as possible; one apparent apostle, Willard Swoop, actually a bodyguard, was as far as the claimant would go. No matter how vulnerable he might be, Jesus had an inexhaustible trust in the kindly qualities of human nature, which seemed utterly at variance with the cynical and worldly background he had just left. Like Faust in reverse, as Meg described it.

I insisted on accompanying Jesus south to listen to some of his addresses to congregations across the Bible Belt, then returned to New York to help Stephen and the R Group as they collated reports and observations from our people in the field.

I was impressed and reassured by Jesus' articulacy and eloquence, and the quiet expression of power driving him like a turbine of the spirit.

Therefore I was unprepared for disaster when Stephen called me in my penthouse from his office at five in the afternoon.

"Yes, Stephen?"

"Nathaniel?" His voice was calm, but I could discern a note of panic. "I think we're in deep trouble. Frankly, I'm not sure how to handle it."

"Tell me."

"He took a deep breath. "Jesus Christ has been arrested.""

"What? What for?"

Another deep breath, before he answered heavily: "Kidnap and child abuse."

"Where?"

"Well, the alleged offence was committed at a farm just outside a small town called Rocky Forge, which is apparently not far from a place called Robertsville, about fifty miles from Montgomery. It was one of the stops on the Luther King Civil Rights march from Selma to Montgomery."

"File a flight plan to Montgomery with La Guardia. I'll go down with Cassie. Is Willard Swoop with Jesus?"

"I guess so."

"I need to know for sure. Find out and have the details transmitted to our plane."

"I'm on to it right now, Nathaniel."

One of Dolphin's Gulfstreams was waiting for us on the tarmac at La Guardia, after I had convened a brief meeting at my apartment with Stephen and Cassie. He was trying to act cool, not very successfully. I thought Jesus was probably alone in a cell in a local jail, with a sheriff who didn't believe a word he said. Kidnap, child abuse—all we needed was a murder charge to persuade God the Father that only His intervention could save his Son from a death sentence. God's notorious abstention from saving his son from crucifixion two thousand years previously didn't augur well for intervention to save him today from Old Sparkie.

231

It had only taken Stephen a few minutes to find out that Jesus was in jail in Robertsville. He had indeed been put alone in a cell. As a witness, Willard was under instructions not to leave Robertsville without the sheriff's permission, and had been installed in a hotel. If he was an archetypal sheriff of the region, he probably had a cosy manner and smoked a pipe. I wondered how he would cope with interrogating the self-proclaimed Son of God.

We taxied fast along the perimeter track, swung on to the runway and after a second's foreground crackling in our earphones against a distorted background were given clearance by Flying Control; the jets screamed as we tore along the runway and thundered into the evening sky.

There was nothing romantic about the sunset which greeted us on the far side of the clouds. It was like a malignant sore eye peering down on Manhattan, the single eye of the giant Polyphemus, perhaps, just before Jason and the crew of the Argonaut put it out.

Chapter 43

The charges against Jesus of kidnapping and child abuse had been laid by a woman called Laura Ernly. It was her fourteen-year-old daughter Ellie who she claimed had been the victim, but Ellie wasn't having any of it. She was staying temporarily at the pastor's house at Rocky Forge, having refused to accompany her mother back to the farm, and denied that Jesus had touched her.

That had put the sheriff in a quandary—he could hardly charge Jesus with kidnapping and abduction when the alleged victim not only pleaded passionately on his behalf, but had ascribed the crimes to her mother, whom she obviously hated.

"I've known Ellie almost since she was born," Sheriff Beamish told us, as we instinctively ducked beneath the still turning rotor blades and shook hands with him. We had landed in the middle of a sports stadium. "She's got a cool head on her and she's not the sort of person to believe someone's Jesus Christ because she wants him to be. I guess even he couldn't guess how much she wants that.

"Been in a kinda cage all her life, you see, but she's not crippled, not yet.

"She's still a free spirit, but I dunno how long she'll be able to hold out if she don't get away soon. What worries me, there may be a killing. Too much hatred and you get an explosion like a firework factory goin' up. You folks hungry?"

"Starving," Cassie told him.

"Thought you might be. Let's go." He ushered us in front of him through a tunnel and out on to a wide macadamed road, where an official car with a woman at the wheel waited behind the sheriff's Buick. Beamish introduced her as his deputy.

"Lola, you can go home now," he told her, "these folks seem peaceful enough." He chuckled. "Judo black belt," he told us, as her tail lights faded into the distance, "wrasslin' with her'd be like wrasslin' a rattler."

"May we see Jesus now, Sheriff?" I asked him.

"Well now, if you don't mind I'd like to get some background first, try to give myself an idea of what I'm involved in."

My impression of him was that he was a good deal more intelligent than he seemed, and more tolerant than I could have hoped. I was right about his pipe and was well aware that, however laid back and bucolic he wanted to be considered, he wasn't a man to take for granted; it wouldn't be so much a case of playing things by ear, as by respect.

I had only met Willard Swoop once or twice, when Jesus had started his campaign; Swoop had the pale blue eyes of a husky and a cleft chin like Kirk Douglas. He had been spared jail but as a leading witness had had to undertake not to leave a Robertsville motel called The Sourdough Inn unaccompanied. He sat beside Sheriff Beamish coughing occasionally as reluctantly shared smoke crawled down his throat.

Cassie and I climbed into the back seat of the Buick and a half hour later climbed out again when we arrived at a roadside diner, where we had a surprisingly good Chicken Maryland dinner.

"Them bananas and yams is sweet enough to kiss," the proprietor's wife told us, as she put the steaming platters on the table.

When, much later, they had been cleared away the sheriff, Cassie, Willard, and I, began our meeting. It was nearly ten o'clock, and the sheriff took his pipe out of his mouth to yawn.

"You're the only one of us was actually there, Mr. Swoop," he said to Willard, "so you give us your version of what happened, and we'll think it over and bring in this fellow claims to be Jesus Christ, in the morning.

"Then Ellie can have her say, and after that we'll go back to her mother's farm and get *her* evidence. Then we'll have a better idea of who's going to stay with who, and what's going to happen next."

"Can I stand bail for Jesus right now, Sheriff?" I asked him. "I really would like to get him out of jail straight away. Willard's already given us an idea of what happened when he called us in New York, and we recorded the call."

The sheriff shrugged. "In that case I don't see why we shouldn't catch up on our sleep now, Mr. ben Ezra. I've checked you and your corporation out on the Web and seems you won't have no trouble finding the bail money." He gave a slight smile of appraisal as he got up. "I'll go see Judge Harkiss and recommend this Jesus fellah spends the rest of the night at your hotel.

"It's your money; if he tries to run for it, you've got the right to stop him trying to break bail."

"I don't think he'll do that, Sheriff," I said, as we walked out to his car.

"Depends on how much he cares who pays and how confident he is of justice in these parts." He levered himself into the driving seat. "Be back soon, folks." He gave a wave that was partially a salute and his tail lights faded into the darkness.

Half an hour later he was back with Jesus, who was pale with some sort of stain on the lapel of his white jacket. A cobweb floated ethereally above his shoulder. We embraced, and Cassie kissed his cheek as Willard seized his hand. The sheriff watched briefly.

"I'll say good night now, folks. See you tomorrow at ten. If you're hungry breakfast time, flapjacks, eggs and dry-fried bacon're pretty good here."

I thanked him. He nodded, and took a battered metal lighter from his pocket. A spear of flame dived into the bowl of his pipe like a fox into its earth with the hounds after it. Willard reluctantly climbed in again beside the sheriff, who leaned out of the window.

"Seems a personable fellow, your Jesus Christ, Mr. ben Ezra."

"Yes. That's what I think too," I told him. He nodded.

"I guess he needs more than that to be accepted as the Son of God." He nodded again, blew a gust of rancid smoke at me and drove off.

Chapter 44

The following morning it struck me that Robertsville would be a good place to commit suicide in. I felt like an egg in a pan as we left the hotel and stepped into the street. The metallic sky was the colour of a skillet, and exuded an overwhelming heat.

Having had breakfast according to the sheriff's recommendation, we were on our way to pick up Ellie from the Pastor's house at Rocky Forge.

Our procession consisted of Willard and the sheriff in his Buick, in which Cassie and I again occupied the back seats, and a down-at-heel-looking Chrysler whose attitude gave the impression of a Muslim on a prayer mat, driven by Lola, the tough-looking black woman who was Deputy Sheriff and a Judo Black Belt.

After a short drive we arrived at Rocky Forge. 'Welcome to Rocky Forge' said a roadside sign, but the place didn't feel welcoming. A few locals were already sitting outside a drygoods store with a tavern alongside in the main square; the wooden church which took up the opposite side of the square had a painted board on one side of the main door proclaiming it to be CHURCH OF THE PRECIOUS BLOOD; PASTOR THE REVEREND DIDIUS ENWRIGHT. After that there was the statement JESUS SAVES, and beside the church the pastor's small wooden house with his name on a brass plate. The sheriff rang the bell and the door was opened by a big, unsmiling black woman with the charm of a mousetrap.

"Sheriff, good mornin'."

"Good morning, Ethelina."

"Pastor's in back, tryin' to talk sense to that stupid chile Ellie Ernly an' make her go back home to her mother. Doubt she'll listen to a word he says." She peered closely at me, then at Willard and Jesus. She was obviously trying to identify which of us was claiming to be The Lord Jesus, and bursting to express an opinion, obviously adverse.

"I'm sorry if Ellie staying here last night caused you any inconvenience, Ethelina."

Ethelina was not disposed to be charitable. "That Ellie, she'd inconvenience a saint." She pouted angrily as a door opened somewhere and a little white man, threadbare as an old carpet, came towards us, a teenage girl with tousled blonde hair following in his wake. We were still waiting to be invited inside.

After exchanging greetings with the sheriff and Lola, he introduced himself to Cassie and me as the Reverend Didius Enright. The crowd went quiet as he stood in front of Jesus. "Are you the one claiming to be Jesus Christ, the Son of God?"

"That is who I am, Pastor."

"But that's blasphemin'!" Ethelina was outraged. "That's takin' the Lord's name in vain."

"Please calm down, Ethelina," the Pastor admonished her, but her voice had reached the men sitting outside the dry goods store and various passers by and we had their attention. A couple of them changed direction, and the men sitting outside the drygoods store stood up. They became the nucleus of the small crowd which began to gather, and it didn't seem friendly.

"Now let's not get het up about this," the sheriff addressed the group. "It may be a sin to take the Lord's name in vain, but it's not a crime. If you ain't careful and start acting savage, you'll be committing a crime and that means I'll have to arrest and jail you."

"I doubt that'll be necessary, Sheriff." The Pastor moved slowly down the steps from his front door to the street. He was old and he was feeble but his voice was still resonant and he knew how to pitch it for effect.

"I can't say for sure yet whether this fellah's taking the Lord's name in vain or not. I was brought up not to make up my mind about something till I knew what it was. Now this fellah says he's the Son of God. I haven't had a chance to prove or disprove anything; I can't think that big. All the years I've worked for God and His Family, the Virgin Mary and Jesus His Son and the Holy Spirit, I've done my best to make people believe in them. I've taken sinners by the hand and tried to help them follow in God's footsteps on the path to righteousness.

"I've preached faith and I've preached love and now I'm so plumb tuckered out I'm not sure if I'm still a believer myself." I heard Ethelina gasp, but there was for a moment no other sound.

"There's talk of this man here, this man who claims to be Jesus the Son of God, being a child abuser. Do you believe that?" shouted a newcomer. He was wearing a bigger ten gallon hat than the sheriff's, and a white and red check shirt. He rode a big black horse which was cropping saw grass before raising its head to glare at us. It neighed loudly several times, arching its neck and showing a mouthful of large yellow teeth: it could have been one of the four horses of the Apocalypse.

Nobody answered.

The rider continued: "Seems to me there's mighty little proof of anything round here. The Son of God here

239

can't prove he's the Son of God, our pastor's just admitted he's near past believing anything, but tells us this Son of God is definitely not a child abuser—"

"He's not! He *is* Jesus! " shouted the tousle-haired girl. "Pastor knows what my Ma's like! She says I belong on our farm, and that Jesus kidnapped me, but I swear I begged him to take me away from Ma and the farm, I begged him to give me a chance in life, I went down on my knees to him and begged him to do that! And he raised me to my feet and he talked kindly to me, like he wanted to make sure I was serious and speaking the truth, and really wanted to leave there, and when I begged him yet again to take me away he said he would.

"Then Ma cursed me and she cursed him, she cursed the whole world, but she had to let me go, because after that she knew I'd never have stayed. If she'd tried to lock me up I'd have broken out, if she tied me up with a rope I'd have got free somehow, and now I'm here and I've got a future and I ain't *never* goin' back to bein' not much more than a slave for Ma! It just ain't true to say I belong with her; I *don't*! I belong here, with Jesus! Where he goes, I go. That's what Pastor in church calls Destiny, when someone can pray to God for a future, for a life, and get it. Then when you've got a destiny, you've got a chance!"

"He claims to be the Lord, let the Lord speak!" shouted a woman standing on a bench. "If he *is* the Lord, you ain't got no right to arrest him, Sheriff."

"That's right, it'd be heresy to arrest the Lord!" shouted somebody else.

The pastor said something to Ethelina, whose body language indicated reluctance to obey. However, she went indoors and came out shortly afterwards carrying a footstool. The pastor held up his hands for

240

silence, although the square was already silent in expectation of an address by Jesus, who stepped on to the footstool and held out his hands. There was a sigh from the crowd as of leaves rustling, and Jesus began.

"I need your faith," Jesus told them. "I need your belief in my claim to be the Son of God. As history has shown, it is not easy to be the Son of God. I have to arouse your faith and nurture it, I have to give you a sense of fulfilment, to guide you back to acceptance of your human spirit. Your human spirit does not feed on the same things as your physical appetites—how could it?

"The spirit and the soul love beauty—can you eat beauty?" The cadence of his voice altered. "Can you drink beauty? Can you swallow a dawn or imbibe a sunset?

"Your body and your soul are two entirely different creations, blending into one. The spirit nurtures the flesh, the flesh gives an earthly home to the spirit."

"Halleluyah!" yelled someone.

"Some of you believe that there's a physical Jesus who will come to Earth to lead and guide you into a life which will be less harsh, without so many cares and hardships, a life which will give you strength and peace of mind and comfort."

He paused. "Others of you believe there is no such person as Jesus, either here or anywhere else. How can I convince you of my reality? A reality based on the compassion and wisdom of my Father? How do I bring you the faith to believe in me?"

"That's right," shouted the man on horseback. "There've been a good many pretenders to the Throne of God, and they died rich. Ain't never heard of a rich man

241

who claimed to be the Son of God, and died poor. Have heard of a passel of poor men who preached the Gospel of the Lord and died rich. Let me ask you, Sir. Are you rich?" He added: "And don't give me none of them political answers what can be taken a dozen ways."

The cry of a mocking-bird assaulted the silence, and the big horse neighed again.

"Yes, I am rich. When I chastised the rich two thousand years ago I did not do so because there is no virtue in being rich and every virtue in being poor. I did it because so many were rich without any accompanying acts of philanthropy or altruism.

"What can a poor man offer another poor man? A poor man can offer kindness, he can offer sympathy, but he cannot offer nearly as many practical gifts as a rich man in order to sustain those who are poor. That is the principal gift of the rich to the poor, to be able to help them."

"My mother's dying, Jesus," interpolated a tall, skeletal man so skinny it made his shirt look like a winding sheet. "She's far gone with breast cancer and the doctors have given up on her. Now I reckon it's all in the hands of God." He flung his arms wide. "In *your* hands, if you're the Son of God. If you'll come with me, I'll take you to her."

There was another thick silence in the square. The skeletal man was not deliberately challenging Jesus, simply fighting for his mother's life, as I had tried to do for mine so long ago through my prayers in the Temple, but a challenge it was. No doubt the raising of Lazarus had aroused a similar tension when Jesus told him to take up his bed and walk, but would the Jesus standing alongside me be able to cure a case of breast cancer?

The sheriff seemed to have similar doubts.

"Wait," he commanded: "I don't want to stand in the way of a cure for Joyce Pilger's breast cancer if Jesus here or anyone else can cure her. But first we got to have another medical opinion, in case it's not cancer but some other sickness that's afflicting her, maybe something doesn't need the Son of God to cure, just an ordinary doctor. I don't want to have to arrest the person I pray to on Sundays for being a threat to public order, but if Jesus cain't cure her, it's public order's likely to erupt."

"He ain't a threat to nobody!" shouted Ellie. "He's Jesus!"

"You arrest Jesus you'll be guilty of heresy!" shouted someone else.

"What about Ma?" yelled the skeletal man. "You goin' to take away the last chance she has to live?"

"I ain't takin' anything, Sam. I just think a second opinion is fair, is all." The sheriff was no orator, and his voice was almost inaudible in the clamour of the crowd.

"We're talkin' about my Ma, Sheriff. I know she's got breast cancer. She's been sick for years and that sickness of hers hasn't ever had no other name. We don't need no second opinion on that."

I found myself hoping desperately that the sheriff would hold out for a second opinion, because if Jesus was unable to heal Joyce Pilger's breast cancer I could sense deep trouble ahead, as the sheriff anticipated. However, he decided to yield.

"All right, Son, Joyce is your mother and I'm not going against you. Jesus, I'm stepping aside."

"Where is she?" Jesus asked.

"Over there. In her rockin' chair on top of the blue stoop yonder." He pointed at a stoop which was one of a row. Instead of grass there was sand in the yard, as if the place was still brand new and the owners were waiting for the landscape people to get to work.

The Sheriff raised an arm and everyone stopped walking.

"She's all yours, Mister Christ."

Nobody said a thing. Joyce Pilger's skeletal son climbed the steps and kissed her forehead. Her hand briefly touched his face in a gesture of love without strength.

Jesus climbed to the stoop and turned towards us. I thought of Martin Luther King and the march he led moving onward not far from here towards Montgomery.

In King's poetic concept his was not simply a march to attain a certain sort of political achievement, but much more. Civil Rights was to include a status identical with that of the persecutors of his people, they were the affirmation of the Liberty, Equality, and Brotherhood expounded by the makers of the French Revolution more than two hundred years previously, before it was so copiously betrayed.

The modern marchers had acquired it, but at the cost of King's life. I was apprehensive about the cost to Jesus if he failed to cure Joyce Pilger's cancer.

Even if she did make some sort of miraculous recovery, would that be enough to convince the crowd of Jesus' Godhead? Somebody would be bound to shout that he was just an ordinary faith healer who had struck lucky, or that she hadn't been nearly as sick as everyone thought?

In today's world there was little reverence, especially where God was concerned. That was one of the penalties of belonging to everybody. One might prate of brotherhood but it was exclusivity that everybody sought after, and there was nothing exclusive about God, only about some of his worshippers.

Jesus stood on the stoop and gazed across the crowd before speaking. As usual, his voice was cast so that it was audible to everyone.

"We all have a time to die. No matter how advanced our medical science, no matter what we can devise to postpone the moment of death, it is simply a waiting game. Death is the garbage cleaner of the universe, and whether you are a man or a ray of light, there is a time to perish.

"Life is the light under a distant door, and that light diminishes, gets feebler the further away from that door we move, and we cannot stop ourselves from moving away. That is because God moves us, we are part of His scheme of things, part of Time." He paused to look round at Joyce Pilger.

"Joyce Pilger's time has come. Because of that I can do nothing to cure her, nothing even to comfort her. All I can do is to bless her and consign her to my Father's eternal protection, for she has just died. May God my Holy Father be with her."

It seemed a lifetime before the stunned crowd uttered its first 'Amen'. Pilger uttered a piercing cry, and fell to his knees beside his mother's chair, which rocked slowly as his body shook with sobs. With his mother gone, his spirit was probably as emaciated as his body.

The death they had just witnessed, even though without realising what had happened, seemed to drain any hostility from the crowd; the mob had returned to individuality. The man on the big horse led the way out of the square, the people who had been sitting outside the dry goods store returned to their places without looking back at us. Silent now, Pilger continued to kneel beside his mother's chair at the top of the stoop and cried quietly, and the sheriff indicated without speaking which vehicles we were to travel in. Jesus and I shared the back seat of the Buick. Ellie rode in front beside the sheriff, her face set. Her eyes would move up to the mirror, and meet Jesus', as if seeking reassurance.

We drove out of Rocky Forge with the dust rising behind us, and headed for Mrs. Ernly's farm to discuss Ellie's future.

And possibly the future of Jesus.

Chapter 45

Ellie's family home was a lonely wooden farm building at the end of a steep and arid lane baked rock-hard by the sun. Our little convoy headed up the lane and stopped outside the farmhouse door, which opened on to a wooden veranda. Round about, scrawny hens pecked at morsels of scattered corn, and it seemed that everything living was melded together under a carapace of blistering heat.

Ellie was as taut as a kitten preparing to fight for its life, her eyes now fixed on the farmhouse door, which swung open. "There's Ma," she breathed. The sheriff opened his door and climbed out. Mrs. Ernley paused. Her hair hung down on each side of her thin, eroded face like some species of kelp. She was wearing a faded gingham dress. Slowly, she continued down the steps and moved towards us.

"Ellie! Come here this minute!"

Ellie cleared her throat. "I'm not comin' back, Ma!"

"Let's talk about this quietly, shall we Laura?" The sheriff stood next to Ellie like a referee.

"Ain't nothin' to talk about, Sheriff. She's my daughter, and she's stayin'!" Mrs. Ernly looked at Jesus, who had also left the car and was moving towards Ellie. Her face twisted with rage, and she screamed. "You're one of them perverts, come with a new line in fancy talk and blasphemin'! You want to take my daughter away an' take her to one of them big cities to lie with strangers for money!" She glared at the sheriff.

"Louis Beamish, why don't you arrest that creature calls himself Jesus Christ, an' take him to jail an' hang him for what he's tryin' to do to my Ellie?"

"I'm hanging nobody, Laura. You're just damaging yourself with that talk. Ellie wants to get away from you, and it ain't a mystery to see why."

"She ain't just damagin' herself! Look what she done to *me!*" Ellie slipped her dress from her shoulders to show some pink welts across her back. "She did those with a window cord! Said I was a lazy little bitch 'cause I walked across the yard with a bucket of eggs instead of hurryin' when she called!"

Ellie turned to Jesus and clutched his sleeve. "Please, Jesus, take me away from here. I'll be useful to you! I can read and write!"

"Well, Laura, seems to me there ain't no gainsaying her." The sheriff took out his pipe and lit it, his clear blue eyes on Mrs. Ernley's face. "I guess Ellie knows what she wants."

"Ellie's a child, she knows nothin'."

"I'm nearly fifteen, Ma. I could get married and have a child of my own if I wanted to. And if there was anyone out here to get married to," she added bitterly. "Jesus, I prayed for you to come and save me, and you answered my prayers. You've come." She sank to her knees, took Jesus' hand and kissed it. He lifted her gently.

"You will take me with you, Jesus? You will give me a chance to lead my own life?"

Jesus looked at the sheriff, then at Mrs. Ernly. "Ellie has to have her chance," he said quietly.

"*Her* chance?" I thought Mrs. Ernly was going to rant at Jesus again, but self-pity had taken over from

248

rage. "*Her* chance? What about *my* chance? I never had none—married a man was killed by a car just outside six months after Ellie was born. Left me nothin', not a cent. Even my looks went, and once I wasn't bad-lookin', so far as I know. Mr. Ernly used to say so. Said I had nice eyes. Said I had pretty hair. But after he went, there was never anybody else said the same thing. 'Cause I had a daughter, an' a young man likes to start with his own children. Soon's they found out I had a child, they ran, an' it wasn't long before my looks ran too. Lookin ' after Ellie, runnin' the farm, tryin' to scratch a few dollars the way them hens scratch for corn—that's all my life's been.

"I ain't believed in God for a long time." Mrs. Ernly put her face in her hands and burst into tears. She wept as if all the years of frustration, solitude and sorrow could be washed instantly away. She sank slowly to her knees, as Ellie had done, her face turned up to Jesus.

"I do want to believe in you, I do. Jesus, If you're the Lord, take me with you as well as Ellie." Her tears poured on to the dust, turning it into mud. "Don't leave me here alone."

Ellie spoke up at once. "No, Ma I want the chance to lead my own life. Please Ma, don't spoil that chance. If you came, it just wouldn't be the same." She gazed down at her mother. "I'll come back an' visit with you, Ma. I promise."

Gently, Jesus raised Mrs. Ernly to her feet. "Believe in me, and you will be comforted."

"I'll be comforted if you take me with you."

I thought that Jesus was going to find out that many people regarded God as being a sort of Father Christmas. Instead of a sackful of toys and a belief in

249

chimneys as a means of access and exit, God had a far wider range of abstract gifts, the essence of which was the same: gratification. Whether the petitioner wanted absolution or a new pedal cycle, the view of Santa God was interchangeable: they were one and the same.

"I can't take you with me."

An immediate reversion to her previous mood: "You're just a pervert blasphemer!" I couldn't imagine any sort of god wasting time trying to redeem Mrs. Ernly. She was beyond redemption, unless she could be returned marked 'damaged' to whoever had made her and issued with a new soul.

Jesus, Ellie and I got back into the sheriff's car, and Lola got back into hers. As we reached the end of the lane we heard a scream. It possessed every element of rage, misery, and frustration.

I wondered if Jesus was equipped to cope with a Satan's Chorus of such screams, if the Day of Reckoning ever came.

Chapter 46

Ellie's mother was determined that Jesus should be tried for a list of offences from child abuse, kidnapping and fraud to alienation of affection and blasphemy. For various reasons—principally the avarice of lawyers and her own malice—she had finally succeeded.

One of the consequences was that Ellie's face looked piteously at us from the screen in an interview with Pentecostal Channel Holy Spirit TV. "He *is* Jesus an' he didn't do nuthin' wrong. All he did was to take me away because I asked him to give me the chance of livin' my own life."

We were in the Alabama governor's office – Horton James, our political liaison officer, who had arranged our appointment to coincide with the interview we had set up with the Channel, Cassie, I, and Pat Armitage the Governor. He was a large man with small shrewd blue eyes in a face the shade and complexion of caramelised cream, and wore a white linen suit with a red silk handkerchief drooping from his breast pocket like a dying bougainvillea.

"Sounds genuine enough to me" he said, when the interview was over. "There's nothing I can do to stop the trial, of course, no way I can be seen to interfere with due process. I wouldn't even dare to have a discreet word with Judge Burnell, as he's a man as jealous of his authority as I am." He switched on a smile, and almost at once switched it off again. "Still, we don't want to give the state a bad name for prosecuting Jesus, especially when there's so much publicity coming down on us." He stared at us as we nodded agreement; we had made sure there would be heavy media attention focused on Jesus' trial.

"Horton here's told me you're friends of the accused, this fellah calls himself Jesus Christ."

"That's right, Governor," I answered.

"And are you a friend or, as maybe I could put it, a dee-sciple?"

"A friend."

"Seems funny, that Jesus sounds like a Yankee. We down here don't somehow expect redemption from the North." His eyes creased until only their shine was visible. Are you saying you believe this fellah is really genuine?"

"He hasn't given us a reason not to believe it, Governor." Cassie's tone was defensive.

"That ain't quite the same thing, Miss Ross".

"Well, it's a question of belief. Either you have faith or you haven't, I guess.

"It's just there's something about him, a kind of holy quality—I couldn't imagine anybody more likely to be Jesus Christ. I don't know how to put it better than that."

The governor looked at her closely. "Reckon you put your feelings well enough, Miss Ross. And you say this is a trumped up charge?"

"Yes, Governor. That's exactly it."

"Ellie was speaking the truth," I put in. "There's no doubt Ellie wanted to join Jesus to escape her mother. She begged to come with him to escape her mother, who's apparently made Ellie's life hell, and Jesus agreed to help her."

252

"Without wanting to get something out of it? Some sexual reward?"

"Definitely without that."

"I've spoken to the witness too," Horton said. "You know me, Governor, I'm not the gullible type. I'm sure Jesus never abused or abducted Ellie."

"I hear you, Horton. Tell me, have any of you seen this fellow Jesus Christ's birth certificate?" abruptly. "Can we prove that's his real name?"

"That's what it says on his driving licence," answered Horton. He was wearing a grey linen suit and black-framed glasses on a black ribbon half-way down a steep nose.

"I understand he was christened Jesus Christo but changed it to Jesus Christ as soon as he could," I put in.

"I see. Well, I sure as hell am not interested in getting my state a bad name through bearing false witness." He gave a grim smile. "I'll maybe have a word with Judge Burnell after all. Seems to me, after watching Ellie and listening to what she and you folks have had to say, this case should never have been brought."

The following day, to the anger, if not anguish, of the media which had been parachuted into Montgomery and sent the town's economy into orbit, the case against Jesus was dismissed.

"Of course," said Governor Armitage, when we thanked him, "you still ain't given us a blind hint of proof your client is really the Lord."

"Could happen tomorrow, when we get back to Rocky Forge," Horton said, "for some unfinished business."

The governor gave a lazy smile. "Would that be for Jesus to cure somebody's ma of cancer?"

We looked at him in surprise. "I just got the news she was dead. Died not long after Jesus' arrest." He screwed up his eyes even more. "You intending maybe to let Jesus raise her from the dead?"

"That will have to be up to Jesus," I answered.

"Turns out she was seventy-eight years old, Mr. ben Ezra. Doesn't seem kind to practise on her, does it? I mean, even if she could be raised, what would be the point?" the governor added. "Of course, it might help Jesus' claim to be the Son of God, but on the other hand he might just be a faith healer, with no claim to be anything else.

"Most of us manage to work some kind of little miracle during our lives, something that's just a bit special, a mite unusual, maybe something that'd normally be beyond us, like hitting a ball clean over the bleachers, or staying underwater for more than a minute to rescue someone who's drowning.

"But does bringing back to life an old sick woman fall into that category? Seems to me it'd be more like self-gratification, to do a thing like that. Damned if it'd do the woman much good." He pushed himself to his feet.

"You know, I'd get a real kick out of believing your friend was Jesus Christ, Mr. ben Ezra. I'd like nothing more. But I don't know what he could do to give me the proof I need. The God up there?" He pointed at the ceiling. "He doesn't have to do anything to give me proof. Looking at things positively, I can maybe accept what I can't see, but my faith is limited.

"I was brought up to worship a god I couldn't see. If there's no shape to the invisible, you can try to imagine it, but if someone looks like yourself and has the shape and substance of a human being , there ain't much to imagine, isn't it so? Logic's not heresy because it's a matter of fact rather than faith. Faith has no truck with logic, but God can get away with inspiring it because faith in a God who's invisible is traditional, it's in the flesh and blood and bone of the believer. That's what we keep coming back to." The Governor gave a feline smile.

"If I'm wrong, and your Jesus Christ is really the Son of God, I'm sure he'll feel real amiable towards me for deciding with Judge Burnell that the best thing for Jesus and everybody else in this state, is his case should be dismissed and that he leave directly."

"I wish you all a very good day."

Chapter 47

The Ellie affair aroused plenty of curiosity, some of it religious and rather more of it prurient. The fact that Ellie herself was so passionately genuine was a great asset in keeping Jesus' reputation intact, but as yet he had convinced few people that he was the Son of God.

Because of the intense heat that blistered Alabama by day, Jesus took to preaching at night. This gave his addresses an extra, almost romantic dimension, as whichever location he spoke in seemed to levitate in a wash of light from moon, stars, and phalanxes of car headlights which burnished acres of sun-dried wire grass into fire-flies.

Jesus' growing reputation as a speaker was matched by the increasing number of those who came to hear him. In turn, this new fame turned many of his competitors—for that is what they were—into enemies. One of the most savage was Foxglove, who apart from envy was unforgiving about our substituting the Church of the Son of God for his own Church on our client list.

Often Jesus would be invited by various evangelists to preach and teach in their churches, but seldom accepted in case he might be accused of becoming contaminated or biased by forfeiting his complete independence.

As a result the competition between the myriad splinters of Southern Christianity inviting him to be guest preacher became intense, and they tried to attract to themselves the lustre they could see he held in the eyes of his followers. Like football or baseball enthusiasts following their teams, many either moved across country with him or preceded him to the next place he was scheduled to speak.

Sometimes he took a hall and preached indoors, but there were few halls big enough to hold the increasingly large gatherings he attracted.

I was back in New York when Cassie, who had stayed down south to monitor events, called me to say that Jesus had accepted the offer of a church that was for rent to any sector of the Christian religion which wanted to hire it. As it was independent and had the seating capacity of a sports centre Jesus had decided to take it for a week: the money for the hire had poured in from his followers. Would I like to attend the first service there? A couple of hours later, I was on my way.

The Church of the Holy Sepulchre was in Alabama, at a small place called Demopolis. Already a cluster of tents had sprouted in front of it, and market stalls manned by farmers with faces scorched by the sun and their families offered produce that had been transported in a cavalcade of refrigerated vans, which glowed in the heat.

When I stepped out of my air-conditioned car, the baking air attacked my lungs like smoke, and after a few yards walk towards the church I began to wilt under the ruthless sky. Cassie waited for me behind the church's square yards of glass doors, in a light cream dress of knitted silk, with white sandals on her elegantly sculpted feet.

"I'm so glad you've come, Nathaniel," after we had chastely kissed. "Jesus is inside with Ellie, who always tries to make herself useful doing odd jobs. She's become very protective of him."

"Good." We began to walk down a corridor between long rows of offices, in which people sat in

257

front of computer screens. The building smelled like the inside of a cigar box, as the roof of the corridor we were in was panelled with cedar. The offices were mostly open plan glass-walled cubicles, but some were enclosed, confessionals in a world which by and large had no secrets.

We emerged into a sort of amphitheatre, chilled by almost polar air-conditioning, with acres of seats of which thousands were already filled with those to whom piety meant less than the need to escape the all-enveloping, claustrophobic heat outside. There seemed to be an equal division between white and black.

The focal point of the amphitheatre was a large circular stage on which a lectern two storeys high reared towards the roof, reached by a small elevator in a glass tube. The organ loft held an instrument like the Wurlitzers which used to rise magically, as if levitating on their music from the depths of cinema auditoriums; alongside it was a glass-walled fully equipped recording studio.

Half a dozen TV monitors whose enormous size was in scale with everything else ensured that whoever was standing in front of the lecturn would enjoy no privacy of feature at all; every spot would turn into a sun and any mole into a black hole. The monitors transmitted every word, every grimace, every shadow of expression in close-up to the twenty thousand people attending the ceremony.

Presiding over the huge hall, a fifty foot high bronze cross was pinned to a fan-shaped, free-standing wall built apparently purely for the purpose of supporting it.

"Jesus hates it," Cassie confided in me, "he told me that although when you're reincarnated you have no

258

memory of what went before, he's only too well aware of his associations with the cross. That's one of the hardest things he has to deal with, the creation of an instrument of torture and execution being turned into a sacred symbol."

There was something about her I hadn't noticed before, or which perhaps hadn't been there, a sense of serenity allied to possessiveness. I would not have thought Cassie and Ellie had much in common, but their feelings towards Jesus seemed similar. I was intrigued.

"I'm interested, Cassie, in any effect Jesus may be having on you. For example, has he made any difference to your beliefs, your way of looking at life?"

"Are you asking me if I believe he's Jesus Christ?"

"I'm certainly interested in what you believe."

"I don't feel any different, I suppose. I was always a happy person in my heart." There was something litanical in that phrase which didn't sound like the Cassie I knew.

"What about faith? For example, do you feel nearer God? Does our Mr. Christ do that for you?"

"I like him very much," Cassie said. "I like him as a man. I don't think of him in terms of being the Son of God or any other deity." She gave a smile I can only describe as lascivious, so perhaps I had imagined the onset of piety.

We went behind the enormous cross and knocked at a small door.

"Enter." Jesus was sitting at a table, listening to a recording of Duke Ellington playing Mood Indigo. "Cassie, Nathaniel! I always find Ellington inspirational." There was a scratch pad in front of him, and an empty glass beside a bottle of Sancerre in a cooler.

"How delightful to see you! May I offer you a glass of wine?" He poured two glasses from the bottle. As we thankfully reached for them, there was a knock at the door, and Ellie and Willard came in.

"Hi, Mr. ben Ezra, good to see you," drawled Willard. "My, that heat outside makes me feel fried."

Ellie and I also repeated that it was good to see each other. Ellie had gained presence since I had last seen her in the flesh in Robertsville, an unwilling guest of the pastor when Jesus was being driven away by the sheriff. She looked at Jesus. "I've made sure folks're goin' to be comfortable, Jesus. I've checked the water-coolers and turned up the air conditionin' and everythin', and –"

"Thank you, Ellie. What would I do without you to look after things?"

She looked at him adoringly. "I'd do anythin' for you."

"I know, Ellie. You're doing all I could ask of you. Willard, any news?"

Willard's smile of greeting had changed to a frown.

"Seems there's a hint of trouble due tonight, Sir. I don't quite know what it is, but I believe it's this Reverend Francis Foxglove wants to do you damage. His headquarters ain't far from here; don't know if you've noticed that big place, the Church of The Loaves and Fishes? Don't look like a church at all, but then neither I guess does this. He thinks you're treadin' on his toes. What's more, he's got the backin' of a number of other religious leaders. Seems like you're threatenin' the Jesus Christ industry in these parts, if you get my drift. Pardon me for callin' it that, but that's how they refer to it.

"They reckon they've all got a slice of him – of you, and that you'll do them all out of a job, 'cause they'll become like surplus to requirement."

Jesus sighed. "How many times do I have to say I've come to unite people, not to divide them."

"It seems to me people often prefer to be divided," put in Ellie. "Cain't be happy if they ain't fightin' like rats in a sack." She added: "Look at the way so many of these folks're leadin' mangled, broken lives. Their lives've been hacked about like meat in a butcher's shop. Can't expect much sense out of a lot of them. They need to be led, and it ain't always the righteous who lead 'em."

"That's why I'm here." said Jesus. " He gave a grim Pauline-type smile.

I stood up. "I'll have a word with Horton James; he can alert the Governor and have the National Guard standing by."

"No, I don't think that will be necessary. I'll defeat these *worshippers* of mine on their own ground. Tonight, I think the time has come to announce who I am." He looked serene, a man who had made up his mind after much thought. "I shall announce that I am Jesus Christ the Son of God."

"Oh no, I don't think you should!" exclaimed Cassie. "I don't think it's time yet. Surely that would increase the danger, as Nathaniel's always said."

"I've abided by what he said, but now I'm ready."

"But there can't be any harm in being prepared if Foxglove and the others do try something."

261

"I shall be all right." Jesus stood up. "Six o'clock – time to start." He waited to give us time to walk into the unnerving glare of spotlights. The great building was so crowded there were hardly any vacant seats, but we eventually managed to find some and sat down.

Chatter calmed into quiet as the organ began to growl the first bars of Poulenc's Organ Concerto; after Jesus had walked on stage, it rose slowly to a crescendo before dying into silence.

All he needed, it seemed to me, was a white gown to look like so many Renaissance representations of him. As it was he wore a plain white T-shirt and black linen short-sleeved jacket with white linen slacks. Slowly he looked round, as the silence intensified.

After a minute or so he raised his arms in an extended blessing before stepping into the one-man elevator and rising slowly to the top of the glass tube, debouching at the top on to the lectern platform. Gazing out over the ranks of followers stretching into the shadows out of sight, he switched off the microphones with an audible click, and began to project his voice, perfectly modulated and with a strangely litanical cadence, rather like that which Cassie had used. It sounded natural rather than recited, yet resonated clearly and audibly throughout the auditorium.

"Many of you believe that Jesus lives in your hearts and minds, and in that you are right," he began. "You have studied the teachings of Jesus, and believe in them. You do your best to live by them, you try not to do evil to your neighbour or anybody else, you try – and it can be sometimes extremely hard – to live unblemished lives.

"Tonight, however, Jesus is not only in your hearts and minds, but in your eyes, for he is standing at this lectern before you." He paused, and a woman in front of me fainted or, as the pious called it in the south, was slain in the spirit.

"This Jesus can be seen and touched." Jesus went on, "I am not an illusion, but the Son of God Himself. I ask you to believe in Me and accept what I am." He paused again. Several scattered cries of 'Hallelujah' broke out in pinpoints of sound in the thick silence, as if belief was challenging disbelief. It was impossible to tell as yet what effect the words had had. There were a few hostile shouts to match the hosannas, which grew louder as more evident believers joined in.

Jesus raised his hands, and the chorus was stilled. "I ask you to believe in me, who stand in front of you and whose voice asks you to believe in me."

"We believe!" someone shouted, and there were more cries of 'Halleluja!"

Again Jesus quietened them. "If you believe in me, what can I offer in return for your faith in me? Can I improve your lives ? Can I guide you to greater goodness and the reward goodness merits?

"Indeed," he went on, "what is goodness? Certainly something that should be too natural to you to arouse pride. And what is evil? It is not merely the opposite of goodness, for evil is not as natural to mankind as goodness. It requires a conscious effort to be evil.

"Be proud, for self-respect is desirable, but not arrogant; Be gentle , not brutal; be kind , not cruel. You have consciences which are the measure of your souls, and if your consciences are at peace the natural savour of life will be increased."

He paused, the monitors showing the concern in his eyes. "However, what about those of you whose lives are miserable? What about those of you troubled by various unhappy circumstances, maybe by sickness, by bereavement, by poverty?

"I have no magic wand, I can only help you as my Father directs. Sometimes it is your destiny to suffer, sometimes to rejoice. You can make much of your own destinies, but it is in God's hands to determine ultimately which way you travel, whether your destination will be sorrowful or joyous, bright or dark. In the balance of life, most of you will experience both."

As he paused again, there was a movement at the main entrance to the amphitheatre through which Cassie and I had come. A tremendous voice boomed through a microphone: "If you're Jesus Christ, the Son of God, give us a sign!"

The huge figure of the Reverend Francis Foxglove marched down towards the stage, hundreds of followers accompanying him down the same aisle, others pacing him down the other aisles, a river of men and women marching towards the confluence at the stage. His followers shouted as they marched: "Give us a sign, give us a sign, water into wine, give us a sign!" They came to a halt, filling the aisles, massed round the stage, above them Jesus peering down like Saint Simeon Stylites.

The little black woman at the organ looked nervously over her shoulder and began to play the Organ Concerto again, a throbbing diapason, whose crashing chords burgeoned and diminished, fortissimo to pianissimo, sinister and discordant, which the woman repeated over and over again, just those chords, as if she were hypnotised by terror at the sacrilege of the insult to the Son of God who was standing almost level with her,

264

two storeys up at the top of the circular shaft, God floating on a pillar of light.

"We want proof!" shouted Foxglove, "we want proof that you're the Son of God!" and the crowd shouted again: "Give us a sign, give us a sign, water into wine!"

"Heal the sick and raise the dead!" yelled Foxglove into the microphone, and the command resounded like a storm in the building, a hurricane of words amidst which Jesus stood, arms resting on the great bible on the lectern, impassive and unmoving: "Heal the sick, raise the dead!" bellowed several thousand people, whilst Foxglove reached upwards with the huge hands that had pushed so many balls into the net, as if to pluck Jesus from his platform and destroy him.

Jesus switched on his microphones to counter Foxglove, but did not raise his voice. Nor did he deign to look down at Foxglove, instead gazing across his disturbed congregation.

"Here you have dozens of churches," he began, "dozens of interpretations of Christian belief. In one thing, though, those churches and sects are united; in one thing, one person, they all share the same belief, and that person, that belief, is myself, Jesus Christ, the Son of God. I tell you, I am the one Church, and every Church is vested in me."

"Give us a sign, then!" screamed Foxglove. He was standing near me, and his bloodshot eyes caught mine.

"Water into wine!" the congregation roared, and I was sure some of them were those who a few minutes earlier had shouted in praise of Jesus. Foxglove hurried over to me and looked at my outstretched hand as if he would rather spit on it than shake it.

"ben Ezra, my my! So you believe this charlatan, is that right ? You're so sure he's the Son of God you want to make sure of a place in Heaven. You choose his Church instead of mine as your client, because you think he's the real thing whereas I'm just preaching the Word of God without claiming to *be* God. What makes you so sure I'm not God? I could claim to be God and I could put up a damn good argument to justify that claim. Or does the Son of God have to be white?"

"He can be every colour of the rainbow," I answered. "Or any colour. We have no idea what God looks like, or even if he looks like anything at all. He's fiction, someone we've invented because we can't explain the universe!"

"You're a heretic and a blasphemer, ben Ezra. If you'd gone on handling my Church's business I'd have been damned to eternal hellfire!"

He turned away from me and shouted yet again for a sign, and again the crowd, now dangerously excited, took up a chant which turned into a roared command: "water into wine, heal the sick, raise the dead!" Foxglove marched on to the stage and pressed the elevator button. The glass elevator began to move downwards with the deliberation of blood in a hypodermic as he stood waiting.

He raised his head and began to bellow threats and promises: "If God lifts you up out of my reach and holds you in the palm of His hand I'll kneel to you, Jesus, and I'll pray for forgiveness. If he raises you that'll be the sign we're all of us here beseeching you for.

"If God doesn't raise you up, we'll get you and lead you out of this building and hold you down outside until you confess your sin of blasphemy and apologise to the Good Lord for claiming to be His Son!"

Jesus did not answer, but continued to stand without moving, an imperturbable expression on his vastly magnified face.

The elevator reached the bottom of the shaft. As its curved glass door slid back and Foxglove leaped inside, there was a lot of distant yelling and screaming as the National Guard arrived.

Foxglove was almost at the top of the shaft of light where Jesus stood when the brittle crack of a shot sounded. Foxglove hesitated now that Jesus was right in front of him, his hands still on the edge of the lectern.

In the gross magnification of the monitors, a red spot the size of a UFO began to spread across the front of Jesus' immaculate white T-shirt. Cassie and Ellie and hundreds of other members of the vast congregation screamed together. "Oh My God, they've shot Jesus!"

The aisles were blocked, people trapped in their seats began to yell. Someone fired another shot, and the next second bullets began flying. I saw Foxglove throw himself across the lectern platform at Jesus, I think in an effort to protect rather than attack him. I pressed the elevator button, and it seemed to take years before I was on my way up to where Jesus lay. Foxglove was holding his head. "Crazy fucking heretic!" he barked.

"My father was with me," Jesus murmured, "it's only a flesh wound," A minute later, slain in the spirit, he collapsed in my arms.

Chapter 48

The air ambulance jet banked steeply on its landing run into La Guardia. Looking after Jesus were a flight doctor and two paramedics, with a neuro-surgeon standing by in case Jesus' spinal chord had been affected, the bullet having entered his body just below the right nipple, and exited beside his left clavicle.

The wound was large, but the impact of the bullet had been lessened by the distance from which it had been fired, probably from the far end of the auditorium. Forensic examination was to show that the weapon was likely to have been a hunting rifle, to judge from the calibre of the bullet a Winchester 270.

As we tilted, one paramedic steadied Jesus on his stretcher whilst the other looked after his plasma and intravaneous drip. The flight doctor monitored his heart rate, with an expression on his face that reminded me of a head chef supervising a couple of sous-chefs.

Tyres squealed and the twin jets bellowed in reverse thrust as we briefly tore along the runway, turned along a taxi way and stopped near a waiting Cadillac ambulance.

As soon as we were installed aboard it accelerated fiercely, siren ushering all other traffic aside. We arrived at Mount Sinai Hospital, on the Upper East Side, in just under nine minutes.

Several hospital staff were waiting with a gurney, on to which Jesus was lifted from his stretcher, to be rushed out of sight through gleaming metal doors.

We were approached by Jesus' parents. Morris Christo's eyes rested on crumpled cushions of shadow, and he looked at me with hatred. A tall, well-groomed and formidable woman came to stand next to him.

Jesus' mother had a handsome face and was wearing a broad-brimmed navy blue hat and a lemon-coloured shantung dress. She came straight to the point.

"Satisfied, Mr. ben Ezra? This is your fault. My husband came to beg you not to take my son as a client, but you went ahead anyway." Hostility came off her like heat off a radiator.

"Mrs. Christo, I told your husband that if your son wanted to end his relationship with my company, our involvement would end immediately. If he wants us to continue now, after this horrifying event, we can't abandon him."

"Abandon him," she said, "and he might live longer." Her glare was feral.

"Mrs. Christo, twenty thousand people in that Church had come to listen to him. I'm desperately sorry there was a nutter among them—"

"There's always a nutter!" Mrs. Christo cut across me. "You have to be nuts to believe my son's the son of God! You think I was a virgin and gave birth to my son Jesus in this very same hospital we're standing in and was still a virgin afterwards? Is that what you think?

"Jesus is my son and his father is my husband, this man here. I'm happily married. I love my husband and I don't need to screw anybody else, not even the God of Israel. Do you understand? My husband's already told you that. You don't believe him, you carry on, my son may be dying in there." She gestured at the nearby metal door.

"Get this through your goddam thick head—my son's a man. He suffers from a delusion that he's the son of god, but that's what it is—a delusion. You'd better believe it, Mr. ben Ezra, because I'm holding you responsible for what happened.

"He comes through this and still wants to carry on with your firm, when next time he's shot and it's through the heart, or a maniac with a bomb goes after him and blows him to pieces, or he's maybe pushed off a high building, you won't claw a way out by saying you believed he was the son of god and you were wrong after all, because he turned out not to be bullet-proof and now he's dead!"

She turned to a passing nurse. "My son is in the operating theatre. His name's Christo. Have you any idea how he's doing?"

Feeling the tension between us the nurse muttered that she would try to find out and hurried away. I couldn't remember having ever been so hated. Morris Christo had moved away to look at a child's painting on the wall of a goat in a pink robe sitting in a chair. Now he turned and came back.

"If our son lives, and decides to get back to his life as it used to be, what happens to his contract with you?"

"If your son wants to cancel our contract, there will be no charge."

"And if he wants to carry on?"

"In that case we shall continue to honour our contract with him."

"Honour? You bastard," said Jesus' mother very quietly. I braced myself for a physical attack, but she had too much dignity. "My husband and I want you to leave."

"Yes, get out of here, ben Ezra!" He tried to echo his wife's tone, but I saw that there was no longer any fury in his eyes, in fact there was no expression at all, as if his spirit had been disconnected. I sensed that he had

270

already begun to mourn, not perhaps for his son, who was still alive, but for the loss of himself.

Co-father with God ? What privilege was there in that? No privilege. Adultery was adultery, whoever committed it. Horns were horns, whether worn by a bull or a man.

Chapter 49

The attempted assassination was of course big news. It was also inevitable that Jesus should acquire a nickname he hated: The Manhattan Messiah. The alliteration and rhythm of the phrase gave Jesus a sort of Wild West persona, as if he were Clint Eastwood galloping across sere landscapes, avenging sin. Furthermore, most headlines across the world included the phrase 'self-proclaimed', making it more difficult for Jesus to retain the dignity and mystique which, together with his oratory, had inspired an increasing number of people to take him seriously.

The most damning comments referred to parables and quotations attributed to Jesus in the New Testament, 'physician heal thyself' being the most frequently invoked. What was the Son of God doing in hospital—surely he shouldn't have been affected by a bullet wound?

Normally, the best way to treat ridicule is to remain quiet and let things die down, but there was a sufficiently large number of people whom Jesus' addresses had convinced, as well as a considerable amount of sympathy for the victim of a gun attack, to keep the public focus on him and his claim.

Although he was referred to principally as prophet, guru, teacher, visionary, seer, and avatar, other names, such as Son of God, Redeemer, and Saviour were in some quarters acceptable, even customary.

After three weeks the doctor in charge of Jesus' case, Dr. Herman Laski, a tall, lugubrious man with the bedside manner of a pathologist, told Jesus he was well enough to be discharged. Jesus was to spend a further two weeks in recuperating, and after a final check-up could resume his religious activities. As Dr. Laski put it: 'the show can go back on the road, but it won't do too good if the leading man's shot again."

I had gone to Mount Sinai Hospital to see Jesus as soon as he was well enough to receive visitors; his faith in himself seemed undiminished, in spite of his parents' views. "I hope they'll come round eventually, but I've got to carry on." He frowned. "I had thought of spending a few days at a country place we've got in Westchester when I get out of here. However, it might be an idea to stay clear of my parents at present, so I wondered if you had somewhere discreet I could use."

"I've got a place a few miles from Greenwich, looked after by a cook and housekeeper at this time of year. As long as you don't go into Greenwich your identity should be secure."

"I shall only want to stay there for a few days. Is there any chance you could come too?"

"There's nothing on my schedule that can't be rearranged."

"Good."

I hesitated : "Will you be coming alone?"

He looked at me quizzically. "There was a woman in my life. Now there isn't."

"I'm sorry. Couldn't she –adjust?"

"We knew each other before I realised the truth of who I was."

"What sort of difference did that make?"

"It made a difference that, sadly, was irreconcilable with my knowledge of my true self and her view of me as a fantasist."

"Jesus, you've only come to believe you're the Son of God quite recently; but that belief has already cost you more than a man should have to pay. Your relationship with your father, your mother, the woman in your life and now very nearly your life itself. "

"Perhaps that's my way of giving up all I have." He smiled, but to me the comment had an unbearable poignancy.

Chapter 50

"You know," I said, after dinner on our first night in my Connecticut house, "what most people want in this world is good health and a reasonable prosperity to make them happy. Pretty banal stuff I suppose, if you regard such requirements as mere catalogue items.

"The majority of people aren't chasing a surfeit of anything. If they have enough, they're happy. They don't have to have so much that it's superfluous to happiness. So I'm not sure where redemption fits in."

"Another catalogue item, maybe?" Jesus said wryly. "Tell me, what's your view of redemption?"

"In Christian terms I'd say it means people have a pretty free hand to do as they want, because Jesus the Son of God has paid in advance for it."

"You mean redemption's giving my Father in Heaven an IOU on behalf of sinners?"

"Not so much an IOU as a blank cheque."

"I wish I'd realised." He spoke with surprising bitterness.

"There's no qualification concerning sin, no grading. You can't define redemption unless you can define sin. Perpetrating a great evil seems to be equated in church terms with using the name of Jesus Christ as an epithet when breaking a glass."

Jesus smiled at me in the dying light. "So redemption of sin should only be true of the major ones?"

"The lesser sins hardly need to be redeemed." I added. "If God is compassionate, and has a sense of humour. He certainly has to have a sense of the ridiculous."

Jesus frowned. "Maybe I should redraft part of the philosophy and concept of Christianity, and, as you say, clarify the meaning of redemption and the sins it should apply to."

"Redemption by its nature surely means that as Redeemer you are as much a prisoner of your universe as a man in a cell. In the name of Redemption you must remain eternally in the orbit of those praying and begging for your attention, because it seems to me that there's no obsession like that of a sinner trying to make sure of his salvation. It's a form of gluttony, demanding time as well as substance, because sin is organic. One perpetration of evil grows from another, even if not intentionally. Still, who am I to rant about sins and sinners to you, of all people?"

"If you don't believe in God you can't be expected to believe in sin, and if you don't believe in sin how can you believe in forgiveness?"

"I suppose it's a question of imagination. I can't imagine a god who can't create a mate for himself." I was about to use the word 'poach' but desisted.

"I can't imagine a god solely in the image of man, but of no other creature or substance in the universe. Why should Earth and its humanity be unique in God's eyes? Why shouldn't there be some other well of creation He can match, something perhaps inanimate?"

Jesus did not at first answer, but his expression was as bleak as tundra.

"Inanimate." He sighed. "Whatever you visualise, would be related to me. What exactly do you have in mind?"

"Does God have to have a mate to beget anything, or to assuage a loneliness he has no need to feel? All-powerful, omnipresent, omniscient—does God have a need to share anything, to enjoy anything with anyone else?

"The God of Israel is an immensely personal god, whose relationship with his people is both intimate and cruel. If we go beyond a personal god we must accept the unimaginable: a mating of fire and rock, the amorphous and enormous shadow of a Black Hole. God the Physicist, acceptable perhaps to scientific thinking, working in a flurry of bubbling crucibles, liquid rock and flame to reach some cosmic deadline whose result will be the explosion of all he has laboured to put together."

"You can believe that God my Father created the world, or that it was an offshoot of an exploding universe, but your belief—or lack of belief—can't embrace both." I could tell I had offended him.

"I'm sorry you feel like that about it. I apologise." I hadn't intended any offence; in fact what I needed to do urgently was to discuss with him the matter that might convince me whether or not he was indeed the Son of God.

"Apology accepted." He smiled, and tension between us faded. I sipped my Makers Mark and took the plunge.

"Jesus, did it ever occur to you that you might die?"

"I don't think so. I didn't consider it."

"Did you think the Son of God could die?"

He scrutinised my face. "Nathaniel, the Son of God did die. And rose from the dead."

"We discussed that when we first met."

"I remember. You spoke of my 'namesake'."

I couldn't afford to offend him again, but at the same time he would lose respect for me if he thought I was not being forthright. "I said too that I didn't believe in the Resurrection, and that reincarnation is something else again."

"You mentioned it as a possible reason for my claim that I am the Son of God. You also suggested that maybe there may not have been such an event as the Crucifixion, and you even said it might have been an elaborate or distorted metaphor. At that point I wondered whether it was worth continuing our discussion and whether it wouldn't be better to walk out of your boardroom."

"Why didn't you?"

"There was a certain empathy between us, and you not only spoke your mind, you had a mind to speak. You were sincere, and told it as you saw it."

"Not quite. You claim to be the Son of God. I claim to have seen Christ on the Cross."

"In a dream?"

"In reality."

His eyes seemed to enlarge as they stared into mine. "If you're serious, it seems we both have something to prove to each other."

"You have a chance to prove something to me. I don't know how I can prove that I'm two thousand years old to you."

"Tell me."

"I'm tired of living. I can't die. Let me."

"Are you asking me to help you commit suicide?" His musical voice held the cadence of shock.

"No."

"You can't be asking me to kill you?"

"I seem to be on a sort of eternal life support machine. I've even been burned alive, and survived. I've fallen thousands of feet into a ravine and survived. I've had my neck deliberately broken and survived. And as I say, I saw Jesus Christ on the Cross, and gave him a goblet of orange juice to drink. I accidentally tasted his blood when it mingled with my own on the crown of thorns."

"I think your story is even more difficult to accept than mine," Jesus said.

"Yes. If you enable me to die you'll have proved your claim to godhead, but you'll have proved it to a dead man, which won't help you with the rest of the world."

"It might be easier to convince you that it was worthwhile to continue living."

"Two thousand years," I said, "should have some resonance with you."

"Belief in each other isn't something we can trade, Nathaniel."

"The Son of God should know whether I'm telling the truth or not."

"That sounds like a challenge."

"To me it's more like a prayer."

He stared at me for a while longer, before standing up. He put a hand on my shoulder. "I have to sleep on this, Nathaniel, maybe not only tonight, but for a lot of nights."

"God would know the truth of it, Jesus."

"Now that's certainly more of a challenge than a prayer," but he no longer looked offended.

Chapter 51

For the rest of our time in Connecticut we kept away from the intimacies we had confided to each other the first evening. We discussed strategy and many other matters, but not Jesus' claim to godhead or mine to be two thousand years old. It was as if he was afraid of our empathy going too far, and of losing it through my death if he gave me what I wished.

Jesus needed friendship in a bleak world in which any step could easily be the wrong one, seemingly firm ground concealing the crevasse beneath. He needed to be able to give faith as well as to receive it. I knew he trusted me, even if he didn't believe me.

As soon as we returned to New York, I received a phone call.

"Mr. Nathaniel ben Ezra?"

"ben Ezra speaking."

"My name is Hatto. Bishop Hatto. Is it convenient to have a word?"

"Certainly."

"I would very much like to arrange a meeting with you and your client Jesus Christ. I am speaking on behalf of His Holiness the Pope."

"I'm sure my client will be very interested in what you have to say, Bishop. When did you have in mind?"

"Tomorrow morning? Say at nine o'clock?"

"I take it this is personal?"

"That is so. Definitely personal. I would be grateful if you confided in nobody else about our arrangements at present."

"Very well. In that case, I suggest we meet at my penthouse, on top of the Dolphin Building. I'll check with Mr. Christ to make sure the time is convenient for him, and call you back."

"Thank you." He disconnected, and I rang Jesus, who agreed the appointment.

It seemed we might finally be starting along the oligarch route. I decided to have a word with Stephen Scott-Harmon.

"Stephen, I've got a bishop coming in tomorrow morning who says he's representing the Pope. Presumably it's to do with Jesus, who has agreed to be there too."

"Do you want me to sit in on the meeting as well?"

"No, not at first, anyway. I just wanted to let you know."

"Thanks. Maybe this is the first step in inviting Jesus to the Vatican." He sounded eager.

"Possibly. I'm not sure that would be a good step, though."

"You don't?"

"One can be suffocated by an embrace," I said, and disconnected.

Chapter 52

There was something sinister about the Bishop's bonhomie. I have always been suspicious of a face too rubicund, with a smile that comes too readily. The Bishop reminded me of too many villains I had met over the centuries who had a similar presence and were equally ready to conceal a solitary soul and evil intent under a gregarious exterior.

After preliminary greetings had been exchanged the three of us sat beside the carp pool with a pot of coffee and the Bishop in an elliptically sacerdotal way began to explain why he had asked for the meeting.

"I am instructed by His Holiness to say how happy he is that you have survived the attempt on your life, which shocked him deeply. I of course would like to associate myself with His Holiness's sentiments." He mopped a drop of coffee from his rosebud lips. Jesus nodded and thanked him.

"His Holiness has of course had considerable experience of people across the world claiming godhead or some sort of allegedly divine connection," Hatto continued. His smile became infected by the unctuousness of his tone, taking over his expression with its glossy insincerity.

"Many of these claimants are, to a greater or lesser degree, insane." He shut his eyes momentarily and abruptly opened them again as though staring at a new dawn, probably a false one.

"The Church which you claim to be yours, Sir," he addressed Jesus, "is by habit slow, its pace attuned to the centuries rather than the rapid rhythms of mere decades. Look, for example, at the time it takes to achieve beatification. We have to investigate possible qualifications for sainthood in the minutest detail, as of course you gentlemen know."

"Indeed", interpolated Jesus drily. The Bishop regarded him with patronising benevolence. "After all, the Pope is my Vicar on Earth," Jesus added, "or so popes have always claimed."

Hatto maintained his equanimity. "Exactly so, Christ's Vicar on Earth. That is, if you will forgive me, not necessarily *your* Vicar on Earth, Mr. Christ. His Holiness is not in a position to acknowledge your claim to be the Son of God without the similar depth of proof required for beatification." A seraphic smile. "Such as commendable stubbornness and the tolerance of an unnaturally high threshold of pain."

"Both of which were frequently tested by your Church to destruction," I commented.

"Alas one has to admit that, Mr. ben Ezra, as an institution we have often been guilty of cruelty and intolerance. There was little excuse for, say, the Inquisition, even in the context of the times."

"True, Bishop," I said, remembering it. "So are you saying that the Pope would need proof, rather than faith, in the matter of acknowledging Mr. Christ as the Son of God?"

"Let me say rather that the belief of the Roman Catholic Church that the Jesus Christ who was crucified two thousand years ago was the Son of God and of the Virgin Mary cannot give way to any claim that is not irrefutable." He gave a small bow towards Jesus and revealed small, pearly teeth sheltering behind the too-red lips.

"Mr. Christ, do you believe you can substantiate your claim?"

"And how would you expect him to do that?" I asked, before Jesus could answer.

"Jesus wasn't above using theatrical techniques when required," Hatto answered. "The feeding of the five thousand in the incident of the loaves and fishes, for example: raising Lazarus, enabling the blind to see. I suppose a twenty-first century claimant to being the Son of God might place an announcement across the Internet that tomorrow everyone suffering from AIDS would wake up free of it. There would be a good deal of scoffing and disbelief, of course, but that would soon stop when every AIDS sufferer was indeed able to take up his bed and walk.

"The onus would then be on the sceptics to find a reason for the cure being something other than a miracle wrought by God or His Son."

"Are you saying that in those circumstances the Pope would accept my Divinity?" asked Jesus. "My guess is he would be more likely to put the end of AIDS down to some celestial coincidence or a Divine Act of Mercy which had nothing to do with me."

The Bishop looked at him blandly. "I cannot guarantee what His Holiness's reaction to the abolition of AIDS would be, apart of course from thankfulness. The identity of the agent of such life-restoring beneficence would occupy his mind after that initial reaction. In such circumstances you would have taken a major step towards proving your assertion as to your Divinity.

"Of course," he added, "such a dramatic claim would perhaps stimulate contradiction among those who would do anything to avoid having to change their allegiance to their previous beliefs."

I found his attitude intensely irritating. "As the widespread practice of paedophilia among your priests has demonstrated," I said.

"One cannot make excuses for the inexcusable," Hatto answered. "That is why we have absolution. When we invoke God's mercy, absolution ensures that we receive it."

"Double indemnity," I put in, "as Jesus redeemed mankind from the sins of the world." The Bishop went on smiling, but I sensed his suavity was rapidly evaporating. Jesus spoke again.

"Why should anyone have to change allegiance to Christian belief, to believe in me? As I am Jesus Christ the Son of God, to believe in me need not change anything at all. After all, don't believers expect a Second Coming? Why should they expect someone else?"

"Given the scepticism of your Church, Bishop," I put in, "proof of divinity has been made impossible for any claimant."

"Not for a genuine claimant, Sir. If this Jesus – he gave his small bow again in Jesus' direction—can eliminate AIDS, I would be at the head of those kneeling to him."

"Without necessarily having the Pope's endorsement?" I asked.

"My soul, Sir, belongs to the Almighty and my allegiance on Earth to The Holy Father. I wonder if I might have another cup of coffee." I poured him one, reflecting that the Bishop knew how to hedge his bets.

"The Mother Church," Hatto went on, "is not so much sceptical as protective. She is responsible for an enormous flock, which has to be protected from heresy, today as it was yesterday. Members of that flock may be more sophisticated than they used to be, but there are still many who can be led astray by, shall we say, tongues of silver whose owners are plausible. However, the tarnish on their shining aspirations becomes obvious when they come up against our request for proof."

Jesus looked sombre. "I agree with my friend here that there is no proof that the Church I founded would ever accept."

"We are an open church with an open mind, Mr. Christ. I have heard you preach, I count myself an admirer of your power over your congregations, and I reported to His Holiness accordingly."

"I didn't realise he thought I was worthy of such scrutiny," said Jesus.

"We could not afford to ignore you, Mr. Christ."

"In case people began to believe in me?"

"In case their souls became damned by an impostor, Sir. Your very power is what makes proof of your claim so vital. The near impossibility of proving that claim helps give the Church security.

"We know that God can impress us, if He wants to, with His truth. He can convince us in ways that could well be beyond our imagination, but which would be incontestable. I am only an emissary of the Holy See, gentlemen, and as such not endowed with the powers of a plenipotentiary.

"My job is much more humble. It is to seek out truth. If for instance there is a rumour of some sort of miracle in the Ozarks—a Vision of the Virgin, say—it is my task to investigate the likelihood of that having actually happened, to find and question the beholder of that vision.

"People have their fantasies for a reason. They find solace in fantasy, which is sometimes all they have. There are people who flinch from life, they suffer from a sort of spiritual agoraphobia.

"In the event of confirmation of a miracle—and I must admit that that is very rare—I write a report to our apostolic nuncio here so that he may confer with the Holy Father as to whether a miracle should be officially proclaimed. I shall also be writing to the apostolic nuncio today, but that will be a courtesy, as I am acting in your case as His Holiness's personal intermediary."

"In case I provide a miracle, Bishop?" I thought Jesus had provided one by keeping his temper.

"One could say that, Mr. Christ."

I decided to obtain a direct answer to a direct question.

"Will you arrange an audience with the Pontiff for Mr. Christ?" I asked.

"Alas, that is beyond my power. I shall of course mention to him that you desire an audience."

"But my request would be granted only when I had offered the requisite proof," Jesus said quietly.

"In which case," I interpolated once more, "your boss would be coming here for an audience with the Son of God." The Bishop winced at my terminology and nodded. He looked at Jesus.

"In which case," he conceded, "we would doubtless proclaim your Divinity, and accept you as the

Founder of our Church." He put down his coffee cup and looked at his watch.

"I will of course pass on your request for an audience to the appropriate authority, Mr. Christ. If the Holy Father's answer to your request is affirmative, I take it you would be prepared to go to see him at the Vatican?"

Jesus nodded. "At present, I don't have the proof which would bring him here for an audience with me."

Bishop Hatto gave an ineffable smile, and I could hear his unspoken words: "Of course you don't, and you never will."

Chapter 53

Contrary to Hatto's scepticism, and I hope to his consternation, the Pope did invite Jesus to the Vatican for an audience. I guessed that, like the bishop and a lot of other people, he too was hedging his bets. Jesus was gaining in power, largely, I suspected, because the factors that might have been expected to be against him —his background, especially—had instead worked for him.

In addition to being able to express his concerns for individuals warmly and articulately, he had shown himself ready to risk his life for his beliefs. He was accepted by his congregations, and by many of those whose bible was the Internet, as being above them without appearing superior. Being rich had also not proved to be a disqualification for Divinity; after all, to escape from poverty was historically an integral part of American cultural ambition.

Therefore Jesus was offered the respect and in many cases reverence, which the people might not have wanted to give someone they thought as being simply their equal. They may not have been certain of his divinity, but he was regarded as having gone a long way towards The Lord, at the zenith of the divine hierarchy.

It was not only in the Deep South that Jesus' influence was growing. Across the world, pockets of believers in him burgeoned into cohesive congregations. Obviously a solely secular world alone had failed to fulfil those who needed more nourishment than purely material things could supply. Believers were probably still outnumbered by cynics, but Jesus' invitation from the Pope to visit him at the Holy See only enhanced his authority.

Stephen Scott-Harmon had hired a sizeable number of people specifically to take care of and develop the New Christian Church account, and we had long ago recovered our original investment, the return of the monies owed by us to Foxglove's Church of the Loaves and Fishes.

Jesus and I had scarcely seen each other since he'd stayed with me in Connnecticut, and it was not until his return from Italy that we were able to get together. We were sitting in my roof garden after dinner, enjoying a cognac; the next day Jesus was scheduled to go to address congregations in Tennessee and Louisiana.

"Did the Pope say anything to indicate he might be persuaded to accept your claim if you came up with whatever it is he requires from you?" I asked.

"Elasticity of thought isn't part of being a pope," Jesus answered wryly.

"Distinguishing between traditional concepts of the Church and contemporary views of tolerance has for some time been enough to keep the papacy intellectually busy."

The mournful canyon-calls of car horns sounded far below, as sharp on the evening air as the faraway bark of mating foxes. In sharp contrast, the extension phone on the table bleeped shrilly.

"Yes, Vanessa? Right, bring him up, will you?" I hung up. "Your father's here, Jesus. He wants to see you urgently."

"I'm sorry. He knew I'd be here this evening—I don't know what could be so urgent."

The doors of my elevator opened and Vanessa, tall and elegant, led Jesus' shrunken father towards us. I thanked her and she went back into the penthouse.

290

Jesus' father continued to approach. His hand reached out towards mine, but his eyes were bright with hatred.

"I told you to leave my son alone but you didn't, you got him shot and now every day I read he's receiving death threats. So you've had your fun and made your money and now enough is enough!" He thrust his right hand into his jacket pocket and brought it up, holding a small gun like a derringer. Jesus shouted and tried to grab his arm but there was the brittle crack of an explosion as he fired straight at my heart.

I felt a thud and staggered backwards, falling into a chair. Jesus' father began to scream, a high-pitched noise bubbling with indecipherable words of anguish and vengeance, as his son, his face the colour of crème brule under its tan, pinned his arms to his sides and looked over his shoulder at me disbelievingly as I groped for the bottle of cognac and poured myself a slug.

Mr. Christ Senior caught sight of me in mid-scream and went abruptly silent, before folding slowly into a faint. Jesus lowered him to the ground, not taking his eyes off me.

"It wasn't a blank," I said, as he straightened up, "and I'm not wearing a Kevlar vest. "I told you I should have been killed several times during my life, but couldn't die. Now do you believe me?"

"I believe you." His expression was still incredulous.

"Take your father home and tell him not to say anything. This is a secret between the three of us."

"For once I'm lost for words, Nathaniel. I don't know how to apologise for what my father did, or how to thank you."

I looked into the depths of his extraordinary eyes. "Jesus, if you really are the Son of God," I said, "you owe me a death."

"Nathaniel." His voice was a whisper. "Oh Nathaniel, my dear Nathaniel." He hugged me, his beard brushing my ear. "You shall have it."

Chapter 54

A week after Jesus' father tried to kill me, I began to feel neurotic about the time, place and manner of my death, or whether after all I was condemned to go on living because Jesus might be a Messiah but did not possess divinity.

I could hardly discuss the matter with him, because he would be embarrassed beyond endurance if he had promised me something he was not equipped to give. I was sure that if he were indeed the Son of God, my death would be as painless as possible. However, something else began to trouble me.

I looked like a man in his thirties, perhaps because that was the age at which Jesus had been crucified, if indeed I owed my immortality to having tasted his blood. One reason I had never been able to believe that was because it seemed so utterly illogical that his blood should have the power to confer immortality on me but not on him, as if I had taken on his mantle and the divinity he had claimed as his. I had never at any time felt like the Son of God, except perhaps when Torquemada had prostrated himself in front of me as I stepped off the flaming pyre and advanced towards him.

What concerns me now is that my true age could be the one prevailing physically at my death. Posthumous vanity seems absurd, but I don't want to turn into a deliquescent, stinking pool of matter, or in a few seconds become mummified, especially if I am to die in a public place.

I shall wait for a month. After that, if I'm still alive I shall have to confront Jesus about the truth of his claim to godhead.

EPILOGUE

From the lead article, front page of the New York Times: 'The death occurred at his Manhattan home last night of Mr. Nathaniel ben Ezra of New York, thought to have been in his early thirties and listed by Forbes Magazine as the richest man in the world. How he became so successful in such a short time and with so little known about him is a major mystery.

'A man of prodigious accomplishment, the deceased billionaire succeeded in building a business empire even bigger than Microsoft, in fact of almost unquantifiable size. The holding company is Dolphin Enterprises Corporation Inc., one of whose member companies is Dolphin Lateral, which is handling the publicity and public relations for the American evangelist Jesus Christ. Mr. Christ, who insists that he is the Son of God, suffered an attempt at assassination six months ago by a person still unidentified.

'An autopsy will be carried out on Mr. ben Ezra because of his death at such a relatively early age, but he is thought to have died of natural causes. The New York Times understands that Mr. Christ, who was close to Mr. ben Ezra, will be giving the principal address at the obsequies, which are to take place at Temple Emanuel, on Fifth Avenue.

'We shall be publishing a full obituary of Mr. Nathaniel ben Ezra in the near future, as soon as the results of the autopsy are known'.

THE END

About the Author.

Godhead is Walter Harris's tenth published novel. Eighty-eight at the time of publication, Harris believes that only an old man would have been able to write it with an appropriate sense of age.

As a young man he joined the RAF in the Second World War straight from Haileybury, served for a year in Egypt immediately after the War in the RAF Repertory Company, and spent a year in England after being demobilised, before emigrating to Brazil. Here he wrote for English language newspapers, sold everything from dried Arctic cod to the Encyclopaedia Britannica, as well as teaching English privately, and wrote and presented a radio series of dance music on Radio Nacional before deciding to go north.

In Canada he sold real estate before becoming accredited to the Canadian Broadcasting Corporation as a freelance interviewer in New York, his first interview being with Ed Sullivan. After a couple of years commuting between New York and Toronto Harris returned to England and continued working as a freelance, adding the BBC to CBC. He also made an ARGO spoken word LP called Theatre 60, with Noel Coward, Peter Ustinov, Albert Finney, Harold Pinter and several others. Going on to sell life assurance for Canada Life, he became a friend of Stephen Ward and motoring correspondent for Penthouse. He also lunched Margaret Thatcher and his novel, The Mistress of Downing Street, about the first female British Prime Minister, was published by Michael Joseph in 1971, eight years before she entered Number 10.

Harris married and had a son, Julian, in 1965, and a few years later took him and his wife to Brazil. In Rio de Janeiro, he recorded an LP for ARGO of Brazilian traditional folk music, Songs From Brazil, with the Coral Palestrina, issued in 1970.

Divorced in 1977, Harris continued to sell life assurance. He made a killing from investing a quarter of a million pounds for two clients but subsequently discovered that at the time he met them they were on police bail for carrying out the biggest cash robbery in British history.

Since his retirement from the life assurance industry in 1990, Harris has contributed articles to numbers of newspapers and magazines and spent several years writing Godhead. When he was seventy-nine he met the much younger Alison, and moved in with her. They have travelled extensively, been chased by pirates off Zanzibar, ridden the zip wire down the Arenal Volcano in Costa Rica and whale-watched from a helicopter over Simonstown.

Harris's first book of memoirs, Deathbed Rehearsals and Other Frivolities, will be published by Patagonia Press in late 2014. Two other books of memoirs will mark his 90th birthday.

Walter's website is www.walterharris.org.uk

www.ingramcontent.com/pod-product-compliance
Lightning Source LLC
Chambersburg PA
CBHW021321250626
47155CB00002B/571